DARK MASTER

DARK MASTER

TAWNY TAYLOR

APHRODISIA
KENSINGTON BOOKS
http://www.kensingtonbooks.com

APHRODISIA BOOKS are published by

Kensington Publishing Corp.
850 Third Avenue
New York, NY 10022

All Kensington Titles, Imprints, and Distributed Lines are available at special quantity discounts for bulk purchases for sales promotions, premiums, fund-raising, and educational or institutional use.

Special book excerpts or customized printings can also be created to fit specific needs. For details, write or phone the office of the Kensington special sales manager: Kensington Publishing Corp., 850 Third Avenue, New York, NY 10022, attn: Special Sales Department, Phone: 1-800-221-2647.

ISBN-13: 978-0-7582-2677-8
ISBN-10: 0-7582-2677-2

First Trade Paperback Printing: May 2008

10 9 8 7 6 5 4 3 2 1

Printed in the United States of America

Acknowledgments

To my wonderful agent, Natasha, may this book be the first of many for us.
To my editor, Audrey, thank you for believing in me.
And most importantly, to my readers. Huge, heartfelt thanks for your support.

1

"I'm sorry, miss." The bank teller glanced down at her computer screen, her smile so stiff it looked like it was chipped out of concrete. "Roslund, I can't complete your transaction."

What? Regan Roslund blinked her confusion.

The woman waited for a moment, then cleared her throat and hit a button, sounding the chime that called the next customer. When Regan, who was too stunned to respond, didn't move, the teller glanced at the gentleman standing at the head of the line, giving him a wordless invitation to step forward.

She couldn't have her money? Why not?

The brush of the strange man's shoulder against hers finally pulled Regan from her shocked silence. Anger shoved confusion out of the way and took over. It burned a path through her body, from her toes up to her forehead, then back down again and sent adrenaline rushing through her body in wild, churning waves.

Had that teller just told her she couldn't have her money? Money that rightfully belonged to her?

Yes, she had!

Ho boy. Look out, little lady, you're about to get an earful. "Now, just wait a minute," Regan said, pulling in a nice long breath so she wouldn't run out of lung power before she'd told this teller a thing or two. Was this any way to treat a valued customer? She'd been doing her banking here since she was in diapers. Her lungs at full capacity, Regan gave the customer beside her an apologetic half-smile, then turned to the teller and let it rip. "What do you mean you can't complete my transaction? I'm only asking for a thousand dollars. I'm not asking to clean out the entire vault. Is there something I need to know? Are you declining all withdrawals today for some reason? Are the computers down? Has there been a bank scare à la the Great Depression?" she blurted in one long tirade, her voice rising with each word until the teller gaped with openmouthed shock, like a goldfish being loved too hard by a toddler, and ran for cover—most likely behind the nearest manager.

Instantly, the customers in line started murmuring their speculations to each other. Was the bank in trouble? Would they be able to cash their checks? They had children to feed! House payments to make! Surely this couldn't be happening in this day and age.

Within seconds, a woman with a sharp chin and a sharper scowl stepped into the teller's position at the faux granite counter and asked Regan to please meet her at a nearby doorway for a private conversation.

Regan eagerly agreed. Now she would get some answers.

Once inside the closet-sized office, Regan took a seat, flopped one knee over the other, straightened her skirt, and waited for the manager's plea to keep her from inciting a riot.

Of all the nerve, holding her money hostage! There had to be a law against that.

The woman sat forward, planted her elbows on the desk between them, steepled her fingers under her pointy chin, and said in a cool voice, "Miss Roslund, I gather this may come as a shock to you, but we cannot allow you to withdraw any funds today because your account is empty."

Empty, empty, empty . . .

The word echoed in Regan's head, snuffing out whatever else the woman said. The manager's red-lined lips were still moving, but all Regan could hear was that one word, *empty.* Her account had no money in it? Where'd it go?

Regan felt her eyebrows bunching up, the tension giving her an instant migraine. Great. She had no money, and now she'd be bedridden for the next twenty-four hours with a migraine. So much for lunch with the girls. So much for lunch, period. "What? How? When?" She shook her head and tried to make her mouth form more than one word at a time. "There must be some mistake. How could my money be gone? Last I checked, there was at least thirty thousand in there. Plus, it's July first. The interest from my other accounts should've been processed by now. They're always transferred on the twenty-fifth of the month."

The woman looked a little forlorn as she shook her head. "There's no mistake. No deposits were made on your behalf last month. And the funds that were in your account were transferred to your investment account a little over a week ago. By your fund manager, I'm assuming, since I'm guessing you didn't request the transfer yourself."

"Huh? That makes no sense. My fund manager, Mr. Davis, has been handling my affairs forever. He's never taken money out of this account, at least not any significant amount. A few thousand here and there, maybe. And he's never missed a deposit."

"Perhaps you'd better take this matter up with him." The woman stood. "I'm sorry. There's nothing more we can do for you today."

"Yes. Okay. Thank you. I think," Regan said, shaking her head and standing. She felt like she'd been beaned in the temple with a brick. Kind of spacey, unstable. She followed the woman from the room, then, her mind bobbing on her churning thoughts like a buoy in the gulf during a hurricane, she walked in a daze from the bank, got in her Jag, and drove home.

She kicked off her Manolo Blahniks at the door, dropped her purse on the console, swallowed a couple painkillers dry, and went straight to the phone in the kitchen. What the heck was this all about? Was Mr. Davis sick? Had he been on vacation and missed the deposit?

Or worse?

Nah!

Granted, she had friends who had warned her not to trust anyone with her money, that she should always know where it was and what it was invested in. But even though she'd tried once or twice to learn about investing, the whole thing intimidated and confused her. Margin calls and stock options. Blue chips and NASDAQ. It was a foreign language. Impossible to understand.

Besides, what did she need to know all that junk for? She had a reliable financial manager. Smart people knew their weaknesses and compensated for them by hiring professionals to handle the things they couldn't. Mr. Davis had always done an outstanding job. He'd been keeping her in Jaguars and Armani for years. He was the best. He was . . .

"Good afternoon, Davis Investments," answered a cheery female voice.

Regan sat on a bar stool, pulled a paper napkin from the holder, and tucked the phone between her shoulder and ear to free her hands. She tore a long strip off the napkin. "Hello. This is Regan Roslund calling. Is Mr. Davis available? I need to speak to him about a rather urgent matter."

"Oh dear," the woman said on the other end. The sudden lack of cheeriness made Regan's belly twist. She ripped another piece off the napkin. "I'm sorry, but Mr. Davis isn't . . . available right now—"

Not available? Darn it! "This is an extremely urgent matter," Regan interrupted. She shredded one of the strips into confetti as she added, "Could you please interrupt whatever meeting he's in and tell him I need to talk to him? Now. I'll hold. Please." She could feel her heart starting to skip a beat here and there. Sweat beaded on her upper lip. She dabbed at it with what was left of the napkin. What was going on? Something had happened. Something big. Something bad.

"I'm sorry," the woman said, sounding extremely sorry. Sorrier than sorry. "I can't do that because . . ."

"Because?" Regan repeated, sensing the woman needed a little nudge. Unable to keep her hands still, she made more confetti.

"Because . . ." The woman sighed. "He's gone."

"Gone?" *Oh God!* "Gone." *Stop it.* She tried to catch her racing breath. Gone wasn't necessarily bad. Gone just meant out of the office. Yeah. Gone didn't mean gone forever. Dizzy from lack of oxygen, she snatched another napkin from the holder and began ripping it apart too. "When will he be back?" Feeling, like the walls were caving in, she abandoned the napkins and bar stool in favor of pacing the floor and staring out the back window. Her cat, Matilda, was doing her best to catch a bird that had dared take up residence in the tree next to the deck. Fortunately for the bird, Matilda was too chubby from overindulging in fresh salmon to do more than howl like a fool at the base of the tree trunk.

"I . . . I don't know. He seems to have . . . vanished," the woman said, sounding quite upset by now. Her voice vibrated like she was sitting on a washing machine during the spin cycle.

"Vanished?" Regan repeated, wanting to be sure she'd heard right. Her brain wasn't registering the facts at the speed they were being dealt her, and they weren't being dealt all that fast.

"Yes, Ms. Roslund. He seems to have disappeared."

Disappeared? Oh God! This was a bad gone. This was the worst kind of gone. Maybe. "Well . . . wow. Okay. Um. Do you think this is a bad thing? I mean, did he maybe just forget to tell you he was going on vacation? Or could he have had a family emergency?" *Please say yes!*

"I doubt it. You see," the woman said. "not only has he vanished, but so has the money from almost all of his clients' accounts. I've been on the phone with clients all morning. The money is gone. Vanished without a trace. The police were here, asking me all kinds of questions. I don't know what it all means."

I do. It means he's gone. It means I'm destitute.

Regan's heart hit the floor. This wasn't happening. It was a sick joke, or a stupid mistake, or . . . or a nightmare. "Mine too? Is my money gone?" she squeaked through a throat that was a hairbreadth shy of closing off completely.

"My guess is if you've called because you're having trouble accessing your accounts, then, yes,. it's gone. I'm very sorry," the woman stammered. "I can give you the name of the police detective—"

Her eyes burned. Her stomach did several loop-the-loops. Her whole body started quaking. Her tongue tied itself into a knot. She struggled to untie it. "No, no. I'll . . . I need to . . . I'll call back a little later. Thank you. Good-bye." Regan didn't wait for the woman to respond; she just hit the END button. She didn't need to hear another word; she knew enough.

For the first time in her life, she didn't have even two nickels to rub together. And no family to turn to.

What the heck would she do if her money didn't show up? No work experience, no skills—unless power-shopping was considered a marketable job skill. How would she keep herself from starving to death? For some reason, she was pretty sure her bachelor's degree in liberal arts wouldn't get her very far in Detroit's tight job market.

The phone still clutched in her hand, she ran to her office and ripped out every financial document she had in her possession. There had to be some money stashed somewhere that

Davis hadn't found. Stocks, bonds, gold? Jewelry? Anything that could be sold to keep a five-foot-two, one-hundred-ten-pound girl in food for a few months. Surely that couldn't take a whole lot. Twenty thousand, maybe?

"Why hadn't I listened to my friends? I'm such an idiot." She dropped her forehead onto the desk, letting it land with a dull, jarring *thunk*. Her brain threatened to burst through her eye sockets. "Why, why, why didn't I listen to them?" She lifted her head, a single piece of paper stuck to her sweaty forehead. She jerked it off and, grumbling, scanned the contents.

What was this? An answer to her prayer? "Thank you, Aunt Rose!"

"You have to."

"No, I don't."

"Yes, you do."

"I'm the king." Shadow Sorenson pushed himself up from the leather recliner and resumed the pacing he'd only moments before abandoned. How had his life gotten to be such a mess in such a short time? Completely out of his control. "I don't have to do anything I don't want to."

Shadow's younger brother, Stefan, rolled his eyes for the third time in ten minutes. "You sound like a bratty kid. What are you, two?"

Shadow clamped his mouth shut, cutting off another obnoxious, poorly thought out retort. By the gods, Stefan was right! He did sound like a brat.

"Aha! You see? You won't even deny it." Stefan puffed up his chest like a peacock.

Whew, he needed to be knocked down to size. And Shadow knew the guy to do it.

He uncurled his fingers from his ready fist and pushed aside the massive framed portrait of his great-grandmother to reveal a small safe mounted into the library's wood-paneled wall. A few mild expletives slipped past his lips as he dialed the combination, shoved his hand into the safe, and withdrew a small box.

"You know you owe it to Father," Stefan said behind him.

"Yeah."

"He paid with his life."

Sharp, hot pain shot through Shadow's chest. Did Stefan have to remind him of that fact every hour of the day and night? Wasn't it bad enough that his own conscience did? "Yeah, yeah. I'm well aware of that. Wish he hadn't, though," he murmured.

"Don't say that," his youngest brother, Rolf, said by way of a greeting.

Shadow spun on his heel and shoved the box into Rolf's hands. "Father always wanted the crown for me more than I wanted it for myself. That doesn't mean I won't do the right thing."

"Good, because my contacts in the western territories tell me that the rebels are gaining support," Rolf said, tucking the box into his jacket pocket. "It's only a matter of time, and we're talking weeks at most, before they're organized enough to be a real threat."

"I won't let that happen. Not again. Our people deserve some stability for a change. I think we've all had enough of the riots and rebellions."

"You're doing the right thing," Stefan said, clapping Shadow on the back.

"Yeah, yeah. I wish it didn't have to come to this. I hate the idea. The fact that I'm literally binding myself to some . . . strange human . . . just to gain a little strength makes me—"

Stefan gave a sarcastic scoff. "A little strength? By binding yourself to a human, you'll gain the power of all the kings before you. So you lose a little personal freedom in the bargain? What a price to pay to be the most powerful vampire in history."

"Power isn't everything." Shadow escorted his youngest brother to the door.

"Says you," Rolf retorted over his shoulder. "But you're the eternal pessimist. I prefer looking on the bright side of things."

"Someday you'll understand what I mean."

"There's nothing to understand," Rolf said. "You marry the Chosen, you gain the Power. The rebellion comes to an instant halt. There will be no way to unseat you, and everyone knows it. To challenge you for the crown would be suicide."

That was true, and Shadow knew it. According to their laws, in order to unseat a king, a ritual had to be followed. A physical face-off. Man to man. No weapons. A test of strength. Once he was married, Shadow would be so strong, he could defeat any opponent without breaking a sweat.

But he still wondered if that would be enough to gain back his people's support. He might still face leading a group of clansmen who despised him.

Shadow tipped his head toward the door in a silent command. When Rolf didn't leave, he said, "Go ahead. Go see Eudor the mage. Get the spells. He will tell you how to find the Chosen, my bride. It's the full moon." He sighed, not bothering to hide his misery, and sunk into the recliner. "A perfect night for a wedding."

His sister, Tyra, swept into the room like a fresh spring breeze. "What's going on, Quinby?"

"I'm leaving in a few minutes. Getting married," he said flatly.

"Oh! That's wonderful." She did her typical Tyra graceful gazellelike dash across the room and threw herself into his arms. "I'm so happy for you. Where are you going? Can I come too?"

Standing, he gazed down at his beautiful sister. Only seventeen. So young and full of life and spirit. "No, Ty. You need to stay here." At her subtle pout, he added, "I promise to bring my bride up to meet you as soon as I return. I have to go now. You be careful. I don't want anything to happen while I'm gone. Stay in your suite."

"Yeah, yeah. You're such a bossy brother." She smiled and sighed as he gently pushed her toward the door. "Act like a king or something," she quipped over her shoulder. Then she pecked him on the cheek and waved a good-bye as she strolled down the hall toward her suite. "Don't be all bossy to your wife. Women don't like that sort of thing, you know."

"That's it. I've died and gone to hell." Regan stood at the front of the most horrific storefront she'd ever seen. In the semidark of nightfall, the building looked like it had been transplanted from a war zone. Crumbling, dilapidated, just plain ugly. Concrete blocks with chipping gray paint. Or was that supposed to be white? A battered wood door painted a deep purple.

A gaudy neon sign in the hazy window shouted BLACK ROSE in flickering red letters, and tacky purple curtains hung in the window, shutting off the contents of the store from passersby. What sense did that make? Wasn't a window supposed to lure customers into the store, not shut them out?

She turned the key in the lock and pushed open the door. A cowbell clunked over her head. How charming.

She flipped on the lights. "Ugh." The interior of the store was no more impressive than the exterior. Racks of black garments cut the floor in long aisles, and more black garments hung on the walls, doing their best to cover the butt-ugly, off-white crumbling plaster walls.

"Oh. My. God. What was Aunty Rose thinking?" Shaking her head at the mystery of why her late aunt would own a store like this—and for willing it to her designer-clad niece—she pulled one garment after another from the hangers to inspect them. "Who—or what—would wear something like this? Martians?"

She slumped onto a pink faux-velvet chaise lounge in the corner to have herself a brief pity party.

Her one and only possession, a closed-down shop of horrors. How could she possibly expect this dump to support her, even for a few months? She was doomed.

It would take capital to get this place looking respectable, and how would she find the money to purchase new stock? There wasn't a scrap of clothing in the place worth selling. It was all black. And shiny. And . . . She stood and inspected the garments on the nearest rack. Were these pants made out of plastic? Ew!

She shuddered and shuffled to the store's front to inspect whatever financial records she could find. Luckily, her aunt had left a ledger under the cash register.

The last entry was almost two months ago, the day before Rose's sudden death. Since Regan had inherited the store, it had remained closed. She hadn't gotten around to doing anything with it. Since her aunt had been the sole employee, there hadn't been any store clerks to keep the shop open. Since Regan's other . . . obligations . . . had kept her busy, she hadn't found the time to come out and pay the store a visit. And since her other holdings had provided her an adequate living, she hadn't needed the money.

But now this dump was her only hope.

Though not a bad one if her aunt's figures didn't lie. Interesting. Much to her surprise, it seemed there was a fairly decent demand for sex toys, bondage gear, black polyester dresses, and plastic pants in Metro Detroit. Obviously, the shop's patrons didn't care about a pleasing atmosphere when they shopped.

Regan glanced around the store with new, granted mild enthusiasm. Sure, she wouldn't be living as comfortably as she had been, but she just might avoid the soup lines if she got this place up and running again.

How hard could that be?

She looked at the jewelry in the glass case next to the checkout counter. There were all kinds of necklaces and chokers, adorned with the most unexpected symbols—spiders, bats, crucifixes. There were long dangly earrings, bracelets, rings. On the case's top sat a plain, white, bald mannequin. Shoulders, neck, and head, that was it. The eyeballs stared blindly out into the store. A bizarre black choker circled its neck. Shiny, with intricate swirls and swoops that met at the center of the throat, forming a low V that plunged between the mannequin's less-than-ample breasts. It was so unique it was almost pretty, in a morbidly ugly sort of way.

Regan ran her fingers over the surface. It was slick, cold, rubbery. As she removed it from the mannequin, held it between her fingers and thumbs, a strange surge of electricity seemed to buzz through it. With growing curiosity, she studied it for a second, then turned toward the small oval mirror sitting on the counter, held it to her neck, and studied her reflection.

Okay, the funky design didn't exactly match her long blond hair, blue eyes, and Armani jacket and blouse. But it was sexy. Maybe she could wear it with that black dress she had at home, if she had a date in the next century. She fastened the choker to her neck and fiddled with it for a moment, vaguely aware of the heat seeping from the curlicues and swirls into her skin. It was only when the heat intensified until it felt like a branding iron that she paid it any significant attention. And by then it was too late.

"Ow, ow, owwwww!" She flipped her head down to untangle the clasp from the hair at her nape and tried frantically to unfasten it. Evidently she was allergic to plastic jewelry. Her skin was on fire! She could practically smell the sweet stench of it scalding. "Oh my God!" she screamed as the pain intensified.

And then it was gone. And the choker was gone. She didn't feel the slight weight of it on her neck anymore.

"That was weird." She looked down at the floor, figuring it had to have fallen. It wasn't there, at least not where she could see it.

Anxious to see if she had a rash, she glanced at the mirror and instantly gasped in surprise. The design of the choker was imprinted on her skin, like a jailhouse tattoo. Clear, clean, black.

Tacky! *I look like I belong in a circus sideshow.*

Her hand on her throat, she ran to the back room in search of a bathroom. Maybe a little soap would wash the mark away. But as she rounded a towering shelf full of folded clothes and boxes, she bumped into a black-clothed mannequin. A big mannequin. A very lifelike mannequin.

A mannequin that moved.

One side of its lips curled into a crooked smile. "Hello, there."

A mannequin with a sexy voice. Who could only be there for one reason, or two. Neither of them good.

"Shit! Don't shoot! There isn't a penny in the store. I swear. It's been closed for weeks. I'll open the cash register and show you if you want. If I can figure out how to. Just don't hurt me. Please." When he reached forward, she stiffened, expecting a blow. "Oh God!" Scared witless, she covered her eyes.

Nothing happened.

Duh! What kind of spineless nitwit was she? Standing there, covering her eyes like a toddler trying to hide from the bogeyman?

But damn if she could get a single muscle in her body to move. Frozen as stiff as a frog on ice.

Why wasn't he doing anything? Had he left? *Oh God, let him be gone.*

She concentrated on the muscles in her fingers. *Move, dammit. Move! I can't stand here forever like this. It's damn idiotic.*

Finally, they cooperated. She spread her fingers to peer through them.

Nope. Not gone.

Her gaze met his, and it felt like some kind of weird invisible arc of energy zapped between them. Her knees went all soft and wobbly for reasons beyond her understanding. Her stomach did a few jumping jacks. His deep blue-gray gaze met hers, trapped it, and held it captive. More zaps charged through the air. The strange energy buzzed through her body. Up to the roots of her hair. Down to the soles of her feet. Spiraled round and round in her belly. She staggered against a swoon and covered her eyes again. She needed to think. That was impossible when her insides were doing calisthenics.

Was she—gasp!—attracted to the robber? Attracted? She uncovered her eyes, and more erotic heat sizzled through her body. Good God, she was! Attracted but also terrified.

What the fuck? She must be scared out of her mind, literally. *I plead temporary insanity.*

"Don't be frightened," he said. His rumbly voice seeped through her skin and vibrated along her nerve endings, making them tingle and zap. "There's no reason to be afraid. I don't have a weapon."

Who was this guy? What did he think he was doing, sneaking into her store like this, scaring the daylights out of her, sending some kind of weird lust vibe through her body? Making her swoon? She'd never swooned in her life! She was not a swooning type of girl. She was a . . . a strong, assured, together type of girl. A girl who didn't cower at the sight of a robber, even if he was sexy enough to turn a better woman into brainless goo.

So, she decided to do what any girl who'd been startled by a sexy robber would do. This was, after all, life or death she was facing here. "Oh, I'm not afraid." Making sure to avoid looking him in the eye, she dropped her hands, donned what she hoped was a disarming smile, and kneed him with all her might. In the vitals. "I'm pissed!"

Like the spineless coward she was, she dashed for the door, screaming at the top of her lungs for help.

2

The agony. The blinding rage. The humiliation.

Shadow dropped to his knees, cupping his injured bits, and growled, "Stop her!" through his gritted teeth. He couldn't remember the last time anyone had bested him in a battle. A hundred years, maybe more. Yet, there he was, rendered powerless. Practically curled up like a helpless fetus. Kneed in the gonads by a weaponless human. A woman.

The Chosen, the one selected to be queen by Eudor, the most powerful mage in the world. His future wife!

A smirking Rolf and a red-faced Stefan escorted the lady (a term used loosely in this case) in question back into the room. She didn't come without a fight, and their crotches were the target of more than one kick, Shadow didn't fail to notice. However, his brothers had learned their lessons the easy way—by his example. Lucky bastards. They weren't lying on the ground, wishing they were dead.

The woman was not only fighting, but also screaming. The only thing between his very sensitive eardrums and a sound that would shred them to confetti was Stefan's hand, firmly pressed over her mouth. He was quite grateful for that, since the woman had a healthy set of lungs. The shriek she'd belted out immediately after attacking his privates had been shrill enough to set every dog within miles into howling, spastic fits.

"Enough," he shouted, straightening himself up to his full height again, which was no easy task. The pain down below was still enough to make his eyes water.

He gave her a warning glower.

She halted. The stifled sound of her cries for help ceased instantly. Her chest rose and fell swiftly as she lifted her chin and narrowed her eyes in silent challenge.

She was a hellcat. Full of life. Full of spirit. Oh yes, she was lovely.

He fought back a smile by reminding himself that she'd humiliated him once already tonight. He could not allow her to see any weakness, or he would lose control of the situation. Not that it was fully under his control as it was. "If I allow Stefan to uncover your mouth, do you promise to keep quiet and give me a chance to explain?"

She stared at the floor for several beats, obviously contemplating her options. Even though he wanted to bark, "What's to think about?" he indulged her, waiting impatiently for the inevitable. The way he saw it, she couldn't take too long. She didn't have any options to consider.

As expected, after several more seconds, measured by the drip, drip, drip of the nearby bathroom faucet, she nodded.

He tipped his head at Stefan, who then slowly peeled his fingers from her face.

Would she yell again? Shadow expected it. His spine tightened as he donned the most carefree expression he could drum up. He would not let her know how much her voice grated. Again, that would hand control to her. He couldn't afford that right now.

She visibly tensed for a moment, like she was about to belt out the scream to end all screams, but then relaxed. She didn't utter a sound. Not a squeak.

A pleasant surprise.

Not that she was falling over herself to make this easy for him. The glare she was sending his way said, *Die*. Her tightly clamped lips said, *I have nothing to say to you*. And her rigid posture said, *Come any closer and I'll make sure you don't stand erect for a week*.

He wanted to laugh but he didn't. She was delightful. The perfect woman to stand by his side as queen. He gave Stefan a slight nod of approval. Eudor had chosen well.

"That's better," he said, crossing his arms over his chest, an intentional movement meant to display his strength and impatience. She needed to learn who was boss, quickly.

"Not hardly," she mumbled, yanking on her arms, which were still being held by his brothers.

He raised an eyebrow to let her know he'd heard her.

She stomped a foot. "Oh, come on! I tried to run away and let you have your way with the store. You could've had all the black plastic pants you wanted. But no," his flushed future bride said between gasps as she struggled to free herself from her captors, "that wasn't good enough."

He watched, fighting a chuckle.

"What's the problem? Why'd your thugs drag me back here? Is it because I can identify you to the police? If so, I tell you, I have the worst memory when it comes to faces." She blinked and tipped her head. "Hello, have I seen you before?" she asked, baring her teeth in what he assumed was meant to be a smile. "See? I've forgotten already. Poof. It's gone." When he didn't respond, she dropped the forced smile and whispered, "Please, let me go. I'll give you anything you want."

"But that's just it. I can't let you go. What I want . . . is you."

Her eyes widened. She shook her head and started fighting again in earnest. "No, not that. Please don't hurt me. Oh God! Tell me this is not going to be a gang rape—"

"Stop," he interrupted.

"—I have AIDS," she continued, ignoring him. "Herpes. My parts down below are absolutely hideous. Riddled with every disease known to mankind, and a few that aren't. You don't want to touch me, or your dick will shrivel up and fall off—"

"Stop," he said louder.

"Ohmygod, I knew this was a bad neighborhood, but I didn't know how dangerous—"

"Stop! It's not what you think."

She kept rambling on and on and on.

He had to explain, ease her fears. Somehow. Psychically, if she wouldn't be quiet long enough to explain verbally. He took a chance and got within kneeing distance, though he stood to the side so she wouldn't have a direct shot at his still-aching parts. He grabbed her by the shoulders and gently shook her. "Listen. To. Me!" he shouted, interrupting her blabbering. He punctuated each word with a shake.

Two bloodshot, tear-filled eyes met his. They were open. Vulnerable. Her mouth snapped shut.

Finally, she'd surrendered to him.

This was his chance. He stared into her eyes and mentally reached for her mind, hoping to form the psychic bond. But he was surprised to find he couldn't remain bonded to her for more than a moment or two. Her mental defenses were surprisingly strong.

Another surprise. He'd never met a human who could resist, who could literally cast him out once he was inside their mind.

Out of stubborn pride, and a bit of desperation, he pressed, but once again, she cast him out. It was no use. Her will was too strong. He couldn't get into her mind until she let him in. That meant he'd have to resort to more traditional means of communication if he was going to convince her to become his wife. There would be no wedding if she didn't ask for one.

Things were looking bleak, to say the least. He was not the most accomplished at verbal communication. Especially verbal communication with females. He heaved a heavy sigh. "I'm not going to rape you. I'm not going to hurt you. I'm going to marry you. If you'll agree to become my wife."

He hadn't thought it was possible, but her eyes grew wider.

"What the hell? You? Marry?" she squeaked, red-faced and gaping, like the chevron tang fish his sister's cat had somehow gotten his paws on last week. "Me?"

"I thought you'd never ask," he said, smiling in triumph. That hadn't been so tough after all!

Okay, so it was a nasty trick, taking advantage of what he assumed was an unintentional utterance of the three words that would make it possible for them to be joined as husband and wife, but who was he to walk away from such a primo opportunity? He needed a wife. She was the Chosen. More than that, he liked her. Until meeting her, he hadn't wanted a wife. But quite unexpectedly, he'd had a change of heart. This lovely little spitfire was perfect for him. He knew it already.

And he knew he'd do everything in his power to make her happy. He'd give her the choice of turning or keeping her mortality. As his wife and queen, she'd have jewels, houses, clothes, shoes . . . power. Everything a woman could want.

Joy of all joys, he'd be married and safe and cozy in his bed, his new bride snug beside him, before sunrise after all. The fates were smiling upon him.

Feeling quite pleased, he nodded to Stefan and Rolf, who mirrored his motion before escorting his lovely soon-to-be wife out the back door.

She didn't exactly come of her own free will, not that he'd expected her to. She struggled against his brothers, kicking, squirming. "Where are you taking me?"

"Outside."

"Why? Why! Let me go, you bastards!" She bent her knee and kicked backward, just missing Stefan's leg. "If you don't let me go right now, I'm going to scream again."

"No! Don't do that." Shadow smashed his hand over her mouth before she let loose. Clearly she needed a bit of an explanation if he was going to make it through the ceremony with his balls and eardrums intact. He added, "I understand you're scared, but I promise we aren't going to hurt you. It's a very nice night. A full moon. I just thought you'd feel safer outside, instead of closed up in a building. Okay?" He looked into her eyes, waited for her to nod before pulling his hand away. He walked across the asphalt parking lot to a shadowy corner backed by tall trees. "This is a nice spot."

"Nice spot for what?" she asked. "I don't understand what's going on. Please, let me go. I promise I won't go to the police."

There was no time for formal ceremonies with fancy dresses and photographers, receptions with bad food, and DJs playing '80s tunes. He hoped she wouldn't mind. Perhaps if she did, he'd let her have a reception later. The reception of her dreams.

His brothers moved their grips higher, to her upper arms, and maneuvered her into position, her back to the moon. He took her fingertips in his, smiled down into her eyes, and said the words of the Joining in the Ancient Tongue.

"What kind of jibberish is that?" she asked, glancing at Stefan and then Rolf when Shadow didn't respond. "What's happening? What are you doing?"

"It's okay." Shadow ran his thumb over the top of her hand as he rooted through his pocket for the choker. "I need your name, love. We're just about through."

"Through with what?" She was breathless, beautiful in the silver-blue light of the full moon. A goddess. The choker between his hands, he lifted it to her neck. "Oh no, not that thing. It burned me."

"It won't burn you any longer." He secured the clasps at her nape, then lifted his hand to palm her cheek. Her skin was so soft, warm. And her sweet scent, carried on a crisp breeze, filled his nostrils. His gaze locked to hers, he traced her full lower lip with his index finger.

He mentally reached for her. The ritual was weakening her defenses. He sent her soothing thoughts. Thoughts of safety. Calm. Peace. He didn't know if they'd completely penetrated, but he kept trying. She appeared to be calming down. The stark terror in her eyes eased. The tension that had pulled her lips into thin lines faded until her mouth was soft and lush and her eyes wide and trusting. "That's it. What's your name, love? I want to make you the happiest woman in the world." He ached to taste her, to complete the Joining. She would make him whole. The dark, empty hollow inside would be filled by her fiery spirit. It had been so long since he'd possessed a soul, hundreds of years. Yet he couldn't wait another second.

"Regan," she answered, still staring into his eyes.

Yes, it was working. "Regan," he repeated. She would be his very soon.

"And yours?"

"I am Shadow." Armed with her name, he spoke the rest of the words in the ritual, but the aching to complete the final steps grew more intense with each word he uttered. By the time he had whispered the last words of the Promise, he was barely able to stand. His limbs felt heavy as lead. His heart as cold as dry ice.

Yet, he was powerless to continue until she said the words that would allow him to. It was agony. Beyond his worst imagining. Once again, he was at her mercy. But he knew it wouldn't be difficult now. "I want to kiss you and take the final step. Ask me to kiss you."

"Step?" she whispered, her eyes locked to his as he mentally reached for her again. Her defenses were almost totally obliterated now. She was completely open to him. Capitulating. He filled her mind with sensual thoughts until her face flushed.

Yes. It would be only moments now. "Ask me to kiss you." He lowered his head farther, until his mouth hovered a fraction of an inch above hers, and her breath warmed his lips. "Kiss me."

"Oh God. What am I doing?" she whispered. "Kiss me, please!" She pressed her lips against his, and a current of energy zapped between their joined mouths. When she parted her lips to gasp, he slipped his tongue inside to taste her. Sweet. Intoxicating.

The electricity sizzled and popped along his tongue as it stroked hers. The energy charged through his body, pulsing along his nerves, igniting miniblazes in its wake. A pleasant warmth gathered deep inside, building until it completely overtook him. Searing, yet not painful. His heart lightened as the chill that had encased it melted away. Profound joy swelled inside until tears pricked his eyes.

He was nearly whole. They were joined in all ways but one.

Now! He couldn't wait. His body cried out for the final step, before the glorious fullness left him again. Remembering now what it felt like to possess a soul, he couldn't bear to think of existing another minute empty and alone. How had he survived for so long?

He broke the kiss, dragged his tongue down the side of her neck. Salty. Sweet. Delicious. His fangs extended in preparation of the bite. They pierced her skin, and his mouth filled with the sweet flavor of her blood. She stiffened against him as her essence rushed down his throat, stirring a different kind of hunger in him.

He wanted her. His groin ached. His erection pressed against the front of his pants. His brothers stepped back, releasing her as he roughly yanked her closer, until her breasts pressed against his chest and her pelvis rested against his leg. As his venom took hold of her, she wrapped her arms around him and clung to him.

She ground against his thigh, stirring his lust to even greater heights.

Her moans filled the night air. She whispered his name, repeated it over and over. It was the most glorious sound he'd ever heard. Each time she spoke it, he soared closer, closer to orgasm. And then she shouted and shuddered against him as a climax quaked through them both.

Sated, exhausted, and jubilant, he lapped at the tiny ribbon of blood running down her neck. It was done. She was his. This dear, spirited woman was his wife. He swept her into his arms and turned to his brothers. "It's done. Let's go home before she wakes. I want to take my time with the Initiation."

Regan woke up in a strange room, in a strange bed, nude. She couldn't say that was a first, but it was the first time in a long, long time.

What the hell had gotten into her?

And then her hazy brain cleared, and she remembered what exactly had happened.

Her hand went right to her neck. She had found that bizarre plastic choker from the store. She moved her hand farther up, to the side. Didn't feel a scab or cut. How weird.

The bastard had done some kind of mind-stealing voodoo on her, then bitten her! Bitten! Like an animal. What kind of freaky stuff was that? And speaking of freaky, what was with the talk about queens and weddings? There weren't any queens in Michigan. And how could there be a wedding without a judge? Or a priest? Or a marriage license? This guy was nuts with a capital *N*.

Time to get out of there!

The room—which was huge for a bedroom—was dark, so she couldn't find her clothes, but she could see well enough to find a closet and the exit. Both were about thirty feet away, on opposite sides of the room.

She carefully peeled back the sheet and lifted the man's heavy arm off her stomach. Almost there. Next, she had to remove the even weightier leg from its position, flopped over both of hers. She did that without a problem too.

Yay! At least it seemed the guy owning said limbs was a heavy sleeper. She did not want to wake him. That would only complicate things. When making a hasty postbite getaway, complicated was bad.

Finally free of the man-trap, she slid slowly off the bed and stood. Yow, she ached. Everywhere. Could hardly move. She felt like the time she'd overdone it at the gym and woke up the next day so sore she couldn't leave her bed. That time, she'd spent a few days lazing around in bed, reading romance novels. She couldn't do that today. She needed to get out of here, go back to that dumpy store, and figure out how she was going to buy food. There was no time for Nora therapy. Bummer!

She limped to the closet and carefully pushed a door to the side, revealing an assortment of men's clothing. Beggars couldn't be choosers. She grabbed a shirt and pair of pants, dressed, then pulled at the shoes tucked neatly into the little cubbies until she found a pair of tennies. They were about ten sizes too big, and she'd look like a clown, but they were better than stomping around shoeless. Of all the nerve—taking her clothes! The guy had *cojones*, she'd give him that.

He had a nicely matching tool to go with them too. She was all too aware of that fact. She'd seen it when she'd accidentally flipped the sheet off him.

What had gotten into her last night? First, she let that scoundrel kiss her. Why had she done that? And then he bit her, and before she knew it, she was rubbing all over him like a cat in heat, begging for his Big One. After that was kind of a blur, like she was looking through the haze of a dozen tequila shots.

Had he slipped her some kind of drug?

She held her head in her hands. Oh, her brain hurt! Thinking wasn't something worth doing at the moment. She'd have to wait until later. Much, much later. Like maybe a year from now. Why relive something that was clearly a mistake? A huge, enormous, gigantic mistake.

Taking long, sloppy strides, thanks to the shoes threatening to slip off her feet with every step, she headed for the exit. She had no idea how she'd get home. No car. No money. And no energy to walk what had to be miles to her house. She was quite certain there were no houses anywhere near her place with bedrooms this huge.

Before pulling the door open, she let herself take a breather against the wall. She did not like living like this! Not only was she feeling like crap physically, but mentally too. She had no money. No job. No future. She'd just woken up next to a guy she didn't know from Adam.

Her life was one big mess.

She thunked her forehead against the wall. "This is all a bad dream—the empty bank account, the creepy store, the guy. All of it. I'm going to wake up now, and my life will be back to normal. . . . Yes, any minute now, I'll wake up. . . . wake up . . ."

She wasn't waking up.

"Hmmm . . ." came a rumbly male voice behind her. Even though the sound came from way over there, across the room, it made her shudder. It wasn't a shudder of dread, either. "It's early. Come back to bed."

Oh, if only she could! There wasn't a cell in her body that wasn't screaming for crisp Egyptian cotton sheets on a pillowtop Serta. However, she wasn't sold on coming back to his bed. A bed, yes. Warm, soft, comforting. A bed full of Shadow the Mysterious? No, not so much.

"Regan," Shadow called from the bed. She heard the rustle of bedding. He was getting up, which meant he'd be closer to her in a heartbeat or two. She was pretty sure that would be a bad thing. Her heart did a funny little hop in her chest. Yes, most definitely a bad thing. "Are you okay? Where are you going?"

She very quickly rummaged around in her brain for her morning-after speech, even though she had no idea what, if anything, they'd done. "Look, last night was . . . Well, I'm not sure what it was. But I need to get home now, take care of some things. I'll . . . er, call you."

"No, you won't," he said from directly behind her. She could feel his presence. The awareness took the form of little tickles that danced up her spine. She shivered.

"Sure I will." Still facing the wall, she reached to the right, expecting to find the doorknob. What she found instead was a large hand.

Not speaking a word, he closed his fingers over hers and pulled. She spun around, her eyes meeting his. There was that funny warm feeling in her head again, and before she knew it, she was following him back to the bed.

He lay down and gathered her to him. The giant shoes fell off her feet. *Thump. Thump.* One of his hands ran up and down her upper arm in a soothing stroke. A few parts of her body decided they liked it. Traitors!

"You're so tense." He nuzzled her neck, and a few other parts joined the celebration.

What was with that? Since when did her body have a mind of its own? "Yeah. I tend to get that way when I wake up naked with someone I don't know."

"Well, then, we must address this matter. We are, after all, married now." With a finger under her chin, he forced her to lift her head and look into his eyes. Felt like her brain was melting. "You have every right to ask me anything."

"Married?" She jerked her head and dragged her eyes from his. "What the fuck do you mean 'married'? I didn't attend a wedding. How could we be married?"

"Sure you did. Outside, in the parking lot. While I admit it wasn't the most romantic—"

"Hold up!" The party inside her body came to a screeching halt. She shoved against his very wide, very muscular, very nummy chest and sat up. She slapped his hands away from her arms before he got a good hold on them and scooted toward the side of the bed. "That wasn't a wedding. It was a . . . a . . . What the hell was that? Whatever it was, I'm very certain it was not a wedding. There was no judge. No marriage license. No rings exchanged or drunk groomsmen doing the Hustle to Stevie Wonder." That was one big fucking bed. Had to be at least double the standard king size. It was bigger than some European countries. When she reached the side, she flopped her legs over the edge and, turning back, added, "By the way, did you bite me?"

"Yes." He didn't look the least bit embarrassed to be admitting that fact. What kind of nutjob was he?

She hopped to her feet, bent over to get the shoes. "Yikes! That's just . . . wrong! Didn't your mommy ever tell you it's not nice to bite? Human mouths are full of all kinds of nasty bacteria. Oh man, I'd better go get a tetanus shot before I die from lockjaw. Come to think of it, I'm feeling pretty achy all over. Could be too late!" Shoes in hand, she headed for the door, but he caught her by the waist long before she got there. How the fuck did he move so fast? "Let me go, dog-boy!"

"I didn't want to have to do this, but you've given me no choice," he said, sounding martyred, like he was the one who'd been bitten and held hostage.

"Hello, I'm the victim here. Why are you acting all put out?" She squirmed and thrashed, once again finding herself overpowered by a male. She vowed right then and there that she'd take a self-defense class if she made it out of this alive.

If . . . if! God, she'd better! She was too young to die. There were so many things she hadn't gotten around to doing yet. And who would take care of her beloved cat and orchids? She fought harder, but all that did was wear her out quicker. Within seconds, she was breathless, nude, flat on her back, arms up, hands overhead, some kind of leather cuffs around her wrists, chains attached to the headboard. Shadow the Monster was working on securing her ankles in matching cuffs, but she was doing everything in her power to stop him.

Unfortunately, that didn't amount to much, either.

Where did that leave her? Spread-eagle, on a bed, with a huge, hulking woman-biter kneeling over her. His very large, very erect cock pointing at her belly like some kind of phallic divining rod. His dark eyes raked over her body, then settled on her eyes. Instantly, sensual images started whirling around in her mind—just like last night!—and, despite the fact that she thought he was a nutcase, he was making her get all warm and girly.

She was weak! Suddenly, gorgeous men who bit women, kidnapped them, and tied them up turned her on?

What was wrong with her? Why did it feel like her body, even her mind, were not her own anymore?

She decided to keep up the strong act, not let him see her faltering, even though her will was now softer than butter left on asphalt in July. Some things were better kept to oneself, especially in this type of situation, however it could be classified.

"Let me go, or the minute I get out of here, I *will* go to the cops. And you'll go down for kidnapping! That's a serious offense, mister. A federal one, I'm pretty sure."

"You won't go to the police," he said, sounding cocky and way too sure of himself for her liking.

"You don't know."

"Sure I do."

"How could you know anything about me? We've known each other for a couple of hours, if that clock over there's accurate," she said, noticing for the first time the alarm clock sitting on the nightstand. "And I spent half that unconscious . . . or . . . or hypnotized or something." That was it! He was hypnotizing her! Sneaky bastard. She tried to shove the sexy thoughts from her mind, but they didn't budge. In fact, they intensified. "Stop messing with my mind!"

"I know this much," Mr. Cojones said, ignoring her demand to leave her brain alone. He levered himself so his chest almost brushed against her nipples. Those very naughty nipples decided they needed to get closer, and stiffened. "I know you've recently found yourself newly broke. That you have no way to get home. No idea how you'll buy your next meal. And no family to turn to for help. I also happen to know . . ." He bent his arms a smidge more so his nose nearly touched hers. Her nipples struck pay dirt, sending happy little surges of energy through her body with every brush against his smooth-skinned chest. ". . . that you like me. So you wouldn't want to see me go to jail."

"Ha! I laugh at your delusions. Ha! Ha! Ha!" She felt her face heating, thanks to all the blood blasting through her body. Her heart rate was out of control. So was her libido, but she was trying hard to ignore that.

Wasn't doing very well in that regard, she had to admit. Didn't help that he was nibbling her neck just the way she liked.

"Delusions, you say?" he asked between yummy little nips.

"Yes, delusions. I'm not broke. I have all kinds of money. Millions of dollars in a trust fund, handled by my very famous, very successful financial advisor. I have a killer house, car, more Manolos than Neiman Marcus. And I do not . . . oh . . ." Her words tumbled down her throat and landed somewhere in her belly as Shadow the Evil One stuck his very naughty tongue in her ear.

"Don't what, love?" he whispered while still torturing her very sensitive organ.

"Stop that and I'll tell you." She had to admit, she sounded stronger than she felt. There wasn't a single part of her body—outside of what remained of the gray stuff housed in her skull—that wanted him to stop. And thanks to his skill at hypnotism, even that gray stuff was marching for the enemy's camp.

Her ears had never been an erogenous zone before. But oh, what this man could do to an earlobe!

"Very well." He stopped. "Don't what?"

She wanted to scream, but she didn't. Why had he stopped? Yes, she'd told him to, but didn't he know that didn't mean she actually wanted him to? "I don't like you. I don't even know you."

"Of course you do! You like me plenty, and I can prove it." He turned his gaze back to her face again.

This time when their eyes met, she didn't try to fight the sensual pulses rippling through her. They felt wonderful. So intense. *Prove it? That could be fun.* "I do not. I am not the kind of girl who runs around falling in *like* with every man who knows the real reason why earlobes were created. And you're not just any man. You're a neck-biting, kidnapping, hypnotizing renegade."

"I'm not a renegade. I happen to live by the law."

"Yeah, right. Didn't anyone tell you that kidnapping is against the law?"

"You're changing the subject." Without removing his gaze from hers, he traced a line between her breasts, down to her belly button.

She gasped. Why did that finger stop? Lower. Lower! "I'm pointing out a fact."

He drew a circle around her belly button, then ran his fingertip back up toward her breast. Wrong direction. "It's insignificant at the moment."

"Kidnapping? Insignificant? Since when?" she blurted between spastic breaths. It was a fingertip. But oh, what it was doing to her skin. Wherever it wandered, a tingly, hot trail was left in its wake. And there was something crazy about his eyes. If she looked hard enough, she could swear there were flames dancing in them. Dark flames. She didn't want to look away.

He gave her an evil smile, ran his tongue over his lower lip. "We're talking about you liking me. That's what's important right now."

Even though all she wanted to do was lose herself in the fire in his eyes, she lowered her eyelids. It was the only way to concentrate, to maintain even a little bit of control. As it stood right now, she was this close to begging him to fuck her. Regan Roslund didn't beg. Regan Roslund didn't sleep with strange men . . . anymore. Strong. She had to be strong. "I don't like you," she said again, forcing conviction into her voice. "How can I put it any plainer? Will you please let me go now?" She opened her eyes.

He sat up, screwed his adorable mug—*I shouldn't be noticing how cute his chin is or how kissable his lips are*—into a mask of deep thought. "If I prove you like me, will you stay?"

"For how long?" she heard herself say.

He shrugged. "Forever."

"What kind of bet is that? Forever? That's insanity. No, I won't accept that bet. Not that I'd expect you to prove I like you. Because I know without a doubt that I don't."

"Chicken?"

"Am not."

"A month."

"A night, and that's my final offer."

"Done." He crushed her mouth with his in a kiss that set off a nuclear reaction in her body.

Ka-plow!

3

"What are you doing?" Regan said around a mouthful of tongue that didn't belong to her. She wanted to squirm but couldn't. She wanted to throw up a white flag and surrender, but she couldn't do that, either. Horny as hell or not, she was not going to let this guy get her all hot and wet and . . . and, oh hell! She was hot and wet already. *I give up! Fuck me! No no, no fucking. No!*

"See?" he said, once he'd reclaimed his tongue. He slid a hand down between her thighs, for which she was mighty grateful, and stroked her very slick pussy. "You do like me." He lifted his hand and held it before her, like he was displaying some kind of trophy.

"That doesn't prove a thing." She lifted her chin. "All that proves is you're a good kisser."

"Why, thank you." He looked extremely pleased by her compliment. "I'm glad you think so."

"That doesn't mean I like you."

"Sure it does. Ever been kissed by someone you don't like?"

She had to think about that one for a minute or two. Then,

she remembered the one time, back in junior high, when Bobby Tanner had cornered her behind McDonald's and demanded she kiss him to get free. "Yes."

"Bet you didn't get wet then, did you?"

"No, but I was also twelve years old and—"

"Doesn't matter. I win! You like me, and now you're mine for the next twenty-four hours." He clapped his hands together and eyed her like a starving man might look upon a broiled rack of ribs. She had to admit, his expression made her rethink her stand on fucking him tonight. "What to do first?"

"How about untie me?"

"No, I think you like being tied up."

"No, I most definitely don't." She tested the cuffs around her wrists as she watched him stand up. It was then that she realized she would not only sleep with the man, but she'd also probably enjoy it more than she'd ever enjoyed fucking in her life.

There was no denying it—Shadow, the man with no last name, had a body straight out of her fantasies. He clearly shaved himself smooth—everywhere—which made all his yummy muscles look tight and defined. Made his cock and heavy testicles look bigger too. Scrumptious.

There was something else too. Something she didn't quite understand. While she should be absolutely freaking scared shitless, chained to a strange man's bed, held hostage, she wasn't. There was something going on between them. Some kind of weird bond. And somehow she knew in her gut he wouldn't do anything to really hurt her.

She attempted to lick her lips, which had become as dry as sand in the Sahara, but her tongue had glued itself to the roof of her mouth. It came unglued when he turned around. Problem was, the sight of him holding a huge dildo in one hand, a whip of some kind in the other sent her tongue straight down her throat—not a good place for it to be. She coughed and sputtered.

He looked worried as he raced across the room. "Are you okay?"

"Yes. Fine." She hacked a few more times, then fought the urge to continue. "See?" She blinked away the tears that had sprung to her eyes during her choking fit. "What are you doing with those?"

"It's the Initiation. Have you ever been spanked?"

A happy little shiver skipped up her spine. "No! At least not since I was a kid. And even then, it wasn't more than a tap of the hand on my fanny. My mother was not into heavy corporal punishment. You're not planning on whipping me with that . . . that thing, are you? It'll strip the hide off my back." She motioned toward his right hand with her head. "That's just plain wrong. This isn't the medieval times, you know." *Whip me, baby. Oh yes! Yes!*

He had the nerve to look disappointed. To add insult to injury, he sighed! "Well, if you feel that strongly about it, I'll wait for a little while."

Damn. You'll be waiting a long, long time. Take my word for it.

His grin was all too smug. "We'll see about that."

What? Could he read minds? "No, you'll see. Now, I've had enough of this tying-up stuff. Let me loose. I have an itch I need to scratch." Boy, did she ever. She didn't bother telling him it wasn't a literal itch. More like a sexual one. There was no way she'd admit to him that this whole whips-and-chains thing was really, really getting to her. In a profound kind of way. "And put John Holmes away while you're at it. That thing scares me."

Shadow lifted a single eyebrow, then looked at the offending item, still clutched in his fist like he hadn't even known he was holding it. He returned his gaze to her, pulled his mouth into a lopsided smile that made her spike a fever. "Sure. Okay. I'll put it away." He crawled up onto the bed, kneeled next to her, and bent over, his mouth on a straight course for her right breast.

We have contact!

Yes, it landed on target, and she yelped. He didn't bother with shy little swipes of his tongue. No, Shadow the Evil One went right for the gusto. He closed his mouth over the tight nub and suckled until Regan was sure she was going to die if he didn't do it to the other nipple. Then he added light nips with his teeth. Oh the sweet agony!

"Shadow . . ." she half-said, half-moaned when he moved to the other breast to give it equal treatment. The man really knew his way around a breast. Another fact she was most grateful for.

"Mmmm?" He appeared to be finished with her breasts. She wasn't so thankful for that, but she was anxious to see what he'd do next. He was heading in the right direction—south, toward her very wet, very warm pussy.

She tried to spread her legs wider, just in case he did decide to check out the landscape between them a little closer, but she couldn't. Stupid chains.

He arrived at his destination, explored her slick folds with a fingertip. It wasn't nearly enough. In fact, his teasing strokes only frustrated her. She wanted big, hard cock. Deep inside. She moaned. "What's wrong, love?" He chuckled.

The nerve!

"Nothing," she snapped.

"Very well, then. I guess I'll continue what I was doing." And that he did. Skirted around her clitoris, which made her increasingly desperate. His naughty finger slipped just inside her vagina, not all the way, just enough to frustrate her further. Then it went about its exploration of her labia again.

She did not like that finger. Not one little bit.

Lost in her need, she lifted her chin, arched her back, and clenched her eyes closed. Tension was pulling her legs, stomach, arms into tight knots. She clenched her vagina closed around its painful emptiness.

Big, hard cock. Now!

She felt something press at her pussy, something large. Something that would fill her completely.

"Open to me," he said.

She tried to pull her thighs apart but couldn't. The hard cock pushed, pushed until it breached her opening. Its entry was slow, wonderful. She heard herself sighing. "Yes. Oh yes." It filled her completely, then retreated, only to make a repeat performance. "Oh God, yes!"

"That's it. Take me. Take all of me."

His words stirred the heat simmering inside her to even greater heights. His cock drove in and out in slow, rhythmic thrusts that carried her swiftly toward climax. He finally found her clit with his roaming finger and drew circles over it, matching the pace of the circles with his thrusts.

Thought fled her mind as her world closed into a pinpoint of sensation. A pinpoint of intense sensation that was almost too powerful to endure. Sight was gone. But sound and touch had taken its place, supplying her system with more than it could handle. Her own sighs of delight mixed with his growls of pleasure. The amazing feeling of his huge cock gliding in and out, stroking every miniscule part of her vagina, including that special place where the sensation made her almost want to cry. His finger dancing over her clit.

Her legs trembled. The knots in her muscles tightened. Her long and even breaths shortened into irregular gulps and hiccups. A flash of heat blazed up her stomach and spread over her chest, and she cried out.

"Open your eyes, love."

Something made her open them, despite the fact that she swore she lacked the strength to drag her eyelids up off her eyes.

"Look down."

She lifted her head and looked between her legs.

It was the dildo fucking her. And she was taking that huge

thing into her pussy. It was wet with her juices. She could see them glistening.

"Isn't it fucking beautiful?"

She watched as he pulled it out and thrust it inside again, and then she started shaking all over as her climax buzzed through her system like a charge of electricity.

"Oh yes!" He quickened the pace of the dildo's thrusts, which made her orgasm more intense. It was glorious. It was beyond words. And eventually, it was over.

Happy little twitches followed. In her legs, arms, pussy. He took the dildo away, set it on the bed, and smiled. "Now it's my turn."

Thanks to the fact that the oxygen hadn't yet reached her head, it took her a second or two to realize what he meant by that comment. It was when he unfastened first one ankle, then the other that his meaning became crystal clear.

He pushed her knees up and out, so her still-twitchy pussy was open wide to him. Then he lifted her hips up off the bed, kneeled at her bottom, and entered her in what she was beginning to believe was his slow, torturous, wonderful inward stroke. The outward one was just as slow. And just as amazing.

His cock filled her just as completely as the dildo had. Her body quickly decided it needed another orgasm and started to heat up again. Waves of desire rippled up and out from her center, from the place deep inside where his cock stroked with each deep thrust.

"That's it, love. You're so hot. So tight. I want to come already. Fuck!" His voice was tense, his words clipped. He slowed his thrusts even further. "Do you know what it feels like to give all control over to your lover? Control of your body. Your passion. Your life?"

Lost in the flood of sensations flowing through her body, she hardly had the strength to respond. "No."

"I will teach you. You will learn the joy that comes from

submitting to your master. Your husband." He increased the pace of his thrusts again. His fingertips dug into the flesh of her hips, and he pistoned in and out of her. "You will be the happiest woman on the face of the planet. I promise you that."

She couldn't imagine being happier than she was at the moment. It was as if their bodies had been made to fit each other. Their minds seemed to fuse as their passion swelled. Every touch, every stroke brought her closer to climax and to the kind of fulfillment she'd never felt before. His thoughts were like whispers in her mind. His building need became hers. And she sensed hers became his. He released her hips, let them fall to the mattress, and changed positions. His cock stroked a different part of her now. A part that she hadn't realized needed his touch. He found her clit and stimulated it with a fingertip.

This time, when the warmth of impending climax buzzed through her body, something else happened. The world behind her closed eyelids exploded as a million colors and images flashed through her mind. Emotions so intense, so overwhelming, battered her system like a raging storm. She screamed, the sound empty and hollow in her ears, and braced herself against the onslaught.

"It's okay, love."

She heard his voice inside her head. Felt it in her belly. In her soul. The colors faded at the precise moment the first spasm of another orgasm gripped her. Vaguely aware of Shadow's shouts as he, too, found his release, she wrapped her legs around his waist to take him deeper. Although this was the second orgasm in such a short time, it was even more intense than the first one, and longer. She enjoyed every spasming second of it until it faded to tingly, twitchy satisfaction. Shadow pulled his semi-flaccid cock from her, crawled to the head of the bed, and released her wrists from the cuffs. Then he settled beside her and pulled her to him in a warm bear hug. She couldn't help but feel safe, cherished. Utterly content.

The need to make a hasty getaway was definitely gone. Whatever had happened just then, right before she'd come, it had done something. Had made her feel closer to this man, this stranger. She felt like she'd known him forever, like he was a part of her. Like she'd wither away and die if they were apart.

It was the strangest thing.

It took some time before Regan was able to repair all the broken connections in her brain. She lay on the bed, snuggled up to Shadow for a while, lost in a haze of contentment and exhaustion, but eventually the thoughts returned, the questions, the doubts.

What the heck had she done? More than that, what the heck was going on?

Granted, she wasn't much for angsting over mistakes. Regret was a waste of time and energy. But in this situation, she had good reason to question her sanity. Who was this Shadow? What did he want from her, besides twenty-four hours of kinky sex? She had more than a gut instinct that he wasn't just about the sex. No, there was more going on here. His words about marriage, words she'd so easily ignored when in the throes of lust, now rang loud like a gong in her head. Married. Wife.

There hadn't been a judge, just a couple thugs. There hadn't been a license. She hadn't signed any piece of paper. No church. No rings. Yet, Shadow seemed pretty convinced their so-called union was legal and binding.

It was time to find out the truth.

She cleared her throat. "Shadow?"

"Yes?"

"About this marriage thing?"

He rolled onto his side and smiled at her. "We have a lot to talk about, don't we?" He nodded. "I was willing to wait a while, let you rest, but if you want to talk about it now, we can."

"Yes, now. Now is good."

"I'm not really sure where to begin."

"How about the part where you sneak into my store, drag me outside, mumble some incoherent gobbledygook, and then bite me? I mean, I'm not one to enjoy rehashing old injuries like some people, but you never did explain. What is this all about?"

"First off, I didn't sneak. The door was open. I walked in. And second, I didn't drag you. You came willingly. Now, the third and fourth things, those I plead guilty to. I did recite some words I realized you wouldn't understand. They are in my people's ancient tongue. And I bit you. That's what my people do during their wedding ceremony. We recite the Ancient Pledge and then we bite."

A million sarcastic quips rushed through her mind, but she dammed them up in her throat. Why bite the bride? Why not shower her with expensive jewels instead? Where was the translator? And why wasn't she given anything to say in the ceremony? She didn't recite any lines. That was plain wrong. All of it was plain wrong.

She waited a few seconds before speaking, just to make sure they wouldn't pop out of her mouth when she opened it. "Okay. How about a definition here so we're both on the same page. Who exactly are your 'people'?" She hooked the first two fingers of both hands to indicate quotations when she spoke the last word.

"I'm a member of a very ancient breed of people whose bloodlines go back thousands of years to a lost culture that predates the ancient Egyptians by centuries."

"Then . . . you're Middle Eastern? It's called race, not breed. Or would that be nationality? Anyway, I know it's not breed. You're not a dog. I've never heard folks from that part of the world identify themselves—"

"Not exactly," he interrupted. "Breed is very accurate. We're not fully *Homo sapien,* human. There are some very important differences, genetically and otherwise."

Regan didn't know what to think about that statement. Important differences? She'd seen everything this guy had, and although there were certain bits that were a little . . . bigger than the average guy, they were still the same danglies she'd seen on every other man she'd slept with. It wasn't like he had two of anything he wasn't supposed to. "I'm probably going to regret asking this, but what the hell? What differences?"

"We cannot go out in the daylight . . ."

"There's a term for that. I've heard about it. Like an allergy. Doesn't mean you're not human."

". . . and we have extremely long life spans . . ."

"What? My great-uncle Lewis lived to be one hundred fifteen. That's like *Guinness Book of World Records* long. He never claimed to be anything but a human. Although, I do admit, he was a little on the weird side—"

"I'm talking hundreds of years, not one hundred."

She felt her bottom jaw fall. Hundreds? That was impossible. She closed her mouth so she didn't look like a landed fish and forced a laugh up her throat. "Oh, now I get it! You're joking! Seeing how gullible I am? Well, buddy, gotta tell you, you had me there for a few minutes with that breed thing. I guess I'm pretty damn gullible for a woman of the twenty-first century—"

"I'm an infant among my people. I was born in seventeen hundred sixty-nine."

"Shut up!" She smacked his shoulder. "You're too funny. But enough's enough. You're starting to creep me out here."

"I'm not joking." He looked as serious as a mortician. "On my next birthday, I will be two hundred thirty-seven years old."

She swallowed hard as the enormity of the situation socked her in the belly.

She just had unprotected sex with a guy who claimed to be a two-hundred-thirty-seven-year-old member of some kind of breed. A fruitcake! Probably delusional schizophrenic. "Oh. My. God." She jumped up from the bed and wrapped her arms around herself. "I . . . I . . ." What to do? What to do? She was afraid to anger him. What if he went all schizo and started hearing voices telling him to murder her? "I . . . need to use the bathroom." She tried to pretend like she had confused the exit for the bathroom, pulled open the door, dashed across a huge living room, and then headed for what she hoped was the apartment's main exit.

The two thugs stood on the other side, blocking her escape route down a narrow corridor. Feeling extremely naked and panicked, she sucked in a deep breath, pretended to be all casual-like (considering she was naked, that was a real trick). When it seemed they weren't buying her I'm-just-out-for-a-leisurely-stroll act, she ran at them full tilt. Maybe she'd catch them off guard.

Didn't work. Not even close.

The thugs caught her and dragged her back into the room with Shadow the Schizo. "But you don't understand," she whispered. "He must've forgotten to take his medicine or something," she pleaded. "He thinks he's a member of some breed. Please, call a doctor. The police. Anyone."

The thugs shoved her inside and left the room, slamming the door before she could dash out again.

"I don't want you to be afraid of me." He stood and strolled across the room.

She backed away until her spine was pressed against the door. If only she could walk through walls! "I'm not scared. I just had to go pee. I told you. I have a very temperamental bladder. It's a girl thing. When I've got to go, I've got to go."

He reached for her, but she cringed and ducked before he touched her.

"Gotta go, gotta go, gotta go." Truer words had never been spoken.

"The bathroom is that way."

"Oh. Okay." Maybe she'd find another escape route in there! A window, maybe. It was worth a try. She hurried past him, locked herself in the very large, magnificent, spalike room, with all the amenities of a luxury hotel. Deep soaker tub for two. The whole bit. Best yet, there was a window. "Yes!"

She took the time to empty her bladder, which was really in need of it, wrapped herself in a towel that was easily the size of a twin-bed comforter, then scrambled over the side of the tub to look at the window's hardware. It was then that she realized two things. First, they were in some kind of high-rise building. No doubt on the top floor. The ground was a long, long way down. Second, she was a whole lot farther from home than she had originally thought. The landscape outside wasn't even remotely familiar. She was guessing they were somewhere in Europe.

So how would she escape now?

She sat on the side of the tub, defeated. Scared out of her wits. Confused. Upset. Pissed off. What could she do? Her out-of-control emotions were not letting her think clearly. "If this was a movie, what would I expect the girl to do?"

The answer came to her. So simple. So obvious. Duh.

Telephone.

She tried to collect herself. If she was going to escape this craziness, she had to keep her wits about her. Panic was not a good thing. Panic was as much a threat as the man out in that bedroom. When she felt a little bit better, she opened the door.

He was dressed in a pair of pajama bottoms. No shirt. Sitting in a large chair, reading the paper. He lifted his gaze when she entered the room.

"Your bladder feel better?"

She attempted to scan the room visually without making it obvious.

She was so not good at this spy stuff.

He turned around to see what she was looking at, then returned his gaze to her. "I have some clothes for you."

"Clothes! Yes. That would be nice. Where?"

He motioned toward an armoire not far from where he was sitting. "I didn't want to buy too much off the rack. Figured you'd prefer to have your clothes altered to fit you properly. But for now, I hope the things in there will do."

"Thanks." When he returned his attention to the newspaper, she hurried to the armoire and opened it. Fresh underwear. Jeans. Tops. Sweats. She opted for the sweats, figured she might be doing some running in the near future. At least, she hoped she would be.

She took the garments back to the bathroom and dressed. Finally fully dressed, she felt more confident. It was amazing what a little cotton blend did for a girl's attitude.

"Better?" he asked when she returned to the room once again.

"Yes."

"Then we will finish the conversation we started." He motioned toward an identical chair, next to the one he was sitting in. "Please, sit."

She hesitated. This guy's propensity for ordering her around really grated on the nerves. But she squashed the temptation to keep standing out of sheer stubbornness when her knees started knocking together. "I suppose I could sit down." She lowered herself into the chair.

He waited for a few minutes while she got herself comfortable. "I want you to just listen for now. Let me finish explaining everything. And then I'll listen to your concerns. That's the only way we're going to get through this."

She saw no phone in the room, which meant for the time being, she needed to stall. When he went to the bathroom—he had to do that sometime!—she'd do a more thorough search. There had to be a phone in there somewhere. "Okay," she said distractedly.

He stood up, started pacing. "Like I said, I'm a member of a rare breed of people. We are known among humans but are considered a legend, folklore. Humans call us *vampires*." He paused, as though he expected her to freak out again. The thought crossed her mind, but she knew it would do her no good.

She nodded for him to continue.

"I am Shadow Sorensen. I am the eldest son of twelve and the reigning king of the *Degenen*. Members of my clan live around the world, which makes it very difficult to maintain control. As a result, we have a history of bloody rebellion. It was only during my father's reign that we have enjoyed peace. With his death returns the threat of upheaval, strife, suffering, death. In order for me to solidify my claim to the throne, and protect my people, I had to take a wife. That is where you come in."

"What does a wife have to do with anything?"

"Her soul—your soul—increases my power a hundredfold. No member of my clan possesses the power to overthrow me. It's a very long and complicated ritual."

She considered his very fishy story for a minute or two, then responded, "But you said yourself that your clan has a history of rebellion. Why would something so simple as marriage be a so-called cure if it didn't work in the past?"

"Because until my father took the throne, our people were forbidden to wed humans, even our monarchs. We did not know the power it would give."

"So, what if your enemies snatched a human wife? Then you're back to the starting block, aren't you?" Was she buying this whole thing? No. So why was she arguing with him? Why listen at all?

She couldn't answer that. Okay, maybe she could. Did she want to believe him? Was this explanation easier to stomach than the possibility that she'd slept with a delusional mental-ward escapee?

"It only works for those with royal blood. Therefore, I have only my brothers to worry about. And they stand firmly by my side."

"You hope."

"I know."

"And we're married? Just like that. You pick me out of the phone book or something, kidnap me, and tell me I'm your wife. No proposal. No wooing. No courtship. No license."

"Not exactly. You were chosen for a reason. But there was no time for courtship, and the license was unnecessary."

"Unnecessary?" She stood up. She needed to face him nose-to-nose, or rather nose-to-chest since he was so much taller than her. It was still better than sitting and looking up at him. Such a weak position. "Let me ask you this—was my consent unnecessary as well? You didn't ask me if I wanted to be married to you. You just assumed I did. I had no choice. Where is my freedom? Hmm?"

"I regret that I had to take that from you. Our ceremony does require you to ask me for marriage. Technically, I did follow the law. But in reality, I admit, I did take advantage of a slip on your part. You repeated what I said, which sounded very much like a proposal—"

"You cheated?"

"But the insurgents are gathering forces. I need to present my bride at our clan meeting the first night of the waning moon—that's tomorrow. You can see I had to move quickly." He dragged his fingers through his hair. "If it makes you feel any better, I feel like I had no choice, either."

She crossed her arms over her chest, gave him a good, long glare, and thought about what he said. It seemed neither of them wanted this marriage. It was only needed to serve one purpose. To make some kind of statement at their big clan meeting.

So, what if she played along until tomorrow night? Then she could walk away and go back to her less-than-thrilling life of poverty. Sounded like a plan. "Fine. I've got a deal for you. I'll stand at your meeting tomorrow, play queen, but then as soon as the meeting's over, I want a divorce."

"You can't—"

"Neither of us wants this marriage. I can see that. Plus, like I said before, I was given absolutely no say in the matter. That's not right. Even you admit it. You cheated. I live to make my own choices."

"Yes, but—"

"Does your so-called law allow for divorce? Or is it like the old British monarchy?"

"Yes, you are free to ask for a divorce. But you are destitute, with no skills, no job." He swept an arm out, motioning about the room. "Surely, you can see you'll have a very nice life—"

"Why aren't you jumping at this? I can tell your heart's not in this marriage. Divorce me and you can pick a more suitable wife, if that's what you want."

"You don't know what I want. You don't understand—"

"True, but you *do* know what I want. You owe me, for tricking me into this marriage. Divorce me or you'll have to tie me up and drag me to the meeting. What kind of peace do you think that would inspire in your rebellious clan members?"

He sat down and silently regarded her for a long, painful minute. What was there to think about? She was an American. No one had the right to force her into a marriage she hadn't agreed to! That was medieval, no better than slavery. She could tell Shadow was feeling guilty about his little faux pas in the parking lot. Cheating was *so* not cool.

"What if we make a deal?" he suggested.

Another deal? She shook her head and gave him her best I'm-so-not-going-there-again glares. "What kind of deal?"

He motioned toward the chair. "Sit down, hear me out. I think this could be a win-win situation."

She had a feeling she was going to regret it, but she nodded, heaved a huge sigh, and plopped into the chair. "Okayyyyy. What you got?"

4

"I'm going to"—Shadow cleared his throat—"woo you," he declared, looking very pleased with himself.

Now that was the last thing Regan had expected to hear. She'd expected something along the lines of financial enticement. Money. Jewels. Deeds to mansions.

She knew her mouth was gaping open again. She had a habit of doing that in this man's presence. He was married to a fishwoman. Not too alluring. She snapped it shut. "You're going to what?"

"Woo. Court. Romance. Whatever you women call it." His neck turned a really lovely shade of pink.

"And then what?" she asked, deciding to humor him for a minute. This was an insane idea. A crazy idea that was making him blush.

Pink was a cute color on him.

"And then you'll decide you can't stand to leave me and you'll stay," he mumbled.

She lifted both brows. "I'm going to what? Decide I can't

live another day without you? Mighty confident of your romancing skills, aren't you, pal?"

"Yes."

She barked out a "ha!"

"Okay, maybe I might be a little rusty at that girly romance stuff. But I couldn't come up with another idea." He visibly swallowed as he waited for her to respond. When she didn't—because she wasn't sure what to say—he added, "So, I take that as a no."

"It's an 'I don't know.' Frankly, I think you're nuts. Why would you want to go to all that trouble when you don't want a wife any more than I want a husband?"

"Because you . . . because if I've gotta have a wife . . ." He sighed, turned, and stared at the wall. "I . . . want that wife to be you."

She sat stunned for a minute, two, an hour, maybe. Who knew how long? "Why? Why me?"

He shrugged and finally returned his gaze to her face. "I like you."

"You don't know me."

"I know a lot." He leaned forward, resting his elbows on his knees. "You remember when we were . . . when we had sex?"

How could I not? Her face warmed.

"You remember what you saw just before you climaxed?"

She couldn't forget! The images had been so intense. The emotions so overwhelming. She nodded.

"We were psychically joined. We shared thoughts, memories, feelings."

"How?"

He leaned back. She wished he'd lean forward again. She liked him being close. It made her feel toasty inside. "It's a very difficult process to explain."

There was no doubt he was speaking the truth about this.

Since the minute she'd met him, she'd questioned what he'd said—his excuse for taking her outside, the story about him being the king of some clan of vampires, the story about their supposed wedding. The excuse he'd given for why he needed a wife.

But she couldn't deny the fact that she'd heard his thoughts, seen his memories, felt his emotions for the briefest of moments.

While that didn't make everything he'd said suddenly incontrovertible fact, it did give him credibility he hadn't possessed a few minutes earlier.

"You're really a vampire?" she asked.

"We don't really care for that label, but yes, that's what most humans call us."

"You drink blood?"

He nodded.

"You sleep during the day?"

He nodded again.

"You can't go outside in the daylight?"

"I'll incinerate."

"You sleep in a coffin full of dirt?"

"No, I sleep on that double California king. It's much more comfortable." He smirked. "Dirt makes me sneeze, and I like to stretch out. Coffins tend to be so . . . confining."

"Yeah. I noticed about that stretching-out thing. And speaking of kings, you're really a king?"

Something flashed in his eyes. Something she couldn't exactly read. "Yes."

She had to ask, poke around. There was something there. Something that wasn't quite right. She sensed it now. She'd also felt it when they'd been making love. What was he hiding? "Aren't you happy being king?"

He dropped his gaze to his hands. "It's what I am. It doesn't matter how I feel about it." He twisted a huge ring around his left ring finger. It had a bizarre stone in it. One instant it was deep, blood red, like a garnet, the next, black, depending on how the light hit it. Funny, she hadn't noticed it until now.

When he raised his eyes to hers, they were heavy with emotion. "My life belongs to my people. I am their king. Their protector. That is my vow. They need me."

They need me. This man's sense of honor was like nothing she'd ever seen before. The sacrifices she sensed he was making. For his people. What kind of man did that these days?

Right then and there, she decided what the hell? She'd give Shadow Sorensen a month. What did she have to lose? If he had a set time, like a few weeks, she'd just have one last hurrah before returning to the life-of-the-penniless. Wasn't much of a sacrifice on her end, as long as she kept things casual.

"We need to set a time limit," she said, holding back a smile. "I can't hang around here forever, waiting for you to figure out how to charm me."

His answering grin made her knees turn to marshmallow. It was a good thing she was sitting down, not standing. "Six months?"

"One week."

"One month."

"Done." She offered her hand. "But understand, I have no intention of letting you win."

He took her hand in his and gave it a shake. "Understood. But there's one more thing."

"Oh yeah? What's that?"

"You'll need to learn what it really means to submit to me as king and master."

"Oh yeah?" she asked, suddenly not feeling as confident she'd made the right decision as she had a heartbeat ago. "Master? What's that mean? Is it what I think it might be?" If so, she had a feeling she was going to have a whole lot more fun these next thirty days than she'd originally thought. Fun, but also a lot more emotionally intense. That was the part that worried her.

"I'll show you. Later."

"Later? Why later? You've got me curious now." She hated surprises. Worse than that, she hated waiting for answers when they were readily available in the present.

"I don't want to shock you. You're not ready."

"I just learned I'm married to a vampire king. Do you think it's more shocking than that?"

"Good point. Okay. Since you insist, come on." He stood and pulled her toward the door. They walked past the two thugs standing outside the door, took the elevator down several floors, then exited. Several hundred yards down identically decorated hallways lined with numbered doors—the place looked a lot like a hotel—around a few corners, and they stood outside a set of double doors.

"You've had a lot of surprises tonight. I'm not sure if you're ready for this."

"Bring it on. I've seen. Heard. Learned worse. How bad could it be?"

He held up an index finger to his mouth to indicate she should be quiet. And after she nodded her understanding, he pushed open one of the doors and led her inside.

She hadn't known what to expect on the other side of those very ordinary doors, but the very out-of-the-ordinary (for her!) scene inside was surely not it.

This was no hotel. At least none she'd ever stayed at. They'd never had a room like this in it.

The room was dimly lit. Dark blue paint made the walls feel closed in, like a cave. But it wasn't the very bizarre décor that made it so shocking.

It was the furnishings, or rather, equipment. And what the inhabitants of the room were doing on said equipment.

She'd been on the Internet, poked around, stumbled upon a

few pictures here and there. Done a little fantasizing too. Okay, a lot of fantasizing. So she knew what she was looking at. But it was much more confusing (and yes, intriguing) in person.

A bondage room, a dungeon.

At the moment, not counting herself and Shadow, there were five people in the room. A threesome—a woman and two men—were in one corner of the room, doing . . . something. She was nude, handcuffed, on her knees, with something strapped around her face. A gag. There was a metal ring in her mouth, holding it open. The two men stood in front of her.

A man and woman stood nearby, seeming to be watching.

Shadow gave Regan a questioning glance before leading her farther into the room. She answered with what had to be a weak smile. He didn't expect her to fall right into the role of slave, did he? Although, she had to admit she'd enjoyed being tied up earlier, despite her complaints. That was sex. Surrendering control in the midst of a passionate fuck was sexy, fun, but living that way all day, every day . . . She didn't think she could do that. Not for a month. And for the rest of her life? Not a chance.

And pain was out of the question!

Was the woman enjoying what the men were doing to her? Allowing Shadow to lead her closer, she studied the woman's features for a sign.

Yes, the woman did seem to be aroused, if heavy-lidded eyes, a flushed face, and erect nipples were any indication.

Both men were attractive, Regan couldn't help noticing. Not quite as handsome as Shadow, but not too far off. And nearly as well-endowed down below. Both their cocks were at full staff, protruding from their well-muscled bodies toward the woman's head. One of the men grabbed a fistful of hair and grinned down at her. "Suck my cock."

The woman nodded.

He wasn't exactly gentle as he thrust his tool into her

mouth. In and out, in and out. It was a little disturbing but also incredibly arousing watching him fuck her mouth.

Despite the niggles of unease skittering around in her body, Regan's panties were getting wet.

As if the man knew the effect he was having on her, he turned and gave her a smile.

Her cheeks flamed so hot, she figured they'd blister.

The other man walked around behind the woman and helped her onto all fours so he could fuck her from behind. One fucking the woman's mouth, one fucking her pussy.

So sexy.

Thanks to the blood being diverted to parts other than her brain, she began feeling a little light-headed. She gripped Shadow's upper arm and held on. Their gazes met. There was that funny hot sensation again. The thought of heading back to the room and jumping his bones flashed through her mind.

Between the weird arcs of sensual energy Shadow was shooting at her and the scene the threesome was performing before them, she was zooming right into the lust zone again. She'd watched porn before, seen two people fucking. Two women. Two men. Even a woman and a pony—now, that was truly bizarre! Porn made her hot, for about five minutes. And then it got boring.

This was not getting boring.

The man fucking the woman's pussy smacked her fanny with his flattened hand. The loud sound echoed off the walls and polished wooden floor. One of Regan's knees gave out.

Shadow caught her before she landed on her rump. He gave her a worried look.

"I'm okay. Sorry," she whispered. God, this was so much to absorb. It was absolutely thrilling but also scary. What did Shadow expect from her? A little kinky sex? An around-the-clock master-slave relationship? Just the two of them? Threesomes? Foursomes? Moresomes?

That wasn't a little spanky-spanky playing going on. Judging by the way those people were carrying on in there. The vast collection of equipment. Shadow and his people were into something a whole lot more intense.

Would she be able to maintain the emotional distance she needed?

"We should leave. Talk about this."

She nodded. "Yes. Okay."

The man fucking the woman's mouth stopped, walked around her, and stood behind the other man.

Regan halted midstride to watch.

He wasn't going to . . . Oh, she'd never seen a man fuck a man before.

Smiling, he pushed on the man's shoulders until he was bent over the woman's back. Then he went for some lube, slicked himself up—watching a man handle his own cock always made her hot—then slowly entered the man's anus. The look on both men's faces was enough to force the air out of her lungs. She gasped to try to reinflate them.

The two bystanders started their own thing nearby on what looked like a weight bench. The woman lay on her back and spread her legs. The man entered her roughly.

Someone cried out. Regan realized almost instantly it had been her.

Shadow quickly escorted her from the room and carefully closed the doors. He didn't speak as he led her back through the maze of hallways to the elevator.

When they returned to his suite, he turned to her. "Now you see?"

Her throat was clogged. She couldn't speak, so she nodded. This was so much more than she'd bargained for. On so many levels.

Shadow was sexy. No doubt about that. But she'd never been the kind of girl to let good looks get the better of her. She liked her men easygoing, undemanding. Compliant.

Shadow was clearly none of those. He'd been tense since that first moment she'd seen him. And undemanding? The man had married her without asking! He was a Neanderthal. A dominant, demanding, muscle-bound bloodsucker.

She'd never let herself fall for him. Lust, yes. Love? Not even close. Well, not as long as she could keep a fair amount of distance from him emotionally. Losing and having to be this man's wife forever was not her idea of bliss. He was too . . . Shadow.

She needed some space. To think. To breathe. If she was going to win, to keep her independence, she needed to keep an emotional distance. If she let herself get too close to him, she knew what would happen. Either he'd annoy her or she'd start to really like him, then her heart would start this achy-yearny thing. And before she knew it, she'd want to spend time with him, start missing him when he was gone . . . exactly the opposite of what she needed. She'd fallen for one too many wrong men in the past.

No way. She wouldn't make that mistake again.

As soon as her tongue began working properly and the haze of raw need cleared from her brain, she crossed her arms. What had she gotten herself into here? She hadn't been in a real master-slave relationship before, but she could tell already that it was a whole lot more intense and emotionally demanding than the average dating relationship. She needed the cards stacked a little more favorably, or she doubted she'd last a week. "I think we need to add a couple of conditions to our little agreement."

"No."

She lifted her chin. "Then I won't be making my guest appearance tomorrow."

He gave her a martyred sigh. "What are these conditions?"

"First, no lying or cheating. You must play by the rules. And no doing that staring-hypnotizing thing like you did out in the parking lot. In the bedroom. Back in that dungeon. Because that's not fair . . . because that's just the way it has to be. Oh, and absolutely no biting! Period."

He didn't look none too happy about condition number one. "What else? You said 'a couple of conditions.' I assume there's more than one, although if you ask me, that first one really qualifies for at least three."

"After the meeting, I'm free to go home, whenever I want. I don't have to live here in this hotel or whatever it is."

He didn't look any happier about condition number two. "Is that it?"

"Yes. For now."

"No. Not 'for now.' If I agree to these very unreasonable conditions—"

She shrugged. "Take 'em or leave 'em. You need me. I don't need you."

"—there won't be any more!" His face turned the color of the woman's paddled behind down in the dungeon. A very interesting blend of purple and red. "You are impossible."

"Which is why you like me." She grinned, knowing she was going to win. She'd put in her time tomorrow and then go home, where there was no dungeon. No moresomes. She'd collect a few gifts, which she could hopefully sell on eBay to get the capital needed to get the store looking decent. Play a little light master-and-slave in the safety of her bedroom. That she could handle . . . she hoped. At least it wouldn't be around the clock. And then she'd kiss the king good-bye in thirty days.

It was the perfect plan.

"You're not the easiest vampire to get along with, either, you know." She offered her hand and tipped her head. "Do we have an amended deal?" She could tell he was really having a hard time swallowing her demands. Poor baby.

That's what you get for tricking me!

He took her hand and gave it an abrupt shake. "Fine."

"So, how about something to eat? I'm starving." She clapped her hands together, flopped into the chair, and kicked up her feet on the ottoman.

Looking extremely cranky, Shadow grumbled, "What would you like?"

"I'm thinking something simple. Filet mignon? With baked potato loaded with the works, tossed salad with ranch dressing. Oh and French silk pie for dessert."

He didn't say a word, just stomped to the door, jerked it open, barked her order at one of the thugs posted outside, then slammed it shut.

"Really, you're being awfully nasty yelling at the help like that."

"You haven't seen nasty. Yet," he growled.

She bit back a sarcastic retort. Like the typical male, Shadow obviously didn't like being outwitted. He wasn't taking it well at all. She could rub his face in it and have some fun, but she figured that wouldn't do either of them any good. So, instead, she decided to explore the very lux suite he temporarily had her held up in.

Being the sole inheritor of a rather large fortune, she'd done her share of traveling. There was a time her accounts were so huge she could've spent to her heart's content and, because of compounding interest, never run out of money.

Those were the good old days—not so long ago.

During her travels, she'd stayed in some top-notch places. This place rivaled the best of them. She went to the wide window overlooking a street crowded with pedestrians, even during the wee hours of the night.

"Where are we?" she asked, still watching out the window.

"Rome."

"Ah. That explains a lot." She turned to face him. "How did we get here so fast?"

"I had purchased a spell from a mage. Like I said, I was operating under a very tight timeline. There was no time for standard travel."

"So, we were standing in the parking lot of my store one minute, and then *poof,* we were here the next?"

"Something like that."

"Is this where you live?"

"No. I live in the States . . . well, at least part of the time. Not far from you. We are here for the meeting."

"Yes, the Big Meeting. You haven't gotten around to telling me yet what I am expected to do during this meeting. Give a little speech, maybe?"

"No. Nothing but stand by my side. It's not so much what you do or say that's important. It's just the fact that you're there. And that we've completed the Joining."

"We have . . . completed the Joining, haven't we? Or am I in for another surprise?"

"No. You're not in for another surprise. We have completed the Joining. However, we have yet to complete the Initiation, but as we discussed earlier, that will have to wait."

"The Initiation? I don't remember that."

His smile was one hundred percent evil. "You had an aversion to the flogger."

"Oh."

That put an immediate end to all conversation. Regan went back to staring down at the street, and Shadow went back to whatever kings did during their downtime. After a while, she heard him get up and leave the room. He closed the door between the sitting room and the bedroom.

Minutes later, her food arrived. She hated eating alone, but at least she was eating good. There wasn't a thing on the tray that wasn't delicious. No sooner had she polished off the pie there was a knock at the door. Shadow didn't come out of the bedroom to answer it, so she figured she was left to do the honors. She opened the door, finding a very pretty young woman standing at the door, dressed in a pair of snug jeans in a size Regan knew she'd never see again, and a plain black knit top. The young woman gave her a brilliant smile, a smile that vaguely resembled one belonging to a certain vampire. "Oh. My. God! You're her, aren't you? Quinby's wife? You're so beautiful." She rushed into the room, moving with an easy grace Regan knew she didn't possess, even after years of studying ballet at Metro Detroit's finest dance studios. Regan wasn't sure if she should admire her or hate her. "Where's that lughead brother of mine? I'm his sister, Tyra, though everyone calls me Ty." She offered her hand.

Regan shook it. "I'm Regan. But who's Quinby?"

"Oh." Ty's eyes widened with comprehension as she turned her head first one direction, then the other. "You probably know him by his nickname, Shadow. Where's he hiding?"

"Quinby, eh?" *It's no wonder he took a nickname.* "He's in there." Suppressing a giggle, Regan pointed at the closed bedroom door. Quinby was not the name for an all-powerful, dark and mysterious vampire king. She was going to have to rib him about that one of these days. "I'm guessing he's busy. He didn't come out when you knocked."

"That's okay. I was just going to congratulate him. It can wait. I'd rather talk to you anyway." She flopped onto the couch and eyed the remains of Regan's dinner. "Wow. Food. I can't remember the last time I saw food." She picked up the plate and sniffed, then screwed her pretty features into a disgusted scowl and set the dish back down. She thought filet mignon was disgusting? "You have to tell me what it's like being mortal. My brother keeps me locked up all the time now. Since Father died, he's had to worry about those silly rebels." She sighed. "I've never talked to a mortal. At least, not in-depth." Ty propped her chin on her fists, rested her elbows on her knees, and looked at Regan like she held the secrets to the universe. "What's it feel like to age?"

Regan's face went instantly red. She could feel the telltale sting on her cheeks.

This girl, who was probably over a century old, thought she was—gasp!—old!

"Sorry!" Ty said, catching Regan's wrist in her hand and squeezing. "Did I embarrass you? I'm so sorry! Oh man, Quinby—I mean Shadow—is gonna kill me. I didn't mean anything by it. I swear."

"I'm not exactly ancient. At least I was born in this century."

"No, no! I know you're not. It's just that our bodies age so much slower than a mortal's, and I've always wondered what it felt like. If you could actually tell the difference over the years. I still feel as young and energetic as I did when I was an infant."

"Can't say I feel that young," Regan admitted. "Especially tonight. It's been a very long night, but I still get around just fine." Yikes, she sounded like her grandmother did before she died.

"Oh! That's right. Mortals sleep at *night.*" Ty emphasized the last word like it was the strangest thing she'd ever heard. She jumped to her feet. "You must be tired. I should go."

Regan stood. "I am a little tired, but I wouldn't mind—"

"No, no. That's okay. I can come back later. It was really good meeting you, and . . ." She lunged forward and gave Regan a very enthusiastic hug and a watery smile. "I'm so happy for you. My brother's a real pain in the butt. So overprotective. But he's a good guy. I'm sure he'll make a great husband and father. See you later." She hurried out the door.

Regan watched her go. The room felt a little empty without the girl's chatty, energetic presence. Regan knew instantly that she liked her. They wouldn't end up friends, because Ty was quite obviously very young yet, but if given the chance, they could end up close. That made Regan even more anxious to get home. She didn't want Ty to get too attached to her. She could tell it might really hurt the girl.

Standing there, the effects of the night's excitement started to hit her.

It was like someone had poked a hole in her and drained all the energy out of her body. She felt as limp as a deflated balloon. She briefly considered going into the bedroom but quickly squashed that idea. Shadow was in there. She didn't want to talk. She didn't want to be tempted to do something else, either. If Shadow just happened to be in that cozy bed, naked, all bets were off. He might be a cheating louse when it came to following the rules of rituals, but he was a sexy louse.

Instead, she made herself comfy on the couch and thought about her plans after she'd gotten her divorce from Shadow and left all this vampire stuff behind.

It didn't take long for her to slip into a deep sleep filled with very happy dreams.

It really riled Shadow to see his bride sleeping on the couch, but he didn't haul her into the bedroom where she belonged, only because he had to leave. When he went out in the hallway, he found that two clan members had replaced his brothers at the door, as he'd expected.

Stefan and Rolf were probably down in their suite. He headed that way, not surprised to find he'd been right. Stefan ushered him into the room and shut the door behind him.

"So, that went well," Rolf said with a smirk. "Gotta say, our new queen has some—"

"Watch it!" Shadow barked.

"Real spunk," Rolf finished.

Stefan doubled over and laughed so hard his eyes watered. "What'd you have to do? Drug her? One minute she was jogging down the halls nude, the next, all was quiet," he said between guffaws.

"No, of course not. I don't need to drug a woman to convince her to remain in the same room with me."

The laughter ceased. Abruptly. "Really?" Stefan asked, looking far too surprised for Shadow's ego to take sitting down, so to speak.

"I'm not a hideous beast." He shoved Stefan aside and headed toward the bar. He needed a drink. Something strong. Something to take his mind off his troubles, if only for a little while. "Women do find me attractive." He gave Rolf a warning glower when he unsuccessfully tried to cover a chuckle with a cough.

His two brothers looked at each other with raised eyebrows.

"She has accepted her role as queen? Just like that?" Stefan asked. "I kind of expected her to put up more of a fight."

"Yeah. She's accepted her role . . . kind of." Shadow poured himself a bourbon and downed it in one gulp. He poured a second one before turning around.

"Kind of?" Rolf asked.

"There were a few conditions to her acceptance."

"Such as?" The left side of Rolf's face was twitching. It always did when he was trying not to smile.

That only soured Shadow's mood more.

He couldn't believe this. His ignorant brothers thought this was funny! It wasn't funny. It was serious. The future of their clan depended upon his ability to make that infuriating woman upstairs cooperate.

He emptied his glass again and refilled it. The liquid slid down his throat easily. Warmed his gullet. Facing the bar, he answered Rolf's question. "She would like me to woo her." This time, he poured himself a double. The laughter pealing through the room was like shards of glass being rubbed over his frayed nerves. He spun around. The bourbon sloshed out of the glass, wetting his hand, the front of his pants. "Enough!" He scooped up a handful of paper napkins and blotted what he could of the liquid from his clothes.

Both brothers clamped their lips closed. Their faces both turned a bright crimson.

"She's a woman," Shadow said, trying to reclaim his self-control. "Women need that sappy romancing stuff. And she's your queen. You should respect her needs."

"In other words, you need our help," Stefan suggested.

"No. I just need your cooperation." He balled up the damp napkins and dropped them into the trash can. "If she's going to stay our queen for more than twenty-four hours, I'm going to have to work fast."

"She's asked for a divorce? Already?" Rolf joined Shadow at the bar, took the bottle of bourbon from his hand, and poured what remained into a glass.

"She will be returning to her home after the meeting," Shadow said, glowering at Rolf.

"But she can't!" Stefan said.

"I already agreed." Shadow took the still-full glass out of Rolf's hand just before he'd lifted it to his mouth and emptied it into his own. "I have to keep my word. Besides, what does it matter whether she's in the same building with me or not?"

"It'll put her in danger," Stefan said soberly. "If the rebels find out she's alone, they can kill her. Then you will be crippled. There was one thing Father didn't tell us. I learned it from the intelligence we've collected from our enemies. Your marriage to her increases your power a thousandfold, but her death will decrease it even more. You'll be as helpless as a fucking newborn kitten."

"Have you verified this information?"

"Yes. I looked it up in *The Book of Shadows*."

That did complicate things. The thought of Regan being in danger, the rebels viciously attacking her, made his belly tie itself into a hard, painful knot. He wouldn't let anyone harm a hair on her head. If he had to, he'd sit on her front porch all night to make sure she was safe. "I'll just have to make sure she's never alone. She asked to be free to go home. I must keep my word."

"You're taking a great risk," Stefan said, pointing out the obvious.

Yes, he was taking a great risk. But he'd already given his word. He'd started their marriage wrong by basically bending the rules to his advantage. To top that with the added crime of reneging on their agreement, he knew Regan would never accept that. For pride alone, she would demand a quick divorce. And he would be alone again, without her.

Empty. Cold. Why did it have to feel so fucking good being Joined with her? So right? Why did it feel like if she divorced him, he'd never recover?

Had that mage cursed him?

He had to take the chance. He would just have to be prepared, assume the rebels would find out she'd gone home.

The bourbon had done nothing to make him feel better. His problems still weighed heavily on his shoulders. And the bitter taste of having been forced into the agreement with Regan in the first place still clung to the back of his throat. He'd wanted it to be simple. Simple was not how it was turning out.

More. More alcohol. He sifted through the remaining contents of the bar for something else. "If I don't meet her demands, she will get her divorce."

"Divorce?" Ty said, doing her usual bounding-hop entry into the room. "Who's getting divorced? Not you, Quinby."

"At least a divorce will spare you from the dangerous energy drain. Your power would simply return to its former state," Rolf said.

"Quinby's wife is adorable," Ty said. "A sweet, gentle lady. She wouldn't divorce him."

Sweet? Adorable he'd give her, but sweet? He wouldn't go that far.

"Better than making you weaker," Stefan added. "Then we can go back to Eudor. See if he can find you a new bride. Someone more . . . agreeable."

The knot in his belly tightened. "No. I will not give Regan a divorce."

His brothers responded with doleful shakes of their heads.

"Quinby, why's your wife divorcing you already?"

"She's not," Shadow snapped.

"Then why not just do what you always do? Make her co-operate?" Stefan suggested.

"Because I don't want to force her. I . . . want to do this her way. I owe her that."

Rolf sighed. "He's gotta charm her. Any ideas, Ty?"

"Oh! Sure!" Ty did a little happy hop. "I can help. Tons."

"You have so little faith in me. I don't need any help. I know how to romance a woman. It's easy. They are simple creatures. A few flowers, some candy, jewelry. She'll be putty in my hands before the new moon."

"I hope so." Rolf didn't look any more confident in his abilities than he had moments before.

He'd show his doubting brother.

"If not, the rebels will take control. You know what that means." Stefan looked more worried than skeptical.

"I realize that. Don't worry. I have a plan"—(a lie)—"I have no intention of losing. Regan is the Chosen. She will be my queen for eternity. You will see. Our people will be safe. As safe as my powers allow."

"I can help, Quinby," Ty repeated.

He gave her a grateful pat on the shoulder. "Thanks, but no thanks. I'll handle this on my own."

He left his faithless siblings to make plans.

The clan meeting would be nowhere near the challenge romancing his wife would be. He'd have to work smart and fast. The longer she was in her home, alone, the greater her risk.

The loss of his kingdom, and possibly his life, would be nothing to the pain of losing his bride.

5

Regan returned home to no air-conditioning (gah!), no power (gahhh!), one pissed-off cat who'd decided to let out her hostilities on the living room curtains (gahhhhh!), and three dead orchids (gahhhhhh!). So far, not the happy homecoming she was hoping for.

But she wasn't ready to call her life over, grab a carton of Bear Claw ice cream from the corner store, drag out her favorite Nora Roberts series, and eat and read herself into a coma. Thanks to the Controlling One, she had a little money in her pocket—not a lot.

She did not accept charity.

A quick phone call was all that was needed. She'd paid her light bill on time. There was no reason for her power to be out. Maybe it wasn't just her house? Maybe it was a bigger power outage? She poked her head out the front door—uck, it felt like an oven out there—and checked her neighbor's porch light. Mrs. Amstadt left her light on day and night.

What do you know? It was on.

"Poop!" She pulled her cotton tank top, stuck to her skin

with sweat, away from her tummy and flipped it up so that only her bra was covered. She couldn't remember the last time she'd been in a place with no air. It was positively inhumane to live like this. How did people not collapse from heat exhaustion?

She peeled the hair off her neck and held the phone to her ear.

Uh-oh. No phone, either.

What was going on? She'd paid the phone bill too. Weeks early, as usual. Hadn't any of them received her checks? She needed answers. She needed an artificially processed, humidity-controlled interior. She was melting.

Cell phone.

She had to admit, she wasn't the best at keeping track of her cell. Normally when she misplaced it, she used her land line to call it and then followed the sound of electronically produced Nachtmusik until she'd located it. That wasn't an option today.

So, instead, she wasted who knew how long digging around her purses, pockets, and drawers looking for the stupid thing. When she found it, some untold hours later—or so it seemed—she discovered that it, too, had been shut off.

Which meant she'd have to go out *there,* into the sunny, sweltering heat, to find a phone. She gathered up the most recent bills for each utility company, returned her tank top to its proper position, and headed outside.

If she'd thought the interior of her house was hot, the hellish heat outside made it feel like heaven. She hurried next door, hoping Mrs. Amstadt was home. She knew the elderly woman didn't go out very often. Chances were good she'd be there.

She banged hard on the front door. Mrs. Amstadt was partially deaf in one ear, completely deaf in the other. Her savior answered on the second round of knocks, gave Regan a toothless grin—she'd obviously forgotten to put her teeth in—and shooed her inside.

It had to be sixty degrees inside. Absolutely orgasmic. She

stood in the foyer, her eyes closed, and let the cool air seep into her skin.

"Are you all right, dear?" Mrs. Amstadt asked as she closed the front door.

"Yes. Fine. Just hot. I was hoping I could use your phone. It seems mine isn't working."

"Sure. This way." She led Regan to the kitchen and pointed at an ancient 1970s harvest-gold number with a rotary dial. People still used those?

Regan thanked her neighbor profusely, got comfy on a steel and vinyl chair, and made her first call. She quickly learned that utility company customer service representatives tended to get hostile when large sums of money were owed and checks for payment had bounced repeatedly. Obviously, her money problems had started long before she'd become aware of them.

She learned something else while talking to Ms. Bitchy, collection agent for the power company. She wasn't going to get her electricity turned back on with a phone call and a promise of payment. Cold hard cash was the only language they were going to understand.

Suddenly the three hundred dollars Shadow had given her seemed like a pittance. She would only have enough money to get the electric turned on and pick up a few groceries.

She ended the call, thanked Mrs. Amstadt for the use of her phone, accepted a small baggie of home-baked cookies, and headed home. Her car's tank was almost empty, but she figured she had enough to get her to the power company's office a few miles away. She spent the afternoon taking care of errands. The power company promised to have her service back on by noon the next day—they sure were slow to turn service back on! She bought some nonperishable goodies to eat and headed home several hours later. She was starving, anxious to dig into a can of Spaghetti O's for dinner by the time she'd pulled into the driveway. However, her appetite did a Houdini and vanished when she got up to the front door and discovered someone had been in her house.

The door was unlocked. She always locked her door. Unless . . . could she have been so distracted about the electric company that she'd forgotten? She thought about going back to Mrs. Amstadt's house and calling the cops. That was the logical thing to do. That was what she always told the stupid heroines in those slasher movies to do when they found an unlocked door or open window.

So, why did she feel like she was being silly for even considering it?

She got halfway across the front yard before she decided against calling the police. She wouldn't walk inside, just push open the door, make a whole lot of noise and wait, see if anyone came dashing out. This was a very safe neighborhood, among the top twenty safest cities in the United States. What was the likelihood that there was a felon in her house? A bazillion to one.

Feeling a little better, she ran back across to her house, pushed open the front door, and hollered, "Honey, I'm home! What's for dinner!" and "Here, Killer! Come get this nice, juicy steak I brought you." Then she held her breath and poked her head through the doorway.

The living room looked like it always did—tidy, with her book collection neatly displayed in alphabetic order. The French doors leading to the deck were intact. The curtains still drawn. She heard no sounds of startled thieves dashing for the nearest exit.

"Hello!" she yelled louder. "Is there anyone here? Answer me, or I'll be forced to shoot. I have a gun." She stepped inside the door but didn't move beyond the small tiled area that served as a foyer. She stomped her feet, opened and closed the bifold closet door, which made an awful scraping noise. She checked the dining room. It looked normal too. The bedrooms. Bathroom. Nothing had been touched.

"Since when did I become so paranoid?" *Since you were ac-*

costed in a creepy bondage store by a vampire, that's when. She headed for the kitchen to put her stuff away.

As she rounded the corner from the dining room into the kitchen, she started sneezing. Once, twice, three times. Her eyes blurred. "What the heck?" She blinked away the tears and walked into the kitchen and halted abruptly.

There was a huge vase of flowers sitting on her kitchen counter.

"Ahhhhh!" she screamed. Someone had been in her house! Scared witless, she dropped the bags of groceries at her feet and made a dash for the nearest exit, on the opposite end of the small kitchen. She wrestled with the locks, threw open the door, and ran outside. She didn't stop until she got to her car.

It was blistering hot inside the car. And the adrenaline rushing through her system was making her tremble and sweat. Before a minute had gone by, she felt like she was going to pass out.

Since she had no phone or electricity, she decided to play it safe. She made a repeat visit to her neighbor's house and called the police. They arrived by the droves—must've been a slow day for crime—lights flashing, within minutes. She explained the situation, and at least a half-dozen of her city's finest went inside to check for intruders.

They came out a short time later empty-handed, all except one, that is. He carried the card from the offending vase of flowers. "Did you know the name on the card, miss?" he asked, making notes in his little spiral notebook.

"I . . . I didn't read it. The point is, it was on my kitchen counter. Which means someone had to let themselves into my house to leave it there."

He handed it to her.

She opened the tiny envelope and swore. "Yes. I know who this is, but he has no business—"

He held out his hand in a silent request to see the card. "Does . . . your husband . . . have a key to your home, miss?"

"No. I mean, not that I was aware of. I know that sounds weird, but it's a long story."

The officer flipped his little notebook shut, gave her a polite shake of the head, and radioed his fellow officers, letting them know the mystery had been solved.

She felt about two inches high.

When she saw Shadow, she'd give him an earful! Once again, he'd acted without permission. Entered her home. Her sanctuary. How dare he! Oh, she was steamed!

She went back inside, picked up the offending bouquet, and, sneezing nonstop, marched over to Mrs. Amstadt's house and presented it to her. Then, blinking at the tears streaming from her eyes and rolling down her cheeks, she went back home and fought her way into the can of Spaghetti O's. Living without an electric can opener was just another in a long list of inconveniences she'd have to endure until that magic hour tomorrow—twelve noon.

She had polished off the last cold little meatball (when she was a kid she'd always saved those for last, some habits were hard to break) when she heard him open the front door.

The locked front door.

She stood up, lobbed the empty can into the trash, set the spoon in the sink, squared her shoulders, and headed toward the front door. Shadow the Sneaky would know in no uncertain terms what she thought of him letting himself into her home. Husband or not, he had to be invited like everyone else. The marriage thing was only a formality. A formality she would make sure was temporary.

There was no way she could remain married to this man.

"How dare you!" she said the minute she caught sight of him. He stood in the middle of her living room, holding a giant red foiled box of chocolates.

He thrust the box at her, a confused look on his face. "You don't like candy? I bought the good kind."

She glanced down at the box. Cordial cherries. She loved them, but they loved her hips even more. They pretty much took up permanent residence there the minute she swallowed a piece. "I'm not talking about the candy. I'm talking about you letting yourself into my house. My house. Emphasis on *my*. Not your house. Not even our house. My house. What made you think you had any right?"

He shrugged. "The front door was unlocked, and I thought I'd surprise you. Thought it would be romantic—"

"You liar! I locked that door. And what about earlier this afternoon? You let yourself in this afternoon too."

"What about this afternoon? I didn't come here this afternoon. I can't go out into the sunlight. Remember? I go up like a pile of gasoline-soaked rags. What happened?" He looked worried. So worried, in fact, that she started feeling a little woozy. He set the candy down and wrapped a hand around her wrist. His fingers tightened so much it hurt. "What happened?" he repeated.

"You're hurting me!"

He loosened his grip. "Sorry." He pulled her toward the couch and more or less forced her to sit. "Tell me."

"What's wrong? Why are you reacting like this? It was just a bouquet of flowers. From you." Suddenly, it dawned on her why he might be so concerned. "You didn't send a bouquet?"

"No."

Suddenly, it felt like all the oxygen had been sucked from the room. "Oh."

"Where is it?"

"I gave it to my next-door neighbor." She jumped to her feet and headed for the front door. "Why would someone else send me flowers but sign the card from you?"

"Lots of reasons." He pushed past her, peered through the

peephole like he expected someone to be standing on the front porch, then slowly pulled open the door.

This time it was she who was grabbing at wrists and yanking. "Wanna tell me what's going on? You're acting like you expect the SWAT team to descend from the roof on ropes or something. What gives? Do I need to be worried?"

He gave her a momentary glance, then pushed open the screen door and stepped out onto the porch. "No. Nothing to be worried about. It's probably just a . . . misunderstanding or something."

"Misunderstanding? If you didn't send those flowers, who did?"

"That's the question I'm determined to find the answer to. Which neighbor?"

"Over there. Mrs. Amstadt." She headed out onto the porch, but he blocked her from going any farther.

"You stay here. I'll go."

"I have to if you want those flowers. Mrs. Amstadt isn't going to answer the door if she sees you. It's after seven. That's late to her. And you're a hulking . . ."

He shot her a questioning glance.

"You have to admit you're a pretty large man. Scary, even. She's like ninety. She'll call the police."

The right side of his mouth twitched. He grumbled something, then nodded. "Fine. But I'll go first."

"We're only walking across the front lawn. I don't think we'll run across any land mines."

"Humor me."

She heaved an exaggerated sigh, making sure he heard it. Then she motioned for him to proceed to cross the big, bad, dangerous front yard. "I've been living alone a long time. Besides, the crime rate in this city is like nil. I think the last crime wave we had here was in the seventies when a couple kids went on a shoplifting spree. They stole Dum Dum suckers like there was no tomorrow." They arrived on her neighbor's front stoop safely without having to dodge a single bullet or grenade. "See? I told you."

He stepped to one side so she could reach the front door. "Just trying to make sure you're safe."

"Safe from whom? The bad guy who sent me flowers? Wow. Now there's an inventive way to off someone. Maybe he knew I was allergic and decided he'd make me sneeze to death. Yeah, that must be it." She chuckled. This guy had obviously been dealing with a lot of death threats, being King of the Undead or whatever he was called. He was taking this way too seriously. "Maybe it was someone in your clan?" she suggested as they waited for her neighbor to answer the door.

"None of them can go outside in the sunlight."

"Then they hired a delivery service to bring the flowers. There is such a thing, you know. Delivery men. Drive trucks. Wear uniforms. Carry packages."

"I just want to make sure."

Finally, Mrs. Amstadt answered the door. In her robe and slippers. What hair still remained on her head was wound round a few rollers on the top of her skull. She eyed Shadow and frowned. "What's the matter, Regan? More trouble?"

"I was wondering if I could show my friend here the flowers I gave you earlier. He seems to think they might be . . ." She hesitated, searching for an excuse to get the flowers back.

"Infested with bugs," Shadow finished for her.

"He's a florist," Regan explained, deciding to play along. His idea had been brilliant. If there was one thing Mrs. Amstadt hated, it was insects. No creature with more than four legs survived within a hundred yards of Mrs. Amstadt's house. She bombed, sprayed, and powered the little suckers to death, no matter what species they were.

Mrs. Amstadt gave him another cautious glance. "A florist? Him?"

"Yes. It does seem like with his . . . er . . . like he'd be more suited to some other line of work, doesn't it?" Regan felt her face heating.

Mrs. Amstadt smiled, revealing her toothless gums. "Yes, it does." She held up a single bent finger, shut the door.

"A florist?" Shadow asked, turning to give her an injured look.

"It was the best I could come up with." She swallowed a giggle and patted his back. It felt like carved stone sheathed in cotton. "Don't worry. I'd say Mrs. Amstadt finds you a most manly man."

"It's not Mrs. Amstadt I'm trying to impress." He gave Regan one of his trademark smoldering gazes. The kind that made her all wet and warm inside. Like molten marshmallows.

"Here you are," Mrs. Amstadt said, opening the door and shoving the vase full of flowers at her. "I don't want insects in my house. Thank you anyway. It was a sweet thought."

"I'm sorry for bothering you so late," Regan said, handing the vase to Shadow. She could feel a sneezing fit coming on. It was like storm clouds whirling around in her sinuses. The inside of her nostrils started to burn. She shoved Shadow, hard, then let loose with the first of about twenty sneezes in a row.

One day she figured she'd sneeze her brains out. Maybe that supposed killer was on to something after all.

Shadow finally got the clue and started toward her house. Mrs. Amstadt said good night and closed the door. Regan waved and followed Shadow at a safe distance.

"Can you open the garage door?" Shadow asked once they were on her lawn.

"Doh," Regan said, pinching her nose to head off another attack. "Dot frob outside." She took a chance and released her nose when he looked at her like she'd sprouted a second head. "I'm trying not to sneeze. No, I can't open the door. The garage door opener is electric."

"And that's a problem?"

"It is when you don't have any electricity."

His face scrunched up into an expression she didn't care to put a name to.

"You can go through the house." She shooed him through the front door.

He stopped in the pass way between the kitchen and living room. "Do you have a flashlight?"

She frowned, hanging back on the other end of the room. "Uh. I might. But it won't do us much good. Forgot to buy some batteries when I was out shopping, and since I haven't used the flashlight in like five years, I guarantee they're dead. I do have some lovely candles." She headed for the bookshelf where she had a lighter tucked away. She lit a taper and held it at arm's length for him. "Here you go."

"I can't search properly by candlelight."

"Why not? Didn't Sherlock Holmes? He lived way back in the good ole days, didn't he?"

"Not that long ago."

"What do you need to search those stinky things for anyway? Just throw them away." She took the bouquet in one hand, pinched her nose with the other, and carried them into the kitchen. She tossed them in the trash, tied up the bag, and, with Shadow at her heels, put it out in the garage, along with all the other garbage. "See? Done." She brushed her hands together, then rested them on her hips. "Why make things so complicated?"

"I suppose it's okay there. For now. Where is the card?" he asked, staring at the black plastic bag.

"Inside." She opened the connecting door and stepped back into the kitchen.

He followed her, and she couldn't help being aware of him behind her, especially when he brushed ever so softly against her buttocks as she stepped through the doorway. "Let me see it. Maybe I'll recognize the handwriting."

"Now, that sounds like a brilliant idea. Why didn't you think of that in the first place?"

"I wanted to make sure nothing would happen to your neighbor."

Talk about being overprotective. At least he wasn't just overprotective of her. He was that way with strangers, even. "I still don't see what you're so worried about. They're just flowers. They're not some kind of terrorist weapon. They're not going to blow up. What did you think would happen to her?" She plucked the card from the counter and handed it to him.

"Hard saying." His eyebrows marched to the center of his forehead as he sat at the kitchen table to read all five words on the card.

Until tonight. Your husband, Shadow.

She kind of leaned into him, reading the message over a wide shoulder. A few of her more sensitive parts urged her to get a little closer. She tried to ignore them. Really. "Isn't anything exactly threatening about that message, is there?"

"I don't recognize the handwriting."

It sounded like he needed some comforting. He was really worried about this, poor thing. Made her realize how difficult it must be for him, being a king of a nation spread all over the world, rebels threatening his life constantly. She couldn't imagine having to live in constant fear, always having to watch her back. "I thought you said being married kept you safe from those rebellious clan members of yours?" She rested just one hand on his shoulder. The happy parts of her body started chanting for more.

"It does."

"Then you have nothing to worry about. You're safe. I'm safe. No one is going to come after me. Why would they? I'm no threat to anybody. There's got to be a logical explanation. When you figure it out, you're going to laugh yourself silly. I figure it was one of your clan members, trying to help you out. Who else knows about our little agreement? Besides you and me?" The other shoulder looked lonely. She put her hand on it so it wouldn't feel neglected. While they were there, her hands decided they might as well give him a shoulder rub. His muscles looked very hard . . . no, tense. Yes, tense. Not hard and yummy and oh so defined.

"Only my brothers."

"There you go. I'm sure if you ask them, they'll tell you they sent the flowers."

"But why would they do that? They know I don't need any help."

She stared at the top of his head and tried not to laugh.

He was supposed to be there romancing her, and what was he doing? Sitting at her kitchen table getting a shoulder rub.

Where was the romance? The jewels? The sappy poems? The candlelit dinners? The expensive gifts she could sell on eBay? A box of candy didn't cut it in her book.

"When you figure out who it is, would you kindly let them know that I'm allergic?"

"Yeah. Sure." He sounded a million miles away, and she found herself tempted to do something crazy to pull him back into the here and now.

Like strip naked and dance in front of him.

That would be fun, lots and lots of fun. But something was bothering her. It was the way she felt right then, looking at him, watching the worry pull his mouth into a narrow line and dim the sparkle in his eyes. She felt bad for him. And that was not a good sign. Feeling bad for a man involved emotion, caring. And in her experience, caring led to other stuff. Bad stuff that she didn't need right now. Stuff like falling in love and heartache and commitment to men who were no good for her. So, in the interest of maintaining her freedom, she had to stick with the no-caring rule.

This was so not going to be easy.

Why, oh, why couldn't she just enjoy sex with this one, appreciate it as an end in itself, and leave her emotions out of things? Emotions were bad, bad, bad.

With Rick the Musician, it had led to six months of misery when he dumped her for some bimbo with big boobs. Musicians had been in the top three of her not-to-fall-in-love-with list. But she'd taken a chance with him anyway and let herself fall for him.

With Gabe the Psychiatrist, it had led to months of therapy for clinical depression when she learned he couldn't go through with their planned wedding—because he was already married and his wife was pregnant. Married men were definitely at the pinnacle of her not-to-fall-in-love-with list.

And most recently, with Jeff the Entrepreneur, it had led to the loss of her best friend, in addition to a broken heart, when he dumped her for Dana. Adding insult to injury, Jeff filled Dana's head with a bunch of lies about Regan and then whisked her away to Florida to start a new life and a new business selling diapers online. Rumor had it they'd been married for about six months now and were expecting to become clients of their own company before Christmas.

Regan had always known entrepreneurs were risk-takers; it was what they did for a living. But Jeff had been so convincing and the sex had been oh so good.

Three unsuitable men. Three disastrous relationships, all begun with the intention of keeping things casual. Until she'd foolishly let herself fall for them. She couldn't afford to let her heart lead her astray a fourth time. It would be plain stupid. If there was one thing she wasn't—or so she liked to believe—it was stupid.

No emotions. That was her final answer.

Too bad her heart wasn't listening. It was going to be a long month!

She dropped her hands and took a giant step backward. What had she been thinking?

Playing with fire. That's what it was. If she didn't quit now, she knew for a fact she'd get burned. Big time.

6

"Oh." Regan sighed. "So much to do, so little time to do it all." She hustled around the other side of the kitchen peninsula to put some space between them. Glanced over her shoulder as she ran the water in the sink. There were no dirty dishes to wash. No food to prepare. No mess to clean. But she wasn't about to tell him that. She needed to act busy, to inspire him to leave. "So, now that you've secured the safety of both me and my neighbor, when does the romancing begin? Tomorrow night, maybe? Do you need to call it a night, do some planning, perhaps?"

Shadow gave her a blank stare. "Begin? It already has."

Clearly, when it came to romance, they were not on the same page. That had to be a good thing. "Oh, that's right. You brought candy. I'm sorry."

"Well . . . yeah."

She heard the chair scrape on the tile as he scooted it out to stand. Busy, busy, busy. She had to get busy. She threw open a cupboard and started rearranging the cans of prepared pasta. Should she arrange by sauce type or noodle?

"And . . . don't you think a man looking out for your safety is romantic?" he asked from much closer.

Realization dawned. "Oh! So that's why you were all double-oh-seven. You were trying to impress me with your brawn and spy-assessing skills." She decided the sauce-type system of organizing wasn't working, since there were only two types of sauce—with meat and without—and started rearranging the cans according to noodle. Just because . . . because she couldn't help it. She glanced over her shoulder again to see how close he was.

Not more than three feet away. He was leaning back against the counter. His thick arms crossed over his chest. That position made them appear even bigger.

His face brightened. He nodded. "Yeah. That was it. I figure all women love James Bond. Sexy, smart, strong."

She turned around and forced herself to shove the image of him standing there looking so incredibly sweet from her mind. Impersonal. Make small talk. Yes, that's it. No deep talk. No serious talk. No revealing-of-dark-secrets talk. "I have enjoyed my fair share of Bond films, though I'm not sold on Daniel Craig as the new Bond. I like my heroes a little prettier."

"That doesn't say much for me." He sounded injured.

Men. Why was it they all got defensive when the word *pretty* was used in reference to their looks? "It's not an insult to say a man's pretty, you know. There are lots of pretty men in the movies. But I don't think they're anything less than manly men."

"I'm not pretty."

She couldn't help laughing. The male pride was so delicate, even housed in two hundred and whatever pounds of lean muscle. She found Shadow's features extremely attractive. They were perfectly proportioned. Striking eyes with thick eyelashes. Long, narrow nose. Perfect lips. Chiseled cheekbones. The perfect-shaped jaw—neither too square nor too soft. The perfect package.

Yes, she'd say Shadow was movie material. He was big. Really built. Like the Rock. But in his face, he had a little resemblance to Ashton Kutcher. She adored Ashton.

Adored? What was she thinking? Adoration of any form was dangerous, even when sort of directed toward another man.

She cleared her throat, slammed the cupboard door, and headed for the one where she stored the glasses. "Something to drink before you head home?"

"No, thanks. Are you hungry?" he asked. Even though she'd stepped a few feet farther from him, he sounded closer. He was following her.

She inched farther down, finding herself at a dead end and standing in front of the cupboards that held the stuff she rarely used. Baking supplies. Cookbooks. "Nope. I had a whole can of prepared pasta product just before you arrived. I'm good. Really. No reason to hang around tonight. No siree."

"Cold prepared pasta does not qualify as a meal. I'll buy you some dinner. Where's your phone?"

"Over there." Seeing a way to get him to walk away, she pointed at the cordless sitting on the far end of the counter. "But it doesn't work, so you're out of luck. Can't order anything. Oh well. Maybe next time." It had been a stupid idea to trap herself inside her kitchen. There was only one way out.

"Batteries?"

"Yeah. That . . ."

He picked it up and pushed the button. "Funny. You have power but no dial tone."

She cringed. "Yeah, well, that might be because the service was turned off."

He frowned. "You must have a telephone. It isn't safe for you to stay here alone without one."

"I'll get it turned on as soon as I sell some stuff and get some cash." She winced, knowing what she'd just opened the door to—wrong door to open!—and tried to hurry past him before he handed her any money. If only she could get him out the front door . . .

Sure enough, he caught her wrist, stuffed his free hand in his pocket, and pulled out a money clip full of bills. "How much do you need?"

"I'm not taking your money. No." Oh God! He was being nice to her. Nice was not allowed. She didn't want to like him. She didn't want to rely on him. She didn't want to remain married to him. She tried to jerk her hand free, but he was holding on tighter than a steel trap.

He pried open her fingers and shoved the whole wad into her hand. "I insist. You can't stay here without a phone. It's not safe. Use the rest of the money to buy food. Pay bills. Do whatever. But make sure you have a phone."

"No." She tried to hand the money back, but he wouldn't take it. Frustrated, she slapped it on the counter, wrenched her hand free of his grip, and pushed past him. "I told you, I don't accept charity."

"My money is not charity! You're my wife. And I need to know you're safe."

"I'm your wife in name only. Quit pretending it's more than a temporary thing. We both know it isn't going to last, so you don't have to be nice to me. I don't want to like you. No emotions. No complications. You and me." She motioned between them. "We're not good together. We clash. You're stubborn as hell, and I'm not any better. Don't you see it? Forget about the whole vampire thing—which I don't even know how to handle. If we decided to make this thing permanent, we'd both be miserable. We'd fight constantly."

"No, I don't see it. What I see is a woman who foolishly refuses to let anyone help her." He caught her upper arms in his fists and held them so tightly his fingertips dug in.

"And I see a man who tries to bully me. Stop it! And stop

hurting me," she shouted. "The manhandling isn't convincing me of anything, outside of the fact that I need to get that divorce as soon as possible."

Well, if that wasn't a stupid thing to do. He was finally starting to scare her off, and she'd gone and told him what he was doing wrong so he could stop. Duh!

"I'm sorry." He released her and looked at her with pleading, doleful eyes that reminded her of Eeyore, the basset hound she had as a kid. "I . . . I don't mean to hurt you. I swear. I'm just . . ." He combed his fingers through his hair. "I'm worried."

"Back to that worrying thing again? Stop it. I've managed to take care of myself for over twenty years now. My folks died a long time ago, leaving me to pretty much deal with life on my own. I'm a lot stronger than I look."

"I'm sorry about your family," he said softly.

"It was a long time ago." She picked up the cash and set it in front of him on the counter. "I refuse to use this. You can leave it here, but it'll sit on my counter untouched. I have a plan, and I have a whole closet of stuff that should get me a few thousand in the next few days."

He shook his head but picked up the money and put it back in his pocket.

Score one for the girl!

"How will you pay your bills?" he grumbled. "You need to pay them now. Not two, three, or more days from now."

"I'll pay the phone bill with the first purchase at the store. I swear."

"Okay." He sighed, looking seriously defeated. She almost felt sorry for him. That made her anxious to shove him out the front door again.

"Are we through arguing in circles, then?"

"Yes."

"Good." She rounded him so he was standing between her

and the door and gave him a sound push toward it. "It's been a real pleasure, but I need to turn in early tonight. I've got a big day at the store tomorrow—"

He dug in his heels, refused to budge, which made her hate the fact that she was like five foot two and one hundred twenty pounds dripping wet. "But how about dinner? I didn't buy dinner."

"I swear I'm fine. I ate."

This time his sigh didn't sound quite so heavy, and his expression didn't look quite so miserable. In fact, a little bit of a smile pulled at the corners of his mouth. "You're not making this easy for me."

"Was I supposed to? I guess I missed that rule." She gave him another push.

"Tonight's not going anything like I'd planned."

Again, she almost felt sorry for him. For some crazy reason, he seemed to really want to impress her. She didn't get it, knowing he entered their marriage not wanting a wife. Was there something more to the divorce thing? A complication he wasn't telling her? Because he was acting like a guy who did not want a divorce.

And while he'd told her he wanted to remain married to her, she hadn't bought it. They'd done that mind-meld thing. And so he did have an advantage over any other man who had known her for little more than twenty-four hours. He knew her. Inside and out.

She would've thought that would make him more inclined to cooperate with the divorce, not less. Even she—despite the postsex muddled brain disease—could see they were not a couple destined to be happily-ever-after.

What the heck?

"You won't let me feed you. Won't eat the candy I brought. What else? What could I do to impress you?"

"You could help me clean that disgusting pit of a store," she quipped, figuring he'd snub that idea and head home before she forced him to cooperate. Surely Shadow, King of the Undead did not scrub floors.

"Excellent!" He grabbed her hand, and before she could explain she had been joking, he had her out in his car (a Maybach!). Call her a meanie, but as she rode in his very lux car, she decided she'd let him help her get the cruddy store cleaned up. After last night, the thought of being there all alone kind of creeped her out. And there was so much work to do that the extra set of hands would be welcome. She'd keep him so busy he couldn't talk. Yes, it could still remain impersonal. Like having hired help.

When they arrived at the store, he went right to work, dragging around heavy racks full of clothes. The man had, like, Superman strength. She had to merely make a peep and he was at her side.

She could seriously get used to this.

It seemed there was one situation under which they did get along—when they were busy at work. Not a single argument arose in the several hours that they sorted, scrubbed, and rearranged. Even more rewarding, working together, they were able to accomplish a lot. By the time Regan was ready to call it a night, the store looked two hundred percent better, good enough for her to open it the next day.

Exhausted, sore, and dusty, she let Shadow buy her a bag of tacos at the drive-through of a fast-food restaurant. They went back to her place, and she munched and slurped her way through a half-dozen tacos (yes, she ate six. She'd have to fast for a week to compensate) and an oversized fountain drink. By the time she'd polished off her last, Shadow had her laughing.

He really was a bizarre man. While he had that surly, bossy side, there was more to him. A fun-loving side that popped out every now and then. It made her wonder what he'd been like before becoming king.

Had the responsibility of a kingdom in turmoil taken all the joy out of his life? If peace did return to his people, would he revert back to this man—the one she'd seen at the store, dancing with the broom and singing absolutely awful renditions of Air Supply tunes?

One thing was certain—he had no issues with making a complete fool of himself. That had been a wonderful surprise. She had a soft spot for men who could act the fool.

Egad! Were his attempts at wooing working?

By three o'clock in the morning, she was seriously in trouble. He was teasing and joking his way right into her panties, and her heart. Sexy double-talk, intentional twisting of her words, innuendo. Even the most innocent of phrases, like "Bring it over here," held a whole new meaning by the end of the night.

She quickly learned that just about anything she said could be twisted around to mean something completely naughty . . . and hilarious. Before long, she started saying things, expecting him to turn them around.

It should have come as no surprise when he kissed her. But it did, mid-belly-busting guffaw. It damn near knocked her to her knees. If Shadow hadn't wrapped his arms around her and dragged her against him, she would've been lying on the floor like a jellyfish out of water. A puddle of molten goo.

She had to give her brain credit. It managed to maintain status quo for a few seconds after their mouths made contact. Thoughts like, *This is not a good idea in your current frame of mind; No, no, bad, Regan, bad!* and *You need to get this man out of your house,* whipped around in her skull like whirling leaves in a maelstrom. But the second his tongue traced the seam of her mouth, the gears in her brain locked up and all thought ceased.

A flurry of sensations swirled round and round inside her body. His amazing taste. The way his hard body felt pressed against her not-so-hard one. The growing ache building inside as the kiss went on and on. His tongue mated with hers, stroking, teasing. He alternated between pressing soft, erotic kisses over her lips and chin and invading her mouth with a tongue that demanded entry, didn't ask for it.

The result was near total meltdown. Three Mile Island had nothing on her.

Now quite overwhelmed in the heat coursing through her body, she lifted her hands to his shoulders, dug her nails into the cotton cloth covering them, and rubbed her heated pussy against his hip.

This felt so right, his hands on her hips as she rocked back and forth against him. His mouth crushing hers. His tongue twisting and wrestling with her tongue until it submitted. She didn't let out a peep when he swept her into his arms and carried her toward the bedroom. She didn't say a word when he shucked his shirt. The sight of his bare torso was awe-inspiring. She didn't even object when he helped her out of her dusty, dirty shirt as well.

His weight felt oh so delightful resting on top of her when he pushed her back onto the bed. His hips fit between her thighs just perfectly. She was in heaven!

While simultaneously kissing her to the stars and beyond, he caught her wrists in his hands and lifted them up over her head, pinning them against the mattress. One hand still securing her arms, he let the other one loose to do some wandering. It started at her neck, tracing a tickly line down to her collarbone with a fingertip. His mouth followed. Tongue and teeth. Lips. He kissed, nipped, and licked up a fierce case of goose bumps before venturing lower. Anxious for more—more of anything, kisses, touches, just more—she squirmed and moaned. Her insides clenched and unclenched in some kind of primitive rhythm, sending ripples of heat through her body.

She ached to feel his thick rod inside. To be filled completely. Her pants were still on. She wanted them off. Now. Her panties were wet, the crotch clinging to her slick pussy.

"Shadow," she whispered. She twisted her wrist, trying to break free.

"No, be still. Give me command of your body. Submit to me. I know you need to."

His words were like a gust of wind, fanning the flames stirring in her body. Her cheeks warmed. Her chest. She couldn't wait another second to feel him inside her. "Shadow."

He pressed an index finger to her lips and gazed into her eyes. "I know your secrets, Regan. They flit through my brain like caged birds. I long to set them free, to make your most secret fantasies come true."

She was trembling now. All over. Her stomach was clenched into a tight knot. Her thigh muscles too. She wrapped her legs around his waist and rocked her hips, tried to rub away the ache. It wouldn't ease. Not a notch. It only grew more and more urgent.

"Say the word, Regan." He lowered his head. His lips barely touched hers. Soft. Fleeting. He whispered against her mouth. His words seemed to slip down her throat and swirl inside her mind. "Speak the word that is even now echoing through your head, and I will give you your reward."

Word in her head? What word?

How she hungered for the reward! She stopped still, her mouth almost but not quite touching his. Closed her eyes and listened to the thoughts drifting in and out of her mind.

What word?

"That's it, my sweet. What is it your spirit is trying to tell you? What is it you ache for more than anything?"

That's easy. A big, long, hard one.

"Concentrate." He pushed a lace bra cup aside and teased the very tip of her nipple with a fingertip.

She dragged in a ragged breath.

"I know you're ready. I can feel it. Say the word."

She was so confused! Ready for sex? Yes, she was definitely ready for that. There wasn't a part of her body that wasn't geared up for the big event. But what word was he looking for? "Please?"

"No. I know it's there. Listen closely. Listen to your spirit. What is it telling you?" He used both hands to press her wrists firmly against the mattress, and it was then, as he held her, his legs pinning her hips, her arms secured overhead, at his mercy, in complete submission that she knew what words she'd been searching for.

"Master." It tasted sweet as it slid off her tongue.

"Yes. Oh yes." He released her wrists and pulled off her pants, her panties. "Part your legs for me. Show me how hot you are," he said as he grappled with his own clothes. His gaze was fierce and scalding as it raked over her burning flesh. It was almost too much to watch. Too intense. She wanted to close her eyes. Needed to. Her eyelids were too heavy.

"Keep them open." He pushed her knees apart and settled between them. He gripped his cock in his fist and gave it one, two, three pumps before teasing her slit with its head. "Don't hide from it. From me. Keep your eyes open."

It was so hard to do! She felt like he was delving into her mind, her very soul. Vulnerable. Yet she fought the urge for him. She didn't understand it, but she felt like she needed to. Like if she didn't, she'd somehow miss out on something special.

He entered her with a slow, deliciously sensual thrust. A fraction of an inch at a time. She held her breath until he'd filled her completely. And only then was she able to pull in a raspy breath.

He remained still for a few racing heartbeats. Her inner muscles tightened around him, increasing her pleasure until it was beyond words. She felt her eyelids shuttering.

"Open," he whispered.

She nodded and lifted her gaze to his eyes. A blade of heat shot through her system, softening when it reached the point of their joining. Her lips parted as a moan slipped up her throat, but for some reason the sound remained trapped inside.

Just as slowly as he entered her, he withdrew, until the very tip of his cock rested against her vulva. She whimpered. It was agony.

"Please, Shadow."

He reentered her with a swifter thrust. It took her by surprise but delighted her at the same time. With his swift entry came a surprised squeal from her lips. She tipped her hips to meet his thrust when it reached its deepest point before receding once again. She realized, as his cock filled her a third time, that she was still holding her arms up over her head, even though he'd released them a long time ago. She moved one arm, intending to trace the line of his tight abs, but he growled a warning not to move. She happily conceded.

There was such an amazing rush in having a powerful, gorgeous man dictate her every movement. It was like flares of white-hot flames blazing through her body.

His hands were on her breasts, kneading, pinching, tugging. He rolled her tight nipples between his fingertips, which sent tense quakes surging through her body. Her pussy pulsed around his cock as the heat of an orgasm flashed up her torso.

He increased his pace, increasing her pleasure, at just the right time. She heard herself scream out in delight as her whole body burned with the heat of a powerful climax.

Instantly her head and spirit filled with Shadow. His presence was everywhere. His thoughts. His needs and wants. His fears. As he fucked her hard, filled her with his cum, he stared into her open eyes. She became lost in it all—his thoughts and feelings, the sensations. She didn't know where she ended and he began. They were one. In all ways.

It was the most wonderful, most awe-inspiring thing. Like she was literally outside of herself and inside him.

But it didn't last long enough. Even though she ached for it to last longer, forever, it faded with the sensations of her orgasm until only bits of thought twinkled in her head like little falling stars. Her body twitched and shook.

He pulled out and settled beside her, gathering her to him in a warm embrace. He kissed the top of her head and she smiled.

This was so right. So wonderful. Why oh why couldn't it last? Why couldn't he be the same man outside of the bedroom as he was inside?

Or was he? She had to accept it—his controlling, demanding nature was what made the sex so incredible. Although she couldn't deny the fact that he knew exactly how to touch her. Where. How much pressure.

It was his words. The intensity of his attention to her that really made the sex so amazing. Those were the same characteristics that drove her mad outside of the bedroom.

Darn it! Did that mean if she wanted this—sex that was beyond anything she'd ever imagined—she'd eventually have to accept the love of a man who felt he had the right to control every aspect of her life?

Was it worth it?

She couldn't think. Her brain hurt.

She snuggled up to Shadow and let his warmth seep into her bones, smiling as he tucked her even tighter to his perfect bod.

She wouldn't ruin the moment with deep thoughts. Just enjoy. Yes, that was the answer. Just enjoy.

He left her sometime before sunrise. Whispered a promise to return, pressed a soft kiss to her cheek, and walked out. She felt a twinge of regret as she watched him leave.

7

Shadow woke the next evening to the sight of both his brothers standing over him with expectation written all over their faces.

Good thing he wasn't the type to kiss and tell or they'd be getting an earful.

"So, how goes the wooing?" Rolf asked, snickering.

"Did you sweep her off her feet, Romeo?" Stefan added.

"It's going fine, better than fine, actually. No thanks to you two," he said, taking a nice long stretch before climbing from his bed.

"What're you talking about? What'd we do?" Stefan asked.

"Which one of you bastards had the flowers delivered?"

His brothers gave each other a surprised stare. "Flowers?" they said in unison.

"I didn't," Rolf said with a shake of his head.

"Neither did I," Stefan said, mirroring Rolf's motions. "Someone sent her flowers?"

"Yeah. And they signed the card in my name. Since only the two of you know about our agreement, I know it's gotta be one of you. So fess up. I swear, I won't hurt you too bad. You only set me back a bit. I managed to overcome it, and things are moving along just fine."

"Wasn't me." Rolf took a couple steps back and gave Stefan a look. "Stefan, what're you lying for?"

Stefan gave Rolf a surprised glare. "Me? I didn't send flowers. I wouldn't waste money on stupid flowers for my own girl. Why would I buy them for Shadow's? You're the guy with the flower fetish."

Rolf's eyes widened until they looked like bulging goldfish eyeballs. "I don't have a flower fetish! You're just jealous because I happen to know how to romance a woman where you think a grunt and a fart is enough to get her hot."

"Shut up!" Shadow shouted. "Dammit, I just want to hear that one of you assholes sent the flowers. If not, I've got something to worry about. So quit pointing fingers at each other and just tell the truth. I won't hurt you bad. Promise."

Both brothers gave him a blank stare. Neither of them stepped forward.

"Rolf?" he asked.

"No. I swear I didn't send them."

"Stefan?"

Stefan shrugged. "Like I said, I don't send girls flowers."

"Fuck."

"What're you thinking?" Stefan asked.

"Someone else sent those flowers. But who? And why?"

"Where are they now?"

"In the garage. But they're wrapped up pretty tight. If there's a bug in them somewhere—not that I think that's the reason why they were sent—I don't think the bastard will hear much out there."

"I don't get it. What other reason would there be?" Rolf asked.

"Don't know. Gonna go find out, though. Maybe there was

something in the dirt. A bomb, even. Fuck. I can't sit outside her door during the day to make sure she's safe. I need her here, where she's protected."

"Then go get her," Stefan said. "Better she's pissed off than dead."

"But she'll divorce me. I promised. Gave my word."

"So what?" Rolf lowered himself into a chair. "Get a new wife. Cut her loose. At least you won't be risking both your lives any longer."

Shadow didn't breathe too often. But this called for a big, drawn-out sigh. Breathing that hard made him a little dizzy. Even though it felt somewhat good, he decided not to do it again anytime soon.

He told his brothers to go, took a shower, and once the sun had set, found himself a willing source of nourishment in the form of one of his slaves, humans who visited nightly to "donate" blood in return for financial compensation; then he headed over to Regan's house. Last night had gone very well, better than he'd expected. Regan was fighting her feelings for him, and he knew why. He just had to chip away at those reasons until they no longer stood in the way of their happiness.

He figured it would take him a week or two, no more. She was open to him, especially in bed, and had shown her willingness to submit to him during sex. The rest would come later, as he showed her she could trust him in all ways to do what was best.

The only problem was whoever had sent those flowers knew she was being left alone during the day. Before leaving home, he'd contacted a security company and would screen applicants tomorrow night. That left her alone one more day. Alone and vulnerable.

He was going to do his damnedest to convince her to come stay with him for one day. That shouldn't be too difficult. He hoped.

He figured a little alcohol might make things go a little more smoothly. Alcohol. Some food. That was the best way to handle women. Fill their stomach. Get them a little tipsy and very often they'd agree to most anything.

Bag containing wine in one hand, a second bag full of Italian takeout in the other, he walked up to her porch, counting the cars lining her street. Someone was having a party. He suspected it wasn't her elderly next-door neighbor. A handful of kids bedecked in black latex with faces riddled with silver studs were gathered around the back end of a beat-up Suburban, dispensing beer from a keg into pop cans. Underage drinkers. Should call the cops.

Shaking his head, he tucked the bottle of wine under his arm to free his hand so he could knock. After last night, he knew better than to let himself in. Whew, had Regan been riled up about that. And here he'd thought she'd left the door unlocked for him.

Wouldn't make that mistake a second time.

He heard the muffled sound of voices through the closed door. Music too. He felt his shoulders droop.

Now he knew who was having the party.

Laughter mocked him from the still-closed front door. He banged harder and forced a smile for the strange young woman who answered. Her heavily lined eyes perused his person for a few beats. She twirled a strand of jet-black hair around her black-tipped index finger.

"I don't suppose Regan's home?"

"Uh . . . who?"

"The lady who owns this house."

"Oh yeah. Sure." The girl stepped aside. "I think she's in the kitchen."

"Thanks." He shimmied through the goth-garbed throng gathered in the middle of the living room, stuffing their faces with chips and salsa (half of which was falling on what was once off-white carpet) and swaying to the sound of cellos performing rock music blasting from the speakers scattered throughout the room. The kitchen was empty (not literally, just devoid of Regan), so he worked his way back around, finding her hefting a platter of sausages wrapped in crescent rolls across the packed dining room.

She gave him a guilty smile when their gazes met. She waved and shrugged.

His temper spiked. Why was she doing this? Intentionally making it difficult for him? How could he romance her in the middle of what equated to a drunken bash with some people who didn't exactly look like her crowd? There was more black plastic worn by partygoers than he'd expect to see outside of a goth convention.

And where had she gotten the money to hold the party? Only yesterday, she'd been scraping together enough money to turn on the lights.

"Hi, Shadow," she said cheerfully, presenting the plate of wieners. "Want a hog? Or is it pig? I keep forgetting the names of these things. Not bad, though." She popped one in her mouth and chewed. "It isn't Russian beluga, but it's edible."

"No, thank you. I don't eat."

"Oh yeah. That's right. How silly of me to forget." She giggled as she whisked away a crumb of pastry from the corner of her mouth.

"Yeah. How silly. Speaking of silly, what's all this?"

She blinked up at him with eyes not even remotely clouded by alcohol. She was as sober as he. "It's a party."

"Yes. Kind of figured that out already. But I'm wondering why you're having a party tonight? You knew I was coming over. And you knew why. What are you trying to do?"

"Nothing. I swear. I opened the store today and kind of decided I needed to have a grand-opening kickoff."

"In your home?"

"Sure. Why not?"

In response, he just simply raised his eyebrows.

"Okay, okay. So they're not exactly my crowd of people. But I'm broadening my horizons. I need to learn who my customers are. What their needs are. So my store will be a success."

"I'd say their needs are simple. They need more body jewelry. More latex. And more black. There. That was quick and painless. So, can we send them all home and get to our evening? I brought lasagna."—he held up the hand still holding the bag—"and a bottle of Barolo."

"Oh. Sorry. I ate already. And wine gives me a headache."

Not the reaction he was hoping for.

"'Scuse me. You know where there's a john in this place?" some guy asked, knocking an elbow into Shadow's shoulder.

Regan pointed. "Around the corner. Second door on the left."

"Thanks." The guy staggered back the way he'd come, bouncing off bystanders like one of those little metal balls in a pinball game.

"Your living room carpet's getting destroyed," he told her, hoping that might convince her it was time to usher the party animals out.

"That's okay." She started working her way back toward the kitchen, offering the contents of the tray to people as she passed them. He followed. "I needed to get it cleaned anyway." She set the now-empty tray on the kitchen counter and pulled a full pan of cooked sausages from the oven, exchanging it for a pan of uncooked ones she pulled from the refrigerator.

"Where'd you get the money for all this?"

She lifted her chin and drew her features into a mask of stubborn pride as she turned to give him a glare. "It's none of your business, but if you must know, I sold some stuff on eBay, and the buyer happened to be a very speedy payer."

"What stuff?"

"Just some old things I had no use for," she mumbled as she transferred the cooked food to the serving tray. "This is business, Shadow. I'm sure you understand. You're a business kind of guy. Tonight's very important." She gave him a half-smile. "There's always tomorrow night. If you want to leave, I totally understand. I get the feeling this isn't your kind of gathering."

"It's not yours, either. You're just trying to scare me off. But I have news for you. It won't work." He stuffed the bag of Italian food into the refrigerator and rounded the kitchen peninsula to trap her in the corner. He raised his arms, planting his hands on the cabinets on either side of her head, and leaned down. "I know what you're afraid of. You can't hide forever."

She visibly swallowed. "You don't know anything."

When would she stop denying what was right in front of them both? It was infuriating! It was dangerous. It was going to drive him crazy. "I do and you know it. Stop playing these games, Regan. I'm getting tired of them."

"Then leave," she barked.

"I can't," he barked back.

"Sure you can. No one's holding you hostage. No one's kidnapped you. Tied you to a bed and is refusing to let you go . . . like some other people have done in the recent past."

She was still sore about that?

"I had no choice—"

"That's not the point. The point is I never asked for this. For you. For marriage. For the queen-hood. Any of it. I was at my place of business, minding my own thing, and you came along, branded me with this stupid choker." She yanked at the piece of jewelry that marked her as his. "I can't get it off. It, like, fused itself to me. Damn thing."

"It's not supposed to come off."

"I hate it. I hate you for coming in and making a mess of my life. I had it all figured out before you kidnapped me—"

"Had it all figured out? Your utilities were shut off. You had no food. You had no job. What did you have figured out?"

She narrowed her eyes at him but didn't answer.

"Hey," someone said from behind Shadow.

Whoever owned the voice tapped him on the shoulder, and it took every ounce of his self-control not to spin around and shout, "Get the fuck lost."

"Hey, what?" Shadow grumbled without bothering to turn around.

"Anyone seen Joe? He was here a little bit ago."

"No." Shadow lifted his hand to Regan's face. Palmed her soft cheek, brushed his thumb over her bottom lip. He knew what it tasted like. And damn if he didn't want to taste it right now.

Regan shrugged away, ducked under one of his arms, and waved at the guy who he assumed had taken the hint and was leaving. "Wait! Was Joe tall? Skinny? With a chain going from his eyebrow to his lip?"

Dammit, he needed to shut this party down. Now. He let his forehead hit the cabinet with a dull thunk.

"Yeah. That's the guy," the pain-in-the ass punk said. "My car's just been repo'd. I gotta go."

"I sent him out to the garage with some trash," Regan said. "But that was a while ago."

"Okay. Thanks. Fucker probably left with some girl, but I'll go check. Maybe he's huffing some . . ."

Shadow twisted his upper body to give the dude his best get-lost stare.

". . . never mind." The guy got the message and headed toward the connecting door to the garage. "Hey. Stinks in here. Joe? You out here? What you got?" He shut the door behind him.

"Where were we?" Shadow asked, gazing down at his very

distracted-looking wife. He gripped her upper arms in his fists and walked her backward until she was standing with her back against the refrigerator door. He stared at that lip, the one he was aching to taste.

"I was getting to the pigs in a blanket before they burn. And you were leaving."

"Oh, no, I'm not." He tipped his head and went in for a kiss.

She dodged his first attempt and shoved at his chest. "Fine. Stay. But let me go. I don't want the whole pan to be ruined. It's my last one." This time when she pushed, he let her go past. If smoke was billowing from the oven, he didn't expect her to listen to what he had to say anyway. He rested a hip against the counter, folded his arms. "I get the impression these people party hard and late. If I were you, I'd call it a night. We can get together tomorrow evening."

"Yeah. Right. I leave tonight, and tomorrow you'll have half the state here for Part Number Two of the Big Drunken Bash-fest. No. I'll stay until the last of your guests either pass out or leave."

"Your choice. It could be past sunrise, you know."

"I'll take my chances. Here," he offered, trying to swipe the tray from her. "I'll help."

"No. Absolutely not. This is my party. You just . . . just stay out of the way."

"Fine." He begrudgingly hunkered down in a corner, safe from the worst of the partiers, and watched Regan run herself ragged delivering food and beverages to people who had no appreciation for what she was doing.

As expected, by a little after three in the morning, Regan's patience was shot. When one guy heaved on her couch, she screeched, "Get out! All of you!" Then, when the last of them had begrudgingly walked out, she plopped on the trampled, trash-strewn carpet and covered her face in her hands.

He didn't say anything. Just waited for her to gather herself together.

She made him wait a long time. Typical woman.

Finally, she peered at him from between her spread fingers. "What a mess."

"Where'd you find those people?"

She gave him a guilty smile. "I gave fliers to a few college kids to pass out."

"You had underage drinkers in your home. You could've been held responsible," he pointed out.

"Underage drinkers? I wasn't serving them alcohol."

"You didn't have to. They brought their own. In the back of a truck. I saw them when I came in. You knew they were drinking."

"I knew they were drunk. Didn't know how they were getting that way." She bit her lip, and he instantly yearned to suckle it.

"Why did you do this?"

"Because . . ." She dropped her gaze, started picking at coagulated bits of tomato stuck to the carpet.

He risked his health—and tested the stain-resistant coating on his slacks—and sat next to her on the floor. "Why?"

"After last night, I needed some space. Some time to sort some things out. And I knew I couldn't do that with you here."

"So you filled your house with noisy, obnoxious teenagers, hoping to hide," he finished for her.

"It sounds pathetic when you put it that way."

He didn't comment. Knew to do so would be nothing but trouble.

"This is all your fault, you know. You're too . . . aggressive. Too pushy. Too . . . char . . . a lot of things I don't want to say right now."

"Why not? You seem to be in the mood for honesty."

"Because my words could incriminate me."

"Does that mean you're falling in love with me?"

"Falling in love?" she asked, laughter lighting her eyes, making them glitter. "Heck no. It means I'm not saying."

"Okay."

She was fibbing. He could tell. She was falling in love with him. Already!

Oh yeah, he was the man.

Fighting a mile-wide smile, he stood and brushed the food off his ass. "I'll help you clean up. You look tired."

"No. You don't have to do that."

"Well I sure as hell am not going to sit on my ass and watch you do all the work. You made me do that earlier. I'm through sitting on my ass."

"I'm too tired to clean. I was going to leave it until tomorrow."

"If that's what you want to do. But let's at least get the garbage picked up."

She crushed a plastic cup in her hand and stood up. "Good idea. Tomorrow's garbage day. I can take this crap right out to the curb."

He couldn't help noticing the corn chips glued to her ass as she walked to the kitchen.

Regan couldn't help acknowledging that, just like at the store, they worked well together when there was a job to do. Within an hour, the worst of the mess had been picked up. What had once covered most of Regan's floors now filled three extra-large Hefties, and she had to admit, she was again more than grateful for Shadow's help. He was proving to be more than the bossy, controlling pain-in-the-ass she needed him to be.

This was so not good!

She sent Shadow out the front door with two of the bags, then cracked open the connecting door to the garage to hit the automatic garage door opener so he could carry the rest of the trash heaped in there to the curb as well. She shut the door quickly to keep the hot, stuffy garage air out of the house and the cool, crisp air inside. Air-conditioning was one luxury she'd never take for granted again!

After tossing the rest of the cold and shriveled sausages down the garbage disposal—to think she'd sold a super-cute Laura Rosnovsky bag to buy that crap!—she headed to the bathroom. She needed a hot shower, some comfy pj's, and her bed. The sooner, the better.

Gratefully, she was so bone-tired, she had a feeling that she'd have no problem nodding off, even if Shadow did a striptease in the middle of her bedroom to Prince.

Just wasn't happening tonight. Her party scheme had worked. Kinda. There was still that whole spending-time-together-while-cleaning thing, and that nice-guy-who-refused-not-to-help thing too.

Grrr! She did not want to stay in this marriage! Bad marriages were torture. For everyone. She knew that. She'd lived it most of her life. Well, until her folks had been mercifully put out of their misery. They'd been tethered to a miserable marriage by too many chains to count, money being the biggest. So they'd spent the better part of her youth making each other miserable. And their child in the process.

Bad marriages were bad, and this marriage was badder than bad. It was a complete disaster.

She shucked her clothes and cranked on the hot water. Glanced at herself in the mirror—always a downer when she was naked. God, she looked awful. Like death. And there was the distinct swelling of PMS bloat going on below her belly button.

She hated hormones!

Just as she was stepping into the shower, a loud knock at the bathroom door made her insides jump into her throat and her heart skip a beat or two.

Damn man! Can't leave me to peace, even in the bathroom? She checked the door to make sure it was locked. "I'll be out in a few."

"Get dressed. Now!"

Huh. Shadow the Jerk had returned. Yay!

"I'm taking a shower," she said, making sure he heard the annoyance in her voice. God, what was wrong with this guy?

"No. There's no time for that. The police are on the way. Get out here. Right now."

Oh man! Had someone called about the underage drinking? Would the police hold her responsible? Even if the kids had brought their own alcohol? If so, what kind of jail term was she looking at? She turned off the water and pulled on her robe. There was no way she'd get back into the filthy clothes she'd been wearing. There were chips glued to her pants, for crying out loud. Not exactly the kind of impression she wanted to give when she answered the door.

She opened the bathroom door and halted midstride when she caught the look on Shadow's face.

She'd seen him looking tense before, but this was beyond tense. He looked like he'd burst a blood vessel if he didn't chill out a bit.

Did vampires burst blood vessels?

"Hurry, hurry," he ordered. "Do you have an overnight bag?"

"What's happening? Am I going on the lam?" She pulled on a pair of sweats and a T-shirt. "I really don't want to live the life of a fugitive. Besides, is it really necessary? I mean, do they send people to jail for holding parties? I didn't serve those kids, although they were drinking on my property—"

"It's not that. You're not going to be a fugitive." He caught her arms and gently pushed her toward the bed. The mattress bumped her rump as he forced her to sit down. "Regan, someone tried to kill you."

"Huh?" Her gaze searched his face. Was this some kind of joke? A trick? "What're you talking about?"

"There are two dead bodies in your garage. I'm not sure what happened. I called the police."

"What bodies? Whose bodies?"

"I think one is the guy you sent out there with the trash. And his friend who was looking for him later."

"What makes you think someone was trying to kill me? Maybe they drank themselves sick? Or . . . or . . ." She scrambled for some logical explanation. Why would anyone want her dead? That made no sense. No. Had to be something else. It hit her. "Huffing! Didn't the one say something about huffing? Doesn't that have something to do with inhaling bad stuff? Stuff that could kill you?"

"Yes, but—"

"There you go! They must've gotten a hold of my Fix-a-Flat or something. God! That's awful! Someone died in my garage." She started walking in circles. Just because she'd convinced herself that she wasn't the intended victim of some crime didn't mean she felt any better.

Two young men had breathed their last breaths. In her garage. Bad karma there.

And so very, very sad. She couldn't help feeling guilty. She hadn't shoved the cans of whatever at those two boys and told them to go to town, but she'd held the party, invited them over as guests, and not paid attention to what was happening.

She felt sick. So sick, in fact, that she had to make a dash for the bathroom. She was absolutely devastated when Shadow followed her in there to watch her hurl.

He held her hair while she vomited. No one had ever done that before. It was . . . very sweet.

Afterward, he ran warm water in the sink, got her a washcloth and towel, then went to answer the door when the first of the police entourage arrived. She stumbled out on wobbly legs a few minutes later to find Shadow standing in the living room giving his account to one uniformed policeman.

A second one went to her and began asking questions. She felt sort of weird, like she was outside of her body, as she answered them.

The first officer asked her the same questions a half-dozen times, and then the cop who'd been questioning Shadow asked her the same questions—didn't those guys swap notes or anything? The two policemen then left her with Shadow inside and went out to the garage to share what information they had with the other half of the police force gathered in there.

She refused to look outside. There was no way she could stomach seeing dead bodies. Especially dead bodies belonging to young people she'd talked to only a little while ago.

God, this was awful!

She sat in stunned silence next to Shadow on the couch. He wrapped a protective arm around her shoulders, pulled her closer until her right side was wedged tightly against his left. He twined his fingers through hers and held her hand gently. She was extremely glad he was there with her now.

More police officers came in and out of her house. They asked the same questions again and took notes. She answered. She waited.

Finally, some of them left. Shadow stood, stretched, and walked outside. She instantly missed him. Despite the fact that the front door was open and the muggy night air was invading her house, she was cold. She wrapped an afghan around her shoulders but stayed right where she was. She didn't trust her legs to hold her.

Shadow returned what felt like a lifetime later. His expression was grim. "They found a dead cat."

What did that have to do with anything? Her brain was really having a hard time keeping up with things tonight. "Oh no! My cat's dead? My sweet Matilda?"

"She was in your garage."

"My poor baby! I hadn't seen her, but I just thought she was hiding. She hates strangers. What does that mean? What's it have to do with those boys?"

"The police aren't saying much, but I think those kids died from something else. Not from drugs."

"What kind of something?" She drew the afghan tighter around her shoulders, tucked it under her chin.

"Not sure." He curled his fingers around her wrist and pulled. "Come on."

"Where are we going?"

"I told the detective you'll be staying with me. At least until they figure out what killed those two boys."

"But . . ." She gave a halfhearted attempt at a refusal, but got no further than a single word. She was exhausted. Scared. Sick. And the thought of spending the night alone in the house after having two people die in her garage was just plain scary. "Okay. But I need to go to work tomorrow."

"We'll talk about that later. Get your bag. We're leaving."

8

Regan woke up momentarily confused, having forgotten she wasn't at home, asleep in her bed. It took only a few moments and the sight of Shadow snoozing beside her to remind her of where she was and why.

Her eyes were hazy from sleep, so she had to squint to read the red glowing numbers on the clock sitting on the nightstand on the other side of the bed.

They were in Shadow's condo. It was dark, thanks to the blinds and heavy drapes covering the windows. The clock said it was a little after eleven.

Shoot! She was late opening the store. Once again, she found herself trying to extricate herself from Shadow's clutches. Even when asleep, the man had a grip like a bear trap. And his limbs weighed more than concrete blocks. She made an attempt at gently pushing his leg off her. When that failed, she used more force.

Naturally, he woke up. "Where are you going?" His voice was gravelly in a very sleepy, sexy way.

"To the store." She wiggled toward the edge of the bed.

Why'd he have to sleep on a piece of furniture that was bigger than some European countries?

"No. You can't go." He caught her around the waist and pulled her backward until her backside was snug against his front side. Some very prominent parts were poking at her not-so-prominent ones.

Shadow woke up with a boner. Why did that not surprise her?

"Of course I can go. I have to. There's no one else who's volunteering to run the store for me."

"Well, for one thing, it's awfully late to be opening your store—"

"Which is why I need to get rolling. So leggo!" She tried to pry his fingers off her, but he held fast.

"No. You don't understand. It's eleven at night."

She stopped her struggling and twisted to look at the clock a second time. "Are you positive? That means I slept like sixteen hours."

"I'm sure. You needed the sleep. You were exhausted."

That was the truth! "Aw, man! I advertised a big sale today." She dropped onto the mattress. It was so soft. So very comfy. Even though she'd slept a bazillion hours, she felt like she could sleep another ten. Or twelve. Was she getting sick? Or just stressed out?

Probably the second. Wasn't every day a girl's attacked, kidnapped, married, freed, hosts a huge party, and then has two people die on her premises.

"Your public can wait another day or two for their sale."

"I have bills to pay."

"They will be paid."

"Not by you they won't. I told you. I don't take charity."

"You're not a charity case. You're my wife."

"In name only."

"I'm so tired of these arguments."

"Me too. So quit arguing with me. Haven't you learned yet that it's an exercise in futility? I always win." She managed to extricate herself from his arms and made fast tracks for the bathroom.

"Where are you going?"

"To get the shower you so rudely interrupted last night."

He threw the covers off the bed and sat up. "Fine." He swung his legs over the side of the bed.

"Where are you going?"

"I'd like to take a shower too."

"Does this suite have more than one bathroom?"

"No." He crossed the room so quickly, he was a blur. Literally.

"How'd you do that?"

"We vampire types, as you so love to call us, have a few special skills."

"Yeah. I'm sure you do," she said dryly.

"Haven't heard you complain yet." He looked and sounded way too proud for her taste.

She tried to hide her embarrassment under pealing laughter as she shoved him hard and stomped into the bathroom.

She doubted she was fooling anyone.

He caught the door just before she slammed it shut, an action that deserved a healthy dose of mean eyes. She gave him her meanest.

He chuckled, the big jerk!

"I need to use the bathroom. And I don't pee in front of anyone." She smacked him in the shoulder. "Go! Get out and give a girl some privacy."

He seemed properly chastised, even a little apologetic. He took a few steps backward. "I'll wait right here until you're through."

"Feel free to go back to bed. This could take a few."

He nodded his head, understanding lighting up his features.

She closed herself into the white-tiled haven and just stood on the other side of the door and heaved a heavy sigh of relief. Good grief, the guy didn't let her take a step without trailing her! It was so annoying, she wanted to scream.

She took care of the more pressing matters first, then started the bathwater. She was very surprised when she didn't hear a rap at the door. Pleasantly surprised. Maybe he'd gotten the hint that women didn't like men in the bathroom with them when they took care of certain issues. She could only hope.

The bathtub was one of those extra-deep soaking tubs with jets strategically placed around the perimeter. A long soak in hot water sounded heavenly. She flipped the lever, blocking the drain, and stuck a toe in the water to check the temperature.

The bathroom door swung open.

She gave the intruding party a scowl over her shoulder. "Has anyone ever told you you're a major pain in the ass?"

"Once or twice." He followed the line of her leg to the bottom of the tub. "Oh goody. A bath."

"Oh goody. You're going to have to wait. There's no room for two in this tub."

He totally ignored her. Stripped down to his little black briefs—sexy!—and bent over to test the water. He frowned. "It's cold." Cranked up the hot water.

Grrr! "Out! This is my bath, and I get to decide how hot or cold I want the water, you behemoth. You're really, really pissing me off!"

He lifted his hands in the universal sign of surrender. "Fine, fine. You take a bath by yourself." He stepped back from the tub but didn't leave the bathroom.

She supposed that was a small step in the right direction. Still grumbling to herself about annoying men, she slid into the warm water and settled herself in for a long, pleasant soak. Closed her eyes to try to mentally shut out Shadow the Barbarian, standing like a big, brainless lug next to the tub.

Too bad the image of his bare torso had somehow become frozen in her mind, so that was what she had to look at when she closed her eyes. Though, she had to admit, the view was pleasant. More than pleasant. It was downright yummy.

She scooted down until she was immersed up to her chin, and tried to relax. The faucet squeaked as Shadow shut off the water. Then a pair of hands landed on her shoulders. He rubbed. It felt nice. Better than nice.

"Ohhhh," she said on a moan, sliding back so he had a better angle to work from. "Now, that feels good."

"Glad you think so." His fingers worked magic on her shoulders, marched up her neck, too, taking away the tension she hadn't even been aware had gathered there. Her skin tingled, fed by a rush of blood, thanks to a very vigorous rub. Those very talented fingers moved higher, to her temples, scalp. She encouraged him to keep going with an occasional sigh or groan of gratitude.

"Aren't you glad I stuck around now?"

"A little."

By the time he finished, every part of her from her collarbone up was feeling like a million bucks. She blinked open her eyes. "Thank you. That was great."

"No problem. But I'm not done yet." He stood up, shucked his Skivvies, and motioned for her to slide forward to let him step in behind her. He sat down, his long, thick legs extended on either side of her. Water, displaced by his bulk, splashed onto the tile floor.

"You're making a mess." She pointed at the huge puddle on the floor.

"You won't be worrying about that in a minute." He went back to work on her shoulders, finding little kinks he'd missed the first time. She slumped forward, resting her left arm on the side of the tub. Her right arm found itself a handy perch on Shadow's bent knee.

Then, slowly, he moved lower, rubbed along her spine until he found her lower back, immersed in the water. He didn't stay there long. He kneaded the upper part of her buttocks, then worked around her hips until his chest was pressed against her back and his hands were between her thighs.

Shadow was one evil man. She was beginning to appreciate that in him. Really, really quickly.

He dragged his blunt fingernails down the sensitive skin of her inner thighs while simultaneously nibbling her neck. The effect was shivering, goose-bumpy delight.

"I love the way you respond to my touches."

"Wish I could say the same," she murmured.

"You're not happy?" He scattered a few tickly kisses over her right shoulder.

"It's not that I'm unhappy . . . it's just that . . ." She really didn't know what she was trying to say. How could she explain it to him? There were so many reasons why she needed to keep this thing between them temporary. But sitting naked in a bathtub didn't seem like the right place to even go there.

"I know you secretly yearn for a strong man. A man who will be your lover. Your master. Take care of you but also respect you. I can be all those things."

"I can't talk about this now. Here. While you're caressing my legs and we're sitting nekked in a bathtub. I will admit this—we have great sex. That I can't deny." She shuddered when his touches traveled higher. His fingertips teased, tormented, until a smoldering fire simmered in her blood. His mouth added fuel to the blaze. "And I can't believe I'm admitting this, but you're right about one thing. I do like the way you take charge in the bedroom."

"Is that so?" he whispered against her neck. He parted her labia and ran a finger along her slit.

She shuddered, dropped her head backward until it rested against his chest. "Yes." She heard the metal-on-metal scrape as

Shadow somehow flipped the lever to let out the bathwater. He stood, scooped her into his arms, and stepped out of the tub.

He carried her so effortlessly, like she weighed five pounds, across the room. As if she were made of the most delicate China, he lowered her oh so gently to the bed, went to the bathroom, and returned a split second later with one thick towel hanging from his hips and a second one in his hands.

He dried her off from head to toe. It was amazing having someone give her such thorough care. Such tender care. Especially from a man who possessed such power, physically, mentally.

When he'd made sure there wasn't a single droplet of water left on her body, he dropped the towel on the floor, then quickly dried himself. His towel landed on top of hers, and he climbed onto the bed with her. He held himself above her with his outstretched arms, one hand on either side of her shoulders. "I've been very patient, Regan." He traced her jaw with a thumb. "I'm not the most patient man."

"Patient about what?" Her gaze followed the bumpy road up his tight abdomen, hulking chest, and shoulders to his face.

"I feel your willingness. It's time."

"Time for what?"

"I've proven I can be trusted. I've shown you the gentle, tender, respectful lover I can be. Now you must respect me for the powerful man and king that I am. I'm through waiting."

"Oh?" A very big lump lodged itself in her throat. What exactly was he waiting for? She knew he had a thing for domination. Was that what he was talking about? If so, hadn't she just said she was okay with that? More than okay? Hadn't she even called him Master?

"It's time for the Initiation."

The air left her lungs in a huff. She struggled to reinflate them. What would the Initiation involve? While a little pleasure-pain could be sexy, she wasn't sure if she was up to something more intense. "I'm . . . not sure . . ."

He sat back on his heels, crossed his arms over his chest. "Haven't I shown you I have complete control over my actions? That I wouldn't hurt you?"

"Yesss . . . That's not exactly what I'm worried about."

"I know how you ache to feel complete abandon, to explore your need to bow at a master's feet, to serve him."

"I'm a little unsure. I don't understand what you expect. I don't know what I expect. I've only done a little reading. A very tiny bit. On the Net. And about all I can handle is a little sensual bondage role-playing . . . maybe. Nothing too intense."

"I will lead you. I won't push too hard, especially in the beginning. There is a reason why I know you want this."

"Oh really? I've been wondering that for quite a while."

"Forget about our psychic connection. There is another reason. It was something you posted on a bulletin board. My brother Stefan saw it."

She felt her cheeks flushing both from embarrassment and anger. "Oh? But I posted on those bulletin boards anonymously. How did you find me? Isn't that illegal or something?"

"No, not really. My brother's a genius when it comes to computers."

She shuddered. "Wow, tells you how safe it is to surf the Net. Any psycho stalker who knows about the Net can track a girl down. That's scary."

"We're straying from the subject. You posted that you wish to find a man who would lead you, teach you, encourage you to explore your deepest, most secret desires. Have you forgotten about that post?"

God, she had written that! One night, when she'd been feeling especially lonely. "No."

"Then, you see? I am fulfilling that wish. I expected you to be much more willing than you've proven to be. You're testing my patience. Did you lie?"

"No, not exactly. I didn't lie. Although, I'm thinking maybe

I didn't use the best judgment when I chose those particular words."

His fingertip skimmed over her skin. Over one collarbone, between her breasts, down the center of her tummy to her belly button. "I can see that complete submission doesn't come to you as naturally as it does to some. You're fighting your own nature at times. A part of you thrills at the feeling of handing over control to a man. The other part fears it. Are you willing to admit that much?"

Couldn't have put it better myself, especially in this case. "Yes."

"We have no secrets. We are Joined. You've known my mind and heart since our first night together. Yet, you've chosen to close yourself off from the knowledge that is there. You're hiding. From me. From yourself. From what you want, what you need. I hate that you're doing that to yourself. It's so unnecessary."

She had no idea how to respond to that. Was it true? Or was he just spewing a bunch of bunk to convince her to do what he wanted her to?

Yeah, yeah. She knew he wouldn't manipulate her like that. Not anymore. He'd kept his word since they'd made their bargain. Hadn't tried that vampire mind-probing thing. Hadn't tricked her or (as far as she could tell) lied. He'd come to her house with the intention of romancing her. He was being Shadow. Without apologies. Without excuses.

Just being Shadow.

Why was it so difficult for her to do the same? To accept what she knew deep down in her heart was true? To trust herself enough to let down her guard and give both of them half a chance?

Being afraid really did numbers on people, didn't it?

"For someone who talks so tough, full of fight, you're slave to a lot of things, fear being the worst." He shook his head, looked down upon her with something she'd never seen in his eyes before.

Pity.

That made her mad, but not at him. Suddenly, the enemy had taken on a new face, a new name. No longer was Shadow, the controlling vampire who wouldn't let her take a bath in peace, the enemy. It was that dark, wretched demon, fear.

How could she be so certain they were bad for each other? That their marriage was doomed? That they'd be miserable forever if they remained married? She had to admit she wasn't certain of that at all. Just afraid of it.

"You're right." She sat up. "You're absolutely right. I've been making excuses why I can't let you succeed at romancing me. Why our marriage must end. Why I can't let you get closer to me. And I've been doing it because of one reason. I'm afraid."

9

"Are you ready to do battle?" Shadow asked.

"Hey, I admitted I'm scared. Doesn't that mean something? Isn't that like the first step in the Twelve Step program?"

"I wouldn't know." He took Regan's hands in his and pulled while simultaneously walking on his knees toward the edge of the bed. "But I do know what the first step of the Initiation is. And you are going to take it. Now."

She dangled her legs over the edge of the bed. "I am?" When he nodded, she mirrored him. "Yes. I am."

"I will teach you everything." As she slid off the bed, he stood and gently pressed on her shoulders. "When you greet me, you kneel. Like so." He waited until she was on her knees, then walked a circle around her. "Bottom off your heels. Knees shoulder-width apart. Arms behind your back. Hands clasped. Head down until your chin touches your breastbone. Spine curved like this." He traced a line up her spine, and out of sheer instinct, she tightened her muscles. "Yes. That's it."

She looked up, waiting for him to tell her more, but he shook his head. She immediately dropped her head again and stared at his feet as he paced a short line back and forth in front of her.

"You may not look at me until I tell you. You must hold your pose until I tell you you're free to move. You will address me as Master, at all times, and only speak when I give you permission. And you will always follow my directives without challenge. You may respond now with, 'Yes, Master.'"

"Yes, Master." He really took this whole bondage, submission thing seriously. A part of her was intimidated by that fact, another part thrilled. Yes, this is what she'd dreamed of. She'd never actually expected to find it, had always assumed it would remain a secret fantasy, something no one would ever know.

"Every part of your body is under my command, including your pussy. You are not permitted to orgasm without my express permission from this point forward. Understand?" When she remained silent, he added, "Very good. You may respond."

"Yes, Master."

"Since we are Joined, I know your limits, and I will not cross them, but I may test them at some point. If you wish me to stop, you will speak the word *courage* loudly and clearly. You never need permission to use that word."

"Yes, Master," she said to his feet. She wished he'd let her stare a little higher, like just above eye level. Now, that was something worth some concentrated stareage.

"You may look up at me now." She wasn't sure if he meant for her to instantly meet his gaze or not, but she found she couldn't help halting at the parts in question for a little look-see.

Yes. Still there and still looking big and yummy and very tempting. She found herself licking her lips just because she couldn't help wondering what it would feel like to have that thick rod in her mouth.

"You will suck my cock. But not yet. Look up."

"Yes, Master." Her pussy twitched when he said she would

suck his cock. It was the way he'd said the words. So authoritative. A little shiver of pleasure danced up her spine.

He reached down, palmed her cheek. "I have something for you." He turned, walked to the dresser, and pulled open the top drawer. "You will wear this when we are together." He carried a small box cradled in one hand, a leather whip in the other, as he returned to her.

Curious, Regan accepted the box when he offered it to her and flipped the hinged top. Inside she found a gold chain with little black loops on either end.

What was it? She knew it wasn't a necklace.

"Let me show you." He set the whip on the bed and lifted the delicate jewelry in his fingers. Much to her surprise, he lowered his head to lave her nipple with his tongue. Then he slipped one of the loops over her now-very-erect nipple.

She gave a surprised gasp when he slid a bead up, tightening the loop.

Wetness seeped from her pussy, slicking her inner thighs. Her legs started to tremble, but she remained in position, her breasts pushed out as he attached the other end of the chain to her other nipple. He tightened them just enough. There was a slight pinching sensation, just enough discomfort to be sexy but not so much it was distracting.

"Two rewards in one day. You've earned them for finding the courage to take this first step." He traced her lower lip with his tongue, teasing her with the sweet flavor before standing up and once again picking up his whip. "Now you may suck my cock."

"Thank you, Master." She started to lift her hands to cup his balls, but he stopped her with a nudge from the tip of his whip.

"Your mouth only."

"Yes, Master." She opened her mouth wide, closing her lips over her teeth, and took him as deeply as she could. She had a wicked gag reflex, always had, so that wasn't too terribly deep.

She just knew he'd be disappointed. Her mouth sliding back toward the end of his dick, she slanted her head to get a glimpse of his face.

Okay, he didn't look disappointed. He looked . . . aroused. There was the glitter of need in his eyes. His features pulled into a tense mask. She was doing okay. Better than okay. She twirled her tongue round the head, then sucked it hard, like a lollipop. She received a low groan as a reward, which only increased her pleasure.

Much to her surprise, she could feel her juices dripping from her slit, warm at first, cooling as they dribbled down her inner thighs toward the floor. It was the combination that was doing her in so quickly. The little bite of the nipple chain tugging every time she moved a bit. The spicy, wonderful scent of Shadow filling her nostrils. The way he murmured sweet, sexy promises to encourage her to keep sucking.

Her cheeks ached. Her jaw was tired. But her body was on fire. She wanted to climax so bad her teeth ached, yet she knew he wouldn't allow her to until he felt the time was right. He tangled his fingers in her hair, holding her head still as he fucked her mouth. In and out, in and out.

She wondered if anyone had ever died from having an orgasm withheld from them. Her bottom was dropping to the floor, her legs too shaky to hold it up any longer.

He stopped fucking her mouth and pulled her to her feet, pushing her over until her chest rested on the mattress and her ass was high in the air.

Would he whip her now? She tensed, dragged in the first deep breath she'd taken in a good long while, and waited. She listened.

Silence.

The chain became caught in the coverlet, and she winced as it pinched her nipple. She plucked the thread out, then stilled. What was he doing?

"Master?" She heard him pulling in a deep breath. Did vampire-types breathe? She hadn't thought about that before. "Master, are you okay?"

"Yes." He caught one of her wrists, pulled it out to the side until her arm was fully extended, then did the same with the other arm. He pushed her feet apart until her legs were wide open, then parted her ass cheeks. "You're so beautiful." He kissed the small of her back, and she tightened it, thrusting her ass higher than it already was. "Oh yes. That's the way." The leather tips of his whips wisped over her skin, tickling and giving birth to a thick coat of goose bumps. Then they slapped down, striking her on the ass and catching her by surprise. She yelped. Not so much because it hurt—it didn't—but because she wasn't expecting it. The second time she was expecting it. The little bits of leather made her ass hot and sent her heart rate into overdrive. She could feel her heart pounding against her rib cage. Her hands started shaking. Her whole body. He struck her a third time, and she tossed her head back. Her hair whipped her skin, giving her chills on top of the heat swirling through her body.

Something was happening. A strange euphoric high that felt kind of like an orgasm but different was building, spreading. It was beyond words. It swept all thought from her mind and narrowed the world to a pinpoint of time and space. All of her senses zeroed in on that tiny speck, but even that was almost too intense. Her eyelids dropped, shuttering out the distraction of sight. She welcomed the darkness.

"See how your body responds? This is what you need, what you've been searching for. Give yourself over to it." He must have set the whip down, because before she knew it, he had that same stinging flesh gripped in his hands and was probing her slit with the head of his dick. She needed him right now, more than she needed her next breath. When just the very tip slipped inside, she rocked backward to impale herself. She cried out in gratitude when he thrust his hips forward.

"You won't come until I tell you," he murmured against her shoulder.

She timed her motions with his, their matched movements a primitive dance that was whisking her away into a place in her mind where only the two of them existed. But after only a few more thrusts, her legs once again became shaky. She gripped the coverlet in her fists, clinging to it, not wanting to stop for anything. A split second later, Shadow pulled out.

"Roll onto your back."

She flipped over, lifted her eyes to his, and once again found herself swept up into his stormy gaze. He lifted her knees with his hands, dragged her to the edge of the mattress, and reentered her in a fierce thrust that nearly sent her over the edge. She was so close now. Her body so tense that she was even gritting her teeth. She shut her eyes.

"You will not come yet," he warned. "Play with your nipples."

Because they were trapped in the loops, they were still painfully erect, so sensitive that just the lightest touch sent blades of pleasure-pain shooting through her body. Her eyes were closed, but she could see in her mind's eye Shadow watching her as she wetted her fingertips with her tongue and teased her nipples.

"Yes. That's the way." The hunger in his voice gave it a low, gravelly edge. "More. More. Touch yourself. Your clit." He pulled her legs wider.

This was so much more difficult than Shadow had expected. He wanted to give himself over to the orgasm that was raging through his body like a fierce storm. But he couldn't. Not yet. This was not about what he wanted. What he needed.

This was about Regan. His wife. Her pleasure.

It was much too soon for either of them to have their release. He had to slow down. Let the tension drop. Then build it up again. Slowly. Slowly.

It nearly killed him to pull out of her, but he did it.

He wasn't surprised to hear her whimper. He'd known how close she'd been. A few more thrusts and she would've come. And it would've been over. Because there was no way he'd have been able not to come with her.

Her face was flushed. Her chest. He could see the pulse at her neck. It called to him. The memory of how sweet her blood had tasted rushed through him, making his mouth water and the hunger inside build until he was nearly blind with it.

He'd promised. Promised not to feed from her. By the gods, he'd keep his word.

Regan's eyelids fluttered like newly hatched butterflies. Her eyes narrowed. "Shadow? What's wrong?"

"Nothing." Even to himself, his voice sounded strained. He pressed a kiss in the crest between her breasts, inhaling the honey-sweet scent of her skin. Followed that one with several more as he made his way down her torso to her belly button. He was very pleased by the sound of her stuttering sigh when he dipped his tongue into the shallow indentation.

She was so responsive. More so than any lover he'd ever had. Every touch, stroke—even look—he gave her seemed to affect her. Made pleasuring her such a joy.

Her skin felt like warm satin. Smooth and soft. Her body was just perfect. Soft like a woman's body should be. With full breasts and hips. A round bottom that pinked up deliciously when he spanked it.

She was perfect. In every way. Perfect for him. Perfect for his people. Perfect.

"I want to taste your honey," he murmured. He parted her swollen labia and dragged in a full breath through his nose. It made him dizzy to inhale that deeply, but he couldn't get enough of the musky odor of her arousal. How she would taste!

He dragged his tongue over her swollen bead, and she trembled under him. Yes, oh yes. The pleasure he would give her. He flickered his tongue over her clit and pressed two fingers at the slick opening of her cunt. She was so hot and ready for him. He wanted to thrust his cock deep inside again but resisted.

Slow. This needed to be slow. Her pleasure was all that mattered.

While swirling his tongue over her clit, he pushed his fingers inside. Her vagina felt like liquid silk. The muscles tightened around his fingers, and he bent his knuckles to increase the friction.

"Oh, Shadow."

She was a million times more intoxicating than his favorite brand of bourbon. More addictive too. There was nothing he wanted to do more than drink her in. All of her. The scent of her skin. The flavor of her pussy. The slick heat of her tight canal closing around his fingers. The sound of her little gasps and moans as he drew her near to orgasm and then stopped a fraction of a second before she came.

With fingers thrusting and tongue dancing, he commanded her body. Every minute rise in temperature was under his control. Heart rate. Shudder. Tremble and moan. Slowly he was bringing her to the ultimate release by teasing and tormenting, coaxing her to the crest and then easing her away.

He gently forced her back over, onto her hands and knees. Her legs and arms wouldn't hold her long. They shook like she'd been running for miles. She looked over her shoulder at him, giving him a beseeching glance through glassy, heavy-lidded eyes.

"It's almost time, my sweet." He took her hands in his and pulled her upright. The nipple chain dangled so perfectly between her full breasts. The loops snug around the erect nipples.

He ached to taste one and leaned down and gave one a light flicker with his tongue. It wasn't enough. Never enough. He opened his mouth and sucked. Hard. His balls ached. Heavy. His cock stiffened even more.

She clawed at his shoulders. Pulled his hair. Murmured his name, over and over. "Shadow, Shadow," she pleaded. "Now, Shadow. Please, now."

Yes, almost time. He suckled her other nipple and reached a hand for her pussy. His fingers probed her slit, plunged shallowly inside in a slow, deliberate rhythm meant to build her need without bringing her to a climax. He let his thumb graze her clit, back and forth.

The evidence of her pleasure coated his fingers as he drew them out. He lifted them to his nose and inhaled until he nearly lost consciousness. Then, with his gaze fixed to hers, he drew them into his mouth.

Her full lips parted. A soft whimper slipped between them, stirring his need to the point of near desperation. "Shadow, now. Please. No more. No more."

He had to see that beautiful ass as he fucked her. He nodded and pushed between her shoulder blades until she was bent over again. He kneeled behind her, took a handful of her smooth skin at her hips in his left hand, and took his cock in the other.

Her hot juices felt so good as they coated the very tip of the head. He dragged it up and down. Up toward her tight little anus, down toward her sodden pussy. Just as he allowed himself to enter her, the telephone rang.

"Oh no!" Regan groaned. She looked over her shoulder at him, her desperate gaze meeting his.

"Fuck it! Whoever it is can wait," he shouted, entering her so slowly, he swore he'd expire from the torture. Yet, he didn't allow himself the pleasure of taking her faster.

This was for her. It was all for her.

When he had completely buried himself inside, he slowly backed out, concentrating on increasing her pleasure by reaching around with one hand to stroke her clit.

She arched her back, thrust that perfect ass up into the air, and tossed her head back. Her hair fanned out over her shoulders and back. It was a fucking beautiful sight.

He allowed himself to increase the pace of his thrusts, working hand with cock to bring her to the pinnacle of release one last time.

"Now? Now?" she whispered.

"No. Not yet." His teeth were gritted from the fierce need churning through him. He wanted to come as much as she did, but he couldn't bring himself to let it end.

While slowly gliding in and out of her, he ran his hands down her legs and then back up to her ass. The flesh was cool under his fingertips. The heat of her spanking all but gone. He gave her a hard thrust, simultaneously smacking her bottom. It bounced delightfully, the sight sending a blaze through his bloodstream, down to his heavy balls.

He couldn't wait much longer. He spanked her again. His control nearly snapping when she started chanting, "Oh yes. Harder, harder!"

He parted her ass cheeks, wetted an index finger in the juices running from her pussy, and pushed it inside her anus. It tightened around his finger, and he couldn't help groaning.

His control snapped.

Regan quivered underneath him and cried out, "Now!"

"Yes. Now."

He came with the first rhythmic contraction of her pussy around his cock. The orgasm was so powerful, every part of his body jerked. He pumped in a frenzy, thrusting in and out of her like a fucking rabbit. The heavy heat pulsed along the length of his dick and left him.

Moments later, he pulled out of her, rolled to the side, and pulled her soft body against his. Her skin was slick with sweat. His too. He counted each gasping breath she took as he cradled her in his arms. Each heavy beat of her heart.

They eventually slowed.

He had given her all the pleasure he could tonight. But there would be more. So much more. Once they were in the dungeon.

10

"We need to talk about some things." Shadow's voice cut through the comfortable silence. "And contrary to my better judgment, I'm freeing you to speak your mind."

How kind of him. She had a sense of foreboding. Whatever he was about to tell her, it wasn't going to be good. "What things?" She could so get used to the Master thing during sex. But after? In between? In everyday life? It would take a lot of getting used to.

"I talked to the detective investigating those kids' deaths."

"Did they figure out what killed them? It was gasoline, wasn't it? I had a tank in the garage."

"Yes, they did figure it out."

"That's a relief. Does that mean I can go home now? Because I need to get back to the store. Sales are better than I expected. And I need the money."

"I told you, you have no need to worry about money."

"Not going there again."

Shadow bit his lip. He looked like he was about to say something that wasn't very nice. "The two boys did not die from inhaling gas fumes. The medical examiner thinks they died from cyanide poisoning."

"Cyanide? Where did they get into that?"

"That's the question. Here's another interesting fact—the dead cat we found in your garage . . . It died from cyanide poisoning as well. Looks like your garage had toxic levels of cyanide gas in it from something."

"That's really strange. Where would it come from?"

"I don't believe it was an accident."

"What else could it be?"

"An attempt on your life. I told the detective about the vase of flowers. They're running some tests."

"But why would anyone want me dead? I haven't done anything to anyone. I've never even received a prank phone call before. This makes no sense."

"You're my wife." He took her hands in his and looked deep into her eyes. For a minute, she thought he might try the hypnotism thing, but he didn't. Her mental faculties remained fully under her control. "Let me explain something to you. Normally, when the king takes his bride, they remain together at all times. There is a reason for this. A reason I wasn't aware of until after we completed the Joining. If you are killed, I not only lose control of the kingdom, but I am also stripped of my power. Both the power I gained by wedding you and what little power I possessed before we were Joined. Someone wants to unseat me from the throne. Enough to try to kill you, since I'm too powerful for them to kill me."

It took a few seconds for what he said to sink in, measured in the steady but increasingly quickening thump of her heartbeat. One second she was fine, staring in his eyes. The next she was reeling in shock.

"Oh. My. Gosh. You mean I'm a target of some power-hungry murderer? Seriously?"

"Couldn't get any more serious."

She was very glad she was lying down right now, or she had a feeling she'd be out cold. Stars glittered everywhere. Those little sparkling pinpricks of light that meant she was about to pass out. She concentrated on breathing for a second. Deep breath in. Hold. Breathe out. "I really, really don't like this. Really. Really. Ohmygod."

"I'm sorry. I was hoping the rebels wouldn't find you, wouldn't find out you'd returned to our home. But somehow they did. I'm trying to discover where the leak is, who is passing the information to my enemies. Until I do, you must stay with me where you're safe."

"Stay with you? I can't go anywhere alone?"

"Nowhere. In fact, we're going back to my home in Europe, where we'll be safer. The security in the palace is impenetrable."

"Your home? The palace? Where's that? I thought you said you lived here in Michigan?"

"Vled, a small town in Slovenia. My palace is there. This is my summer home."

"Slovenia?"

"A small country between Italy and Croatia. It's beautiful. I'm certain you'll like it, especially this time of year."

"I've been to Europe but never heard of Slovenia. Murder attempt or not, I'm not sure I'm sold on just packing up and heading for parts unknown. This is my home. My store. If (had she just said *if*?) we're divorced, this is all I'll have to come back to. What if it's gone when I return?"

"I can hire someone to keep up your home and the store, if that's your wish. We can't risk someone making another attempt on your life. If they were to succeed—"

"Yes, as you said, you'd lose your power."

"It's more than that." He sounded injured. "We can't leave quite yet. If there are some preparations you need to make first, you have a little time to take care of them."

"This is absolutely necessary?"

"Absolutely."

"There's no other way?"

"This condo is not secure. There's no security in the lobby. Anyone can come up here at any time."

"And you're sure the cyanide was meant for me? What did the police say?"

"They are running tests, keeping pretty quiet. I think until you're cleared as a suspect, they aren't going to say much. It took a lot to get from them what I did."

"Yes. But I know all about your powers of persuasion." She motioned toward his eyes. "That voodoo hypnotism thing."

"That voodoo hypnotism thing doesn't work over the phone. Have to make eye contact."

"Ah! So that's the secret. I'm storing that one away for future reference."

"I am injured by the suggestion I haven't kept up my end of the bargain. I haven't used my 'voodoo hypnotism' on you since we struck our deal and you so unfairly determined it was against the rules. Left me with so little to work with."

"Take my word for it—you're doing just fine without it. Though I'm still not ready to accept the mantle of forever Queen of the Undead."

"Maybe soon."

"Keep dreaming."

"I'm nothing if not an optimist."

"Yeah, and I'm the queen of England." She waited for his laughter to die down to a low chuckle before asking, "Can I at least call my voice mail and check messages?"

"Yes, you may."

It was a small measure of freedom but one she appreciated after having him dictate just about every move she made for the last several hours. She punched the number to retrieve messages. She had two.

The first one was a telemarketer trying to sell her vacation tickets to Disney World. Ha! Like she needed an artificially created fantasy land when her real life was like a carnival ride.

The second was from the police department. She assumed it was about the investigation. After listening for a few seconds, she was surprised to find out it wasn't.

Her store had been burglarized. She needed to go down there at once to see what was damaged or missing. Damn! That store was proving to be the source of one headache after another. No wonder her aunt had left it to her. She'd be willing to bet every other family member had threatened her with bodily harm if she dared will it to them.

She set the receiver on the cradle not so gently. "Shadow. The store."

Shadow lifted his head. "What's wrong?"

"My store's been robbed. I need to go—"

"It's almost daylight. I can't come with you. And I put off interviewing the private bodyguards, thinking we'd leave in the next few days."

"I have to go. They need an inventory of what's missing. My insurance company will need a list of damages. Isn't there anyone you trust who can go with me?"

"I don't want to trust anyone at this point."

"Then I'll go by myself."

"No. I forbid it!"

"I can call the police. They'll meet me there. I can't just leave this undone. You must understand that. It's all I have."

"I understand only one thing—someone tried to kill you."

"You don't know that for a fact yet." She stomped across the room in search of her shoes. "I'm going. It'll only take a little while. Besides, if your rebels are vampy types like you, they can't go out in the sunlight, either. I'll be safe from them, right?"

"If the flowers prove to be the source of the poison, then we have to assume they're working with humans."

"I'll be careful. Who's going to know? The only ones who know I got this phone call are you, me, and the police department. I'll call them right now and tell them I'm on the way."

"It's too dangerous."

"Shadow, if we're going to have any hope of getting along, you're going to have to learn to give me a little space. Master and slave, dom and sub or whatever, you have to learn to back off sometimes. You can't expect me to turn into the perfect submissive queen overnight. I've been alone, taking care of myself, for so long now. I'm trying. I really am. Because even though I'm not sure this dominant and submissive stuff will be a long-term thing, I'm ready to admit it's something I've been curious about for a while now."

He studied her for a moment, then shook his head. "No. Now come to bed."

"Shadow."

"Now!"

She knew from his tone that there was absolutely no chance she'd get him to give in. That left her with only one other option—she'd have to wait until he was asleep and then sneak out.

At least she knew she wouldn't have long to wait. A glance at the clock told her the sun had risen. Shadow the Dom might want to control her twenty-four-seven, but Shadow the Vampire couldn't stay awake during the daylight hours.

He'd be out like a baby in minutes. She just hoped it wouldn't be too late. She'd need some help, and there was only one other person there she even half-trusted. Ty was a vampire, too, probably as apt to sleep during the day, but she was Regan's only possible ally.

Sure enough, Shadow's head had no sooner hit the pillow than he was out cold. Knowing he was easiest to wake in the first hour or so he was asleep, she very slowly and carefully extricated herself from his embrace, crept across the room, and headed for the door. A quick search of the living room and she had Ty's phone number. Shadow had it programmed in his cell phone. Within minutes, she was able to connect with Ty's condo, conveniently located in the same building. She sounded sleepy but still awake and aware enough to comprehend what Regan was telling her.

After discussing a few options, Ty made arrangements to distract the guards posted outside Shadow's condo door while Regan slipped out. She took Shadow's car keys, a handful of twenty-dollar bills, and stuffed them in her purse.

Ty met her down in the building's lobby, near the exit. "Good luck. You're mighty brave, sneaking out. I did that once. I got caught. And I'm warning you, the consequences weren't so great."

"I'll take my chances."

"Be careful. I'd hate myself forever if I helped you sneak out and something happened. And I don't even want to think about what Shadow will do to me."

"I promise I'll be very careful. If anything looks fishy, I'll hightail it back here. The detective said this should take no more than an hour. I'll come right back."

"Here." Ty pulled a cell phone from her pants pocket. "Take this in case you need help. I'll program my room number in." She punched a few buttons, then handed Regan the phone. "I don't sleep as deeply as my brother. And I know who to call if there's trouble."

"Thanks for your help. I'll be back as soon as possible." She dashed outside to the parking lot and found his car.

Man, a Maybach! She was going to drive a Maybach. Yes, there were some things about being the Queen of the Undead that she could get used to. Although she'd had a pretty good lifestyle, she'd drawn the line at buying uber high-priced luxury cars. Now she wondered why she'd denied herself.

She settled into the buttery-smooth leather seats, made a few adjustments to the mirrors, seat, steering wheel. Checked out the sound system—absolutely killer!—then pulled away.

Felt like she was literally riding on air.

Unfortunately, she didn't have far to drive. She arrived at the store before the police detective did, so she sat in the car and listened to some tunes while she waited—satellite radio, yay! It was tempting to go check and see if she could get inside without him, but she figured that might be stupid on a number of levels, least of which being there might be some murdering vampire rebel hiding in the storeroom. Poor Shadow. Having to live in fear for his life had given him a very bleak picture of his fellow clansmen, as well as humans. He suspected there were bad guys practically around every corner. Just waiting for the right opportunity to pounce. Sorta like a tiger lying in the jungle grasses.

She just knew that once the police were through with their tests, they'd find out the kids had died from overdosing on spray paint of something. And the cat . . . Well, maybe for kicks they'd stuck the stuff in the cat's face too. Who knew? Teenagers were apt to do some pretty strange things, especially when they were under the effects of drugs and alcohol. She just hoped they'd figure it out sooner rather than later. Although she'd planned on taking a trip to eastern Europe before she'd lost all her money, she wasn't exactly jumping up and down at the thought of being dragged onto a plane, flown to some "small" town in some country she'd never heard of, and locked in a castle with "impenetrable" security. What little smidge of personal freedom he was letting her cling to now would be absolutely gone. No home. No job. No car.

She was pretty sure she'd go absolutely insane living like that.

Finally, she caught sight of the police car as it pulled around the corner. It was one of those unmarked-but-you-can-still-tell police cars. Black. No stripes or signs but with a bazillion extra lights and mirrors and stuff.

She was out of the car and standing next to the door before the detective had put his car into park.

Okay, so she was a little anxious to get this over with. Despite the fact that she'd been back to the store several times since that first night with Shadow, the place still gave her the creeps. Even more so now that she knew some real criminals had been inside doing God only knew what.

"Looks like you've had a little run of bad luck, eh?"

She recognized the detective immediately. He'd been one of the many policemen who'd come to her house.

He pulled a business card from his pocket and handed it to her. "Thanks for returning my call. Tried calling the number where your husband said you'd be staying, but there wasn't any answer."

"Oh?" She tried not to blush. "Must've been when we, I mean, I was in the shower. My husband likes to sleep during the day, so he turns off the ringer."

"I see." He produced a key from his pants pocket and unlocked the ugly padlock that had been slapped on the front door of her shop. So not the look she was going for. "Try not to touch anything. I just need you to tell me if you see anything missing."

"Okay."

He pushed open the door and motioned for her to proceed inside.

It didn't take a genius to see that whoever was responsible was a complete ass. Had no respect whatsoever for the work it took to arrange garments by color and size. Just about every fixture in the place was empty, all the clothes having been thrown on the floor.

"It's hard to tell what's missing. It's such a mess."

"Just do your best."

"Once I get in here to clean it up, will I be able to give you a revised list?"

"Yes, no problem."

"Okay." She tried not to step on the clothing—which was impossible since the stuff coated the floor—as she wandered through the store's interior. She stopped at the checkout counter and glanced at the cash register. She'd left only fifty bucks in it for the next day's change. Looked like the thieves hadn't bothered trying to get at it. The jewelry cases were all intact, the contents all still in their places. "Frankly, it looks like there's nothing missing, just a big mess."

"Are you sure?"

"No. How could I be? My inventory's heaped on the floor like dirty laundry. But the cash register hasn't been touched, and the jewelry's all there. Vandals?"

He nodded, pulled out the little notebook all policemen seemed to carry, and scratched down a few notes. "Okay. Then we're done here. Unless you want a few more minutes to look around."

"Yes, sure. Can you stick around a few minutes longer? We haven't checked the back room." After receiving a nod of assent, she headed toward the storeroom, hidden behind a wall of plastic beads. Just like out front, the back was a mess. What little stock she'd left back there was thrown all over the place. "What in God's name is the purpose of breaking into someone's store and making this kind of mess?"

"It's hard to say, madam."

Did he just call her madam? She was only thirty-one years old. Not nearly old enough to be called madam.

"Could've been a bunch of teenagers, just looking for something to do."

"Couldn't they go roller-skating or something? Wouldn't that be more fun?"

He shrugged. "In this neighborhood, unfortunately, we see a lot of this kind of thing."

"So, when can I get in here and clean up?"

He handed her the key he'd used to unlock the padlock. "Here you go. I'll give you this key. I have a duplicate at the office if you need it. You're free to go ahead, get things back in order. If you find anything missing, just give me a call. You have my card."

"Okay. That's it? No dusting for fingerprints or anything?"

He shrugged again. "There's nothing missing. Probably a bunch of juveniles. The store's going to have hundreds of fingerprints in it anyway, since it is open to the public. We did collect a few samples from the door and found the crowbar they used to break in. If either of those lead to something, I'll be in touch."

She wouldn't hold her breath.

"Good luck." He did a high step back through the store, clearly trying to avoid stomping over the clothes. She followed him to the front door, figuring she'd head back to the condo and return tomorrow to start cleaning up. But then she took a second look around. This was a huge mess. It would take days to clean up. She couldn't afford to have the store closed so long. So, she did the best she could to secure the battered front door and went to the counter in search of a phone book to find someone to repair the door.

She had no idea how she'd pay for it, but she had to have it fixed. Having only a cheesy-looking padlock to secure it on the outside was not an option. The entire frame was messed up. After making a few calls, she found someone who could make it out in a couple hours. She'd just have to wait for him.

After bracing herself for the argument she just knew was coming, she called Ty to let her know she'd be a while.

She didn't answer the phone. That was a small relief. Probably sleeping the sleep of the undead, as she liked to call it. During the middle of the day, she'd learned it took a natural disaster to wake the vampy types. No biggie. She left a message, letting her know she was safe and sound, no need to worry. And she'd be back before sundown. Then she went back to work putting the various and sundry latex, polyester, and lace garments back on their hangers and racks.

She worked for at least two hours with nary a vampire rebel or poison-laden floral arrangement to be found. The door guy came, took measurements, gave her a staggering quote, then took the cash she reluctantly handed him and promised to return in two days with a new door. About the time he headed out, she discovered she was starving and walked over to the counter to look up a local restaurant that delivered. Found a menu for the Italian place down the street tucked under some papers on the counter. Evidently, Aunt Rose ordered from there. It was well marked. The veal parmigiana sounded downright yum. She called in an order and went back to work. A little over a half hour later, a delivery boy showed up at her front door with a paper bag and extra-large Diet Coke. As she was tipping him, a scrubby puppy straggled into her store. Skeletal, filthy, the little dog looked too pathetic for her to toss out onto the street, although she suspected it carried at least a wicked case of fleas and ticks. Not the kind of thing she needed in a clothing store, especially a clothing store in which the vast majority of her inventory was lying in piles on the floor.

She opted to trap the pathetic animal in the back room with a carefully placed unused shelf, then opened the foam container of food. Ripping the top off, she dispensed half of it into the top and set it down for the dog to eat. Okay, it wasn't Eukenuba, but the poor thing was starving. She figured it was better than nothing.

While the dog ate, she took a few bites here and there as she worked. She wasn't starved anymore. The caffeine in the diet cola took the edge off. So she did more working than eating.

About an hour later, just as she was getting ready to call it a night, she heard a sound at the front door. Feet shuffling, scratching. She knew she had the CLOSED sign hanging outside, in clear view, but figured maybe a customer was poking around, trying to find out why she was closed. She started toward the front door, but the sound of it being kicked in kind of made her change her mind about the wisdom of doing that.

What the hell?

She ran for the back room, figuring the back door was her only way out at this point, then tripped over the sleeping dog, who didn't stir a bit when she kicked it.

That bothered her, but there wasn't any time to ponder the reason why it hadn't moved at the moment. She had to make her getaway before whoever was at that door got his way in.

Evidently they weren't through doing whatever they'd started last night.

As she slipped out the back, she suffered a brief moment of regret. She'd left Ty's cell phone sitting on the counter. That was a bummer! Without the phone, she couldn't call the cops and let them know the bad guys had returned. And since she'd parked in the back, she wouldn't get a look at the bastards who trashed her store.

But she wasn't ready to get all Charlie's Angel and start whooping bad-guy ass yet. Unarmed, a wimp who admittedly threw a sissy punch, she had no reason to think she'd succeed.

No, better to be safe than sorry. She'd call the detective when she returned to the condo.

As she pulled out of the driveway, she craned her neck, looking for a waiting vehicle, anything that would be useful to the police. Unfortunately, there were dozens of cars lining both sides of the busy street in the fairly brisk shopping area. Dozens of people walking up and down in front of the store. No way to know if any of them were there with the bozo who'd kicked in her door.

Grumbling about jerks who weren't happy if they weren't destroying someone's property, she drove back to the condo. She'd worked damn hard and was seriously whipped. The first thing she was planning, after placing a quick call to the cops, was a nice, long bath.

She let herself into the suite, kicked off her shoes, and quietly tiptoed into the guest bathroom, which was thankfully connected to the living area, not the bedroom. Ran some hot water, stripped, and lowered herself in.

Ahhhh. Heaven. She closed her eyes, let her head drop back, and settled in for a nice, long, peaceful soak.

Unfortunately, the door crashing open a split second later kind of put a damper on the peaceful aspect of her bath. And the entry of one obviously furious vampire king didn't help matters, either.

He didn't rush toward her. That made her more nervous than anything. She instinctively slid down into the water. Like that would shield her from an enraged vampire. Not!

He towered over her, glaring. His nostrils flaring. A veritable inferno burning in his eyes.

She didn't know what to say. It seemed like anything she managed to stammer out at this moment might make things worse. Obviously, he'd somehow found out that she'd left.

Unable to meet his furious stare anymore, she dropped her gaze to the water.

He reached down, snatched her wrist, and yanked. Pulled her clear out of the tub. Didn't even wait for her to get her feet under herself before he started walking out of the bathroom.

She tripped and slipped behind him, held up only by his pythonlike grip on her arm until he literally tossed her onto the bed.

Never had anyone manhandled her like that before. Never! She was a firm believer in women's rights. No man had a right to hurt a woman because he was angry, no matter what she did.

Didn't appear that Shadow the Barbarian shared her world views. He rushed to the dresser, pulled out a little whippy-looking thing, and was next to the bed in the time it took for her to drag in her next breath.

He was not going to hit her with that! No way!

11

Regan scrambled toward the head of the bed, wrapped the covers around her body, and gave him her best death glare, shouting, "Get the hell away from me!"

It seemed he had a moment's thought about how he was acting, because he didn't move for a few seconds. His mien changed, but not a lot. Just enough to not be so damned scary. At least it didn't look like he was about to whip her to death with that thing anymore. "You defied my orders," he said in an icy, clipped tone that told her things were nowhere close to being okay.

She knew she'd be in big trouble if she tried to lie her way out of this. The only thing left to do was try to talk him out of his snit—if that was possible—by being calm and honest and mature. "Yes, I did. But we're both adults here. I told you I had to go take care of this issue. It couldn't wait. The store is all I have." His face was like a stone mask. No emotion whatsoever. "You do understand, don't you? It's . . . all I have." She knew she was repeating herself, but gosh darn it, he wasn't speaking. She wasn't sure which was worse (or more dangerous)—Shadow the Furious or Shadow the Silent. Her gut instinct told her it was the latter.

"I know. But I said you couldn't go. I said it very clearly. And I said it for a good reason, not because I was trying to be unreasonable." He crossed his arms over his chest, which made them look bigger, made his entire upper body look bigger. "I won't wrestle you. I won't chase you. You will come here and take your punishment like an adult." He pointed at the floor in front of his feet with the whip end of his weapon, a weapon he clearly meant to use on her.

"I will not. At least, not if what you're intending to do is hit me."

"You have forgotten already. I am your master and king. You will do as I say."

Oh, he was begging for some heat! Pulling this master shit on her now. "No one hits me, mister! That master stuff is for the bedroom. That's it. I never signed up to be anyone's slave around the clock."

"We're in the bedroom."

"That's not what I mean!"

"On your knees, slave. Or you will suffer even more at my hand!"

This time, the thin veneer of his control cracked, and she saw how truly angry he was. Saw it in his eyes, the tension rippling along his shoulders. Heard it in his voice.

Was it wise to kneel within striking range of a man who was about to snap? Probably not. But she knew for a fact it would be even more foolish to try to fight her way out of this situation.

If he seriously hurt her, she reasoned, she'd find a way to leave. Immediately. She'd hide if she had to. She'd file abuse charges too. That would be the end of that.

She scooted to the edge of the bed and slid to the floor. The last thing she wanted to do was assume the slave position, but she knew that was what he expected. She did it, with the covers still wrapped snuggly around herself. Let him get a clean crack in through layers of cotton and quilting!

Naturally, he wasn't about to let her get away with that.

"Remove the covers."

Her eyes still focused on the floor, she released the material and let it fall from her body. She was nude. On her knees. Completely vulnerable. It was humiliating!

"Arch that back," he demanded sharply.

She gritted her teeth and did as he asked, knowing full well it would make her breasts stick out. How dare he get all hot and bothered over her breasts while making her sit on the floor and grovel for his forgiveness?

This slave thing was so not for her!

Then, she heard a soft smack, like a small piece of leather striking skin. And before she knew what had happened, she felt the pain, white hot, blaze across her shoulder blades and razor up and down her spine. She yelped out, jerked.

Another strike. This time on the other side of her back. Tears ran unchecked from her eyes as the blistering sensation shot across her upper back.

She trembled, waiting for another. Her breaths came out in sobs. She lifted her hands to her face and rubbed away the wetness.

"You will never—never!—disobey me again."

She lifted her head to look at him just before he turned away and strolled across the room.

He headed out to the sitting room. She heard him open the suite's main door and speak to someone outside. A minute later, he closed the door and sat on the couch. Kicked up his feet on the coffee table and turned on the television.

Okay. Now what? Was she supposed to stay there, on the floor? Wait for him to tell her she could get up? Or was she free to go about her business? She was mighty tired. She opted for staying put, even though she was ready to conk out right there on the floor.

Couldn't have been more than a couple minutes later when there was a knock at the door. She watched as Shadow stood, hit the POWER button to cut off the TV, and went to the door. He opened it and let in a stunningly gorgeous woman. A stunningly gorgeous woman who just happened to have the world's perfect hair, face, and body. She knew this because the woman also happened to be nude, with the exception of some cute little dangly hearts from her nipples and a black choker that looked a great deal like the one permanently affixed to Regan's neck. She was clean shaven. Everywhere. Suntanned. Trim and amazing. Everything Regan felt she was not.

No sooner did the woman enter the room than she was on her knees, her gaze down, her perky, suntanned breasts pushed out, her arms behind her back.

Ass kisser.

"My king," the woman said, sounding awestruck.

Shadow closed the door. "You may stand. Come. This way." He motioned toward the bedroom. "Tonight I have something special planned for you."

What did he have planned? She was not into girl-on-girl stuff, if that was what he had in mind.

He gave Regan a vicious glare as he led the beautiful woman into the bedroom. Then his expression turned icy, his smile almost a sneer.

Whatever he had up his sleeve, it was pretty safe to assume it wasn't going to be pleasant for her. This assumption was reinforced when he shifted his gaze to the other woman and his expression immediately softened to obvious adoration.

Well, hell! If he liked this Little Miss Perfect so much, why didn't he marry her?

"On your knees, slave," he commanded, pointing to a spot no more than a few inches from where Regan was kneeling.

The woman seemed unfazed by the fact that she'd just been told to kneel next to another naked woman. Made Regan wonder how often that sort of thing was asked of her.

"You will see now what rewards come to those who are obedient," Shadow said in clipped tones that told Regan he was speaking to her. She didn't lift her gaze to his face to double-check, though she did let it wander slightly to the left. It kind of skipped up the woman's lean torso to her head. She had a nice profile. Not a flaw that Regan could see anywhere.

Regan hated Miss Perfect Slave already.

"You, my sweet, may suck my cock. Until I come," he cooed. He unfastened his pants, pulled out his penis, which happened to be at full staff already, and grabbed a handful of streaked blond hair.

"Yes, my king," the woman said with such awe, she sounded as if he'd just asked her to be the mother of his children.

Okay, Regan had sucked cock before. It wasn't that big of a deal. In fact, to her it wasn't much of a thrill at all. Her cheeks tended to ache after a while, and she had an overactive gag reflex, so if the guy happened to thrust a little too hard, she was ready to lose it. So why was this woman so thrilled to take Shadow's dick in her mouth?

She'd tasted it already. Wasn't coated in chocolate or anything.

Sounds of oral pleasure ensued. Regan dropped her gaze. It was just plain weird watching another woman suck Shadow's cock. He was holding her hair and really fucking her mouth hard. She was slurping and "mmmmmming" like he was feeding her Godiva chocolates.

"Watch, Regan. See what kinds of rewards a woman receives for being obedient?"

She kept her thoughts to herself about who she thought was really getting the reward. And it wasn't the red-faced blonde with a mouthful of Shadow's meat.

"Touch her pussy, Regan."

"Huh?"

"My slave will have her reward. Touch her pussy, Regan. Slave, spread your legs."

The slave dutifully scooted her knees apart as she continued to slurp and lick and suck.

Regan hesitated. She'd never touched a girl. At least, not down *there*. On the arm, probably. Maybe a shoulder. But never, ever below the belly button.

"Do it!" he shouted.

Regan jerked. He wasn't messing around. No siree. She'd clearly pushed him by leaving today. Darn it! Would he forgive her? Lighten up a bit? Or would he continue this tyrant act for the rest of their time together?

Suddenly a month seemed like an extremely long time.

She reluctantly inched her left hand over until it met the silky skin of the slave's thigh.

God, this was weird!

The slave trembled slightly under her touch.

Regan glanced up at Shadow's face. He was watching. His eyes were fierce, reminded her of a pit bull before it attacked. She couldn't hold his gaze, so she let hers fall back to her lap.

If she had to touch another woman, she wasn't going to look. And she wouldn't think about it too much. Just let the fingers do the walking.

She leaned a bit to reach down around the inside of the slave's thigh until she found the warm juncture between her legs. Her labia were as smooth as the skin of her legs. Regan tried not to think about the fact that she was touching the woman's genitals. That little fold of skin was just . . . an elbow. Okay, it was a mighty strange elbow. And wet.

Oh, this was too weird for her!

The slave gave a little whimper.

"Fuck her with your fingers, Regan. Fuck her hard. Two fingers," Shadow barked as he thrust his dick in and out of the slave's mouth. His stomach and thighs were coated in a thin sheen of sweat. She guessed he was about ready to come.

She scrunched up her face, closed her eyes, and slid her fingers into the slave's canal. The inner muscles instantly tightened around them. Slick and slippery. Tight and hot. Regan couldn't see what guys saw in it. She withdrew her fingers, then plunged them in again and again, attempting to match Shadow's rhythmic thrusts.

The slave seemed to appreciate her efforts, if all the trembling and shaking was any indication. The woman's pussy was dripping wet. Tightening around Regan's fingers, then slackening in time to her thrusts. Regan hazarded a glance to her left and sucked in a gasp.

The sight of her hand between the other woman's legs did something really strange. She couldn't explain why, but for some reason, it sent a little lick of heat up her spine. And then another. And another.

To her utter astonishment, she felt her own pussy getting wet.

The slave's whimpers were getting louder and more frequent. Her right thigh was trembling under Regan's arm. She could feel it. And she could feel the woman's skin heating.

"Regan, touch your own pussy with your other hand."

She didn't have to look at either one of them to know they would not be staring at her. Both were flush-faced and so close to coming, Regan could literally smell it. The scent of sex hung thick in the air. Her inhibitions were gone, lost in the haze of wanting what the sights and sounds and scents were building inside her body. She pushed her index finger inside her own pussy, then dragged the dampened tip up to her clit. She drew slow, lazy circles, round and round in time with the in and out thrusts she gave the other woman. The simmering heat slowly increased. She dropped her head back. Her hair brushed her shoulder blades. Tickled. She shivered. Her breathing quickened. Her stomach tightened.

"Slave," Shadow said in a hoarse voice. "You may come."

Instantly, the room was filled with the husky moans of release. The woman's vagina pulsed around Regan's fingers. Hot liquid coated them. She continued to thrust them in and out and waited, holding her breath, for Shadow to tell her it was her turn.

"Regan," he said. "Stop now!"

What? Stop? Oh. That's what he meant. Stop touching the slave. She pulled her hand away.

"No. Stop touching yourself."

That wasn't right! She'd just started enjoying herself. Even though she'd joined in the fun a little late, she was almost caught up with them. Wouldn't take more than a minute or two.

"But—"

"I said stop! Do not question me. Hands behind your back."

Frustrated beyond words and a little confused, she did what he asked.

"I'm going to come now, slave." He pulled his hips back, then drove them forward hard, sending his cock down her throat. "Oh yes, that's it. Swallow it all." He gave her several hard, fast thrusts, then pulled his dick out of her mouth and smiled down at her. "Did you enjoy your reward, my sweet?"

"Very much, my king."

"Good." He pulled her up until she stood before him, gathered her hair into his hand, and laid it over one shoulder. Then he tipped his head and smiled, flashing a set of elongated fangs that rivaled the canines of a dog. He stared into Regan's eyes as he lowered his head to the slave's neck and bit.

A tiny trickle of deep crimson ran down the slave's skin as she bucked against him. She threw her arms around his neck, looped a leg around his, and cried out. Her hips ground against him as he sucked. Her head dropped back. An expression of profound sexual ecstasy swept over her features.

Regan watched in horror for a minute, maybe not even that long, before dropping her eyes to the floor. The slave sounded like she was in absolute heaven, screaming out, "More, more!"

but Regan still felt awful for her. A vampire was feeding on her. Yuck! And double yuck! The woman looked boneless and limp when he was through with her, though she somehow managed to stagger a step or two away from him.

He simply pointed at the door and she nodded. Like a zombie, she turned dead eyes to Regan, then walked out of the room.

"Come." It wasn't an invitation. Evidently a couple wicked lashes with a whip and a little erotic teasing weren't enough to soothe his riled nerves. He watched her stand with arms crossed over his chest and dark eyes. "I'm through being nice. I tried it your way and you didn't respect me. From now on, I'm going to do things my way. Obviously kindness isn't going to get me anywhere."

She started to open her mouth to shoot a sarcastic comment about how beating people was not the best way to win friends, but he stopped her with an upheld hand and a meaningful glare. No, sarcasm would probably not be well received at the moment. She sure didn't want to feel the bite of that whip anytime in the next millennium.

"Our agreement remains. I have just under a month to convince you to remain with me as my queen."

She almost laughed out loud at that insane idea.

"I'm just going about wooing you in a different way. I made a mistake. I should've known you wouldn't respect me for my kindness. That you'd take it for granted. It's human nature to do such a thing." He walked a circle around her. "But I've seen the error of my ways, and I am acting now to correct things. You will be treated as the slave you are. You will earn everything, from the food you consume to the privacy you so vehemently demand in the bathroom. Clothes. Water. Nothing will be given to you if it hasn't been earned." He halted in front of her. "You will stay with me at all times. You will not leave my side, which in a few hours will not be an issue any longer. We are leaving for Slovenia. Do you have any questions?"

"Leaving? What about my store? My home?" Her eyes and nose stung with tears threatening to gush out like a waterfall held back by a couple of twigs and a handful of mud. The dam was breaking. Despite her best efforts to hold it back, hot, salty water leaked from the inner corners of her eyes, dribbled down her cheeks. This was not fair! What was in this for her? What had started out as a give-and-take kind of thing was now all take—on his part. No give whatsoever. No understanding.

"Your home and store will be looked after. I know you don't understand right now, but this is for the best. For everyone concerned. I can't have you out traipsing around unguarded. It's too risky."

"Yeah, because if something happens to me, then Shadow the Great Vampire King becomes a pile of worthless decrepit old undead flesh," she muttered under her breath. "Can't think of anybody but himself."

Something scary flared in his eyes. Then it was gone. He looked at her coolly for several seconds, then swung, just missing her left cheek. Shock blasted through her body. He'd almost hit her! In the face. She staggered backward and gave him a glare of hatred. "I see you heard that."

"It's your choice," he said, turning away. "You want to make this difficult, I am fully capable of making the rest of your month pure hell. Doesn't matter to me either way."

"Why? Why not just divorce me and get it over with now?"

"Because we have an agreement, and I'm holding myself—and you—to it."

"How honorable."

This time the look he gave her was so icy, so fucking cold, like he was looking down at some filthy piece of shit he'd stepped in, it yanked the air out of her lungs, made her dizzy. How dare he look at her like that? When she was there doing all this as a favor to him! She took another step back and battled rage so fierce inside her it threatened to snuff out what little remained of her humanity. Pure animal instinct battled inside for control. She wanted to leap on him like a cat and smack him silly. But before she'd eliminated the last bits of doubt in the wisdom of that action, he left the room and slammed the door. So, instead of doing the catwoman thing and making him sorry for what he'd done to her, she fell on her ass and started blubbering like a baby.

Crying was such a useless pastime, but every now and then, she had a need for a good, long cry. This was without a doubt one of the most miserable, frustrating, and terrifying positions she'd ever been in. No control. Not a shred. The idea of being completely dependent upon someone else like this was so foreign to her. It was absolutely horrifying.

She paced the floor, trying to think of a way out of the mess. She could call the police and tell them she was being held hostage. Yes, that sounded like a great idea.

She ran to the phone. The line was dead. Fucker was always one step ahead of her, obviously had the phone cut off. She jerked the cord from the wall outlet and threw the useless thing across the room. It left a nice dent in the wall. Hit with a satisfying plastic-cracking smack before falling to the floor.

He'd see. Instead of beating her into submission, he'd riled a caged tiger. Now, there was no way in hell that she'd submit to him by her own free will. Not a chance. He could take his stinking "Master" and whips and chains and shove them where the sun didn't shine.

He returned to the room just as she was clearing all the art from the walls. The room was a jail cell. What the hell did she need fricking pictures on the walls for? The paintings landed with a crash, the glass shattering as each one fell.

He didn't say a word. He just walked up to her, scrambled to catch her wrists in his big luggish fists—she didn't make it easy for him—and jerked them behind her back. He held them so tightly, her fingers went numb. Her arms were stretched straight, pulled together to the center of her back. Standing behind her, he pressed the front of his body against her and leaned down to nibble on one side of her neck.

She was breathing like she'd just run full speed for twenty miles. How dare he! What did he expect? She'd fall to her knees and beg him to fuck her now?

Goose bumps popped up all over the right side of her body. Stupid nerves! Why'd they have to be so fricking sensitive? She clamped her eyelids shut and stood rigid. Maybe he'd succeed in setting off a few chemical reactions in her body, but he wasn't going to succeed in penetrating her mind, her heart. Those were hers, and it'd take more than a little stroking to turn them to his side.

He shifted hands so that both her wrists were held by one, then lifted the other one to her breast. She flinched, knowing what he was about to do. Her nipples had always been sensitive. Even a light touch drove her crazy.

He pinched her right nipple, and little sparks of desire flickered here and there. In her tummy. Where his body pressed up against hers. Between her legs.

Didn't matter. She wasn't going to fuck him. She wasn't going to kneel before him, either.

"My little wildcat," he murmured in her ear, just before he thrust his tongue in it.

Oh, he was so not playing fair.

"I adore your spirit. Your strength. You just need to learn how to use them to your full advantage." He lifted his fingertip to his mouth, dragged his tongue over it, and dropped the moistened digit to her nipple. Round and round, he drew slow circles. Faster and faster beat her heart. "Submission isn't done out of a position of weakness but one of strength. You will learn that."

Like hell. Strength? How could kneeling at a guy's feet and having no control over any aspect of one's own life be a position of strength? He was so full of shit. Oh no, the other end of the whip was definitely the position of power.

"You will see. Before the month is through."

In your dreams, buddy.

Half pushing her, half carrying her, he walked her through the room, out the door.

"Where are we going?"

"Our flight leaves within the hour."

"I'm naked. I can't go to the airport naked." She dug her heels in, not that it did a bit of good. With two hundred and whatever pounds of Super Vampire propelling her forward, she didn't stand a chance of not going where he had decided she'd go.

He jerked back on her wrists until she dropped to her knees as they stepped into the hallway. "I didn't give you permission to question my decision, did I?"

"No. But—"

"Would you like to be whipped again? Am I still being too easy on you?"

"No." Too easy! He'd whipped her. And was now dragging her outside with no clothes on. In pain. Humiliated beyond words. Could it get worse? She hated to find out. She bit her lip until it bled.

He pushed her into a waiting Hummer limousine. There were no other people inside. No thugs. Not even his sister. A few minutes later, the truck pulled away. Sitting snug up against Shadow—and not because that was her idea—she watched as the truck carried her away from her hometown toward the airport. Instead of pulling up to the normal terminal, though, it headed down a long, nearly deserted road to a big steel building. A small jet sat just outside. The limo stopped beside it. The door opened and Shadow exited. He pulled her out and ushered her to the plane.

Despite being furious over being literally dragged away

from her life and everything it contained, she had to admit the plane was nice inside. The interior was narrow, with a couple of swiveling captain's chairs, a couch, and a desk in what could best be described as a living area or office. Shadow steered her toward the back of the plane, where a small bedroom was hidden behind a closed door. He pushed her onto the bed. "You need to sleep." Before she could object, he shut the door.

Naturally, she tested it. Naturally, it was locked.

She plopped on the bed. She knew she should be panic-stricken about now. She was on a plane. No identification. No clothes. Nothing to even indicate she'd been boarded. What if what Shadow had said was a lie? What if he didn't face losing all his vampy powers when she died? What if he decided he was sick and tired of her and escorted her to the door while they were up around thirty thousand feet while they flew over the Atlantic? That was one helluva long fall! And she'd completely vanish without a trace, unless she left some evidence. She briefly considered plucking a few strands of hair and scattering them around.

But all of those what-ifs seemed so unlikely. She felt only a twinge of worry. A lot of anger. But not much fear. Despite the fact that he'd been a little heavy-handed today, he hadn't done anything to really hurt her. Strong as a freaking ox, he was certainly capable. The lashes on her back only stung a little now.

She lay back as the plane's engines hummed, setting the vehicle into motion.

Like always, she'd worn herself out. The fight was gone, replaced by achy exhaustion. Maybe after a little nap, things would look better. As the plane launched into the air, she rolled onto her stomach and settled into the bed. Soft. Comforting.

She wondered what part of the world she'd wake up in.

12

"We're here," Shadow whispered in her ear. "Wake up. You've slept a long time."

Regan slipped from a deep sleep into a semisnoozing state. Aware of her surroundings but not fully awake yet.

Her mouth was hanging wide open. How appealing. She snapped it shut and blinked open her eyes. She felt awful. Rundown. Achy. Nauseated. "Where are we?" She lifted her head and slid up the window shade to peer outside. They were rolling toward a building that looked a lot like the one they'd left behind in Detroit. Still, the mountains in the background sort of gave it away. They definitely weren't in Michigan anymore. But from past travel, she knew flying over the Atlantic took many hours. They couldn't be in Slovenia yet.

"We're in Ljubljana. At the airport."

"Ljubljana? What happened to New York? Wouldn't we need to stop? Fill up the gas tanks?"

"You've been sleeping for a while." He pulled open a small door to the right of the room's entry—if you could call it a room. Produced a mid-thigh-length white terry-cloth robe. He handed it to her. "It's a little cooler here than in Michigan. You may wear this."

She shrugged into the robe and tied the belt. It felt nice wearing clothes. Granted, it was short. Didn't cover much but her arms, ass, back, and stomach. But it still beat being ferried around nude.

He took her hand in his and led her through the plane. When they stepped out into the crisp air inside the metal building where the plane was parked, she was extremely glad she had that flimsy little robe. It wasn't a parka, but it did keep the cool air off her more sensitive parts.

They entered a car parked inside the building. The windows were shaded and tinted, probably to keep the sun out. When they pulled out, she couldn't tell whether it was daytime outside or night. She had no idea how long she'd slept. That travel time-zone thing. Totally confusing.

They drove for only a short time, maybe a half hour, before pulling up to the most amazing building. She'd seen European castles before. And she'd found every one of them breathtaking. But this one beat them all. Not so much because of its construction. It was made of rough-hewn stone blocks with a pair of round turrets flanking either side of a two-story tall rectangle topped with a clay roof.

It was the location.

It was twilight outside, either predawn or presunset. She couldn't be sure, since she didn't know which direction was which. But one side of the sky was purple with streaks of salmon pink. The castle perched high on the top of a craggy cliff overlooking a lake. Tree-covered hills lined all sides of the lake. It was stunning.

"We need to get inside now, before sunrise." Shadow pulled on her arm as she climbed from the car and walked on shaky legs across the stone-tiled courtyard, past several armed guards.

The castle had a very Mediterranean feel, both inside and

out. The interior walls were white. Heavy wooden beams held up the high ceilings. One wall was painted with a huge, stunning mural. Buildings. People. Trees. Absolutely lovely.

She glanced up at Shadow as she followed him through the main living room area and across another courtyard completely enclosed inside the castle's walls. Past more guards. A set of very steep stone steps led up to a second floor. Bedrooms.

"This is our suite. You will stay with me at all times."

No surprise there. She sighed and took a look at her new prison cell. It was gorgeous, as far as prisons go. All velvet and posh and formal. Just the kind of interior she loved. But it was still her prison.

He removed her robe, folded it, and set it inside a huge dark-stained armoire. "It's nearly sunrise, and you know I am unable to stay awake while the sun is up. I have requested some food be delivered. It should be arriving shortly. And I have informed the guards that you are not permitted to leave this suite. Should you try, they will make certain you're unable to make a second attempt. Do not make me regret letting you roam free while I sleep. I am fully capable of securing you in a space so you have no chance of escape."

"I can't go anywhere anyway. Not unless you thought to bring my passport. And from the looks of it, it'd be a long walk to the nearest tourist trap."

He smiled. Ooh, she hated him for that smile. "No. I'm afraid I didn't think to bring your passport. What a shame."

Yeah.

No denying it any longer. He had her exactly where he wanted her. There was no chance she'd escape. And if she did, she had no money. No papers. She couldn't buy a plane ticket and just hop on the next commercial flight for the States.

Like it or not, she was indeed his prisoner. She lacked the energy to fume and rant. So, she sat and waited for her food to arrive. Somehow, she'd have to make it through what remained of her month. Then she'd be free again, to live her life. It was only a little over three short weeks. If soldiers could make it through nine or twelve weeks of hell the U.S. government called boot camp, couldn't she make it through three in this place?

God, she hoped so!

Then again, if there was a little reward at the end, something to make it all worthwhile, to give her something to look forward to, she figured it would be that much easier. If she had something really great to work toward, she could play his little submission game.

Yes, a reward. That was the ticket. The gears started turning. . . .

Shadow hung up the phone and turned to his sleeping wife. Tell her or not? It wasn't an easy decision to make. Tell her there'd been a second attempt on her life? Who knew what kind of reaction he'd get? She could somehow blame him and turn hostile again. She could become fearful and suspicious of everyone. He was willing to bet whatever reaction she gave, it would take him by surprise. If anything, he'd learned his wife was full of surprises.

Clearly, they'd needed this, leaving the States. Not just for security reasons. They needed someplace quiet. Remote. Where they could simply spend time together. Get to know each other. Where she'd have no distractions. No store. No house. No parties. Just the two of them in this big, lonely castle.

Didn't feel so lonely with her here. For the first time since his father had died.

He admired her as she slept. Stroked her silky hair and listened to the slow but steady sound of her breathing. She brought life into this place. And into his very soul. Life and energy and warmth.

Yes, this was a very good idea. Here, in a place full of cherished memories, he'd make a new life with his bride. He'd make her see they were meant to be together. He'd help her discover the part of her inside that hungered for a strong man to take control. And he'd show her the strength of submitting to him.

No, he decided. He wouldn't tell her about the poisoned food and dead dog the security guard had found at the store. Not yet. He'd let the detectives do their job. Already, they'd found a lead. The restaurant did receive an order from Regan that day, but minutes after the order was placed, the restaurant clerk had said she'd called back and cancelled it.

He knew she hadn't been the one to make that second phone call. And that meant a woman was allied with his enemies. A woman who sounded enough like Regan to place a call in her name.

The detective also had a description of the car that had made the delivery and a partial license plate. Shouldn't take much time at all to track down the fake delivery driver. From there, it would be smooth sailing.

Yes, this was the best for everyone. He'd let his wife know about the attempt when the police had more information. Until then, he'd continue with the training. He'd seen it in her eyes when they'd walked into the castle. She'd finally accepted her role as slave. There was a sense of surrender. She'd given up the fight. They would move forward now. It would be so much easier.

Tonight, she would be rewarded. Tonight he would fuck her exactly the way she liked it. Slow and gentle. Hard and fast. But first, he had to feed.

He caressed her shoulder. "Wake up, Regan."

He received a grunt in return. She rolled away from him and tugged the blanket up to her chin.

"Regan, it's time to get up." This time he didn't wait for her to grunt or roll away. He snatched the blanket away, scooped her into his arms, and carried her into the bathroom where he deposited her on her feet. She was unsteady, since she was barely awake, so he held her waist gently and waited for her to fully awaken.

She blinked her heavy-lidded eyes at him. "What time is it?"

"Doesn't matter. What matters is I said it's time to get up." He turned and walked out of the bathroom, passing the unhinged door as he returned to the bedroom. He sat on the bed and stared at her. It would make her uncomfortable. He knew that. But she needed to get over it. It was a little bit of urine. She was a mortal. Those things happened.

Her face turned a bright shade of pink. She settled on the commode, her knees pressed tightly together. A moment later, he heard the telltale sound of water striking water.

Very good.

She wiped, flushed, and went to the sink.

"Take a shower. I want you clean."

She blinked a few more times. Her lips thinned but all she said was, "Okayyyy." She turned on the water. Since she was already nude, she didn't have to undress. Merely stepped into the shower stall.

He wanted to go in there with her, wash her up, but he decided against it. He was starving, and he knew without a doubt that if he went in there with her, it would be a while before they got out.

While she cleaned up, he called for one of his favorite slaves to meet them down in the dungeon. Then he dressed in his favorite leather pants and went into the bathroom to hurry Regan along.

She looked absolutely mouthwatering, all wet and slick with fragrant soap. Her saturated hair hung in heavy waves down her back. Mini rivers of water streamed from the ends, down her back, over the curve of her ass.

Maybe he wasn't as starved as he thought. . . .

Regan cut off the water and reached past him for the towel sitting on the countertop. He watched as she wiped away every last droplet from her chest, shoulders, stomach. The bloodlust was rising, threatening to strip away his ability to think.

No, he needed to get down to the dungeon. Now. Before he broke his promise to Regan and fed on her.

"This way," he said with a voice that sounded tight even to him. "Leave the towel." He handed her the nipple chain he'd given her in the States.

"Okay." She sounded fearful as she fastened each end to her nipples.

He watched, his mouth watering at the sight of her fingering her own nipples. "If you behave like a good slave, you have nothing to fear."

She didn't respond, merely stepped ahead of him when he motioned for her to and preceded him out the door and down the stairs. He noticed the way her shoulders tensed when they walked past the guards at the foot of the stairs.

"They've seen more women undressed than dressed in this castle," he explained.

Her shoulders didn't relax, but she nodded and followed his directions through the castle and down the steps that led to the dungeon.

This was his absolute favorite dungeon. It didn't have all the equipment one might find in a modern dungeon. It had the real stuff, the kinds of equipment designed to torture prisoners. He hadn't had a prisoner down there in a long time, though. The mostly wood and iron apparatuses had been put to new uses. Stocks. A rack. Torture tables. A garrote. Ropes, chains, and suspension devices. The room was painted a dark color. The floor was stone. Cold under bare feet. The air was damp and chilly. There was without a doubt a very ominous feel about the place.

Regan stopped just inside the door, giving a startled gasp.

He watched as her eyes darted from one piece of equipment to another. She didn't speak. Didn't have to. A coat of goose bumps coated her skin. The fine blond hairs on her arms stiffened.

The slave he'd called for was kneeling in place at the far end of the room.

"Kneel there." He motioned for Regan to kneel beside the slave. He couldn't help noticing her trembling. That was okay. A little fear would make her appreciate the reward that much more.

"You. Stand." He pointed at the slave. She stood, looked up at him with eyes already dark with need. She hadn't been fed upon for a long time. He could tell.

That was the thing with slaves. Once they became a regular source of nourishment to a vampire, they began to need it, crave it. If their vampire died or deserted them, the need would eventually overtake them, drive them mad, if they didn't find a new vampire to take the last one's place. This slave was nearly there.

He caressed her long, ink-black locks. Straight and silky smooth. "It's been too long."

"Yes, Master. Much too long." She tipped her head to the side, exposing her jugular. "Please, Master." There was such desperation in her voice, he didn't have the heart to tease her, torment her. She'd clearly had enough of that already. He pulled her to him until her nude body was flush with his and bit. Her blood was so sweet. Spicy too. Absolutely delicious. He drank his fill as the slave sighed and writhed in his arms. She ground her slick pussy into his hips. He reached down with one hand and thrust two fingers into her slick, hot depth.

Regan was still kneeling on the floor. In his current position, he couldn't see her. But every now and then, between squeals of delight pouring from the slave's mouth, he could hear her little gasps, her teeth chattering.

When he had his fill, he gently pushed the slave away and commanded her to leave him, with the promise to return for a feeding the next night. The slave kissed his feet and left.

Now that he'd satisfied his need for nutrition, he could turn his attention to the fun part of the night. His wife's training.

"Does it make you hot, watching me feed?" he asked.

She shook her head. Her eyes were so wide with fear. Her face so pale. "No, M-Master."

"Ah. You're afraid." He glanced meaningfully at her nipples, which were jutting out in tempting little pink points. "Yet, I see there are at least two parts of you that found my feeding more than just terrifying."

She followed the direction of his gaze. When she lifted her eyes to his face again, he noted the adorable pink tint her face and upper chest had taken.

"Yes, Master. It would seem they did."

"Stand."

She followed his command. Though she didn't take a pleasing position. Her shoulders were stooped, her spine weak.

"What do you suppose it is?" he asked, circling her. Prodding various parts until she straightened her posture. "That's it. Spine strong. Stomach in. Breasts out." He stopped directly behind her. Admired the slope of her back down to her derriere. One fine ass, his wife had. Perfect for spanking. "What part of my feeding did your nipples find so appealing?"

"I-I'm not sure."

Still standing behind her, he traced the line of her neck down to where it sloped to her shoulder with a fingertip. That was a sexy spot on a woman. The nape of her neck and shoulder. He leaned down and inhaled. The scents of shampoo and soap filled his nostrils. But the spicy scent of Regan's arousal lingered below the surface. That was the scent that he hungered for. And he would have his fill of it. Tonight.

Even though he'd just fed, he longed to taste her. To feel her blood rushing down his throat. His fangs elongated. He flickered his tongue over her collarbone, pleased when she shuddered slightly and leaned into him. She was so responsive . . . so delicious. His mouth hovered over the pulse on her neck. He closed his eyes. Fierce temptation swept through him but he battled it.

He couldn't bite her. He'd made a promise. Now was not the time to back down on his word. He needed her trust more than anything.

He forced himself to pull away before the last strings of his self-control snapped like overtightened violin strings. Time to start the training.

He motioned toward the dong stand in the far corner.

She looked reluctantly at him for a moment, then nodded. She obviously had no idea what pleasures were awaiting her. After tonight, he expected she'd be quite the tame kitty. Might even admit defeat and accept her role as queen. He would do everything in his power to make sure that happened.

Regan eyed the contraption Shadow was leading her to with caution, a little curiosity too. It wasn't a particularly complicated piece of equipment. Nor was it overly frightening. Not like some of the stuff in this place. The room was the dungeon of dungeons. Dark, chilly, creepy. Like a real honest-to-goodness dungeon. And a good portion of the equipment looked like genuine medieval torture devices.

If it wasn't for the heat simmering in her veins after watching Shadow feast on that girl, Regan knew for a fact she'd be shivering. Cold. Scared. Completely turned off.

Somehow, Shadow made this place . . . sexy.

The thing she was now standing next to was simply constructed. There was a flat square-shaped wooden base fixed to the floor. Upon the base were attached two chains with leather cuffs at the ends, one chain on either side of a metal pole standing straight up. The pole ended at about mid-thigh height.

"Do you know what this is?"

Feeling her cheeks color, she nodded. "I have an idea. I've seen things similar on the Internet."

"Good." He turned from her. Went to a tall wooden cupboard, opened the door, and pulled out a huge dildo.

A lump about the same size became caught in her throat. She swallowed a few times as she watched him attach the dildo to the top of the pole.

He'd expect her to stand on that base and impale herself on the dildo. The thought made her tremble. In a good way.

He pulled a tube of lubricating jelly from his pocket and greased up the dildo, then tucked it back inside and wiped his hands on some tissues he'd pulled from his other pocket. "Come now." He offered a hand to her. "Come and take your reward. You've been such a good girl since we've arrived."

The "good girl" bit rankled a little, but she decided not to make a federal case out of it. Things had been rather pleasant since they'd arrived, granted, they'd been at the castle for less than twenty-four hours, but still, already she'd seen that there were ways to influence Shadow. Ways that worked a whole lot better than screaming at him and calling him names.

She placed one foot in position and waited for him to fasten the leather strap around her ankle before moving over the top of the upright dildo.

Since she was short, at least an inch or two of the toy would be inside her at all times once she was standing in position, legs spread, feet on either side of the pole. With a slight bend of the knee, she'd be able to take the dildo in all the way. And he'd be watching her.

So sexy!

"Mount my cock, slave," Shadow demanded.

A rush of warmth pulsed to her pussy. She looked down, gripped the shaft in one hand to steady herself, and lifted the leg that hadn't been tied down yet. The dildo's head slipped between her labia and sank into her pussy. Not all the way in. Just enough to tease her. Immediately she wished she was shorter.

"Foot down."

"Oh God," she whispered, tightening her legs.

He buckled the strap around her second ankle, then stood and crossed his arms over his chest. He looked extremely pleased by what he saw. That made her internal temperature rise a couple degrees. Her inner muscles clenched around the tip of the dildo, increasing the torment.

"Are you enjoying your reward?"

Was she ever! But she'd enjoy it even more if she could bend her knees just a smidge. He'd let her. Soon. She knew it. No reason to press the issue. She nodded, pulled her hands behind her back, and pushed her breasts out. "Yes, Master."

"Nice. Look at you, my sweet pet." He circled around her like he'd done earlier. She felt the heat of his gaze searing her skin. Little tingles buzzed up and down her spine. He pressed his body against her back and wrapped an arm around her waist. "Would you like to sink down on that dildo? Take it deep inside?" he whispered.

"Y-yes, Master."

"Very well," he said against the side of her neck. Little frissons of pleasure danced up and down along her spine. "But you will move as I command." He tightened his grip around her waist, letting her know he meant to control her movements.

"Yes, Master. May I move now?"

"Yes."

She started to bend her knees, but he halted her downward motion by lifting up on her waist. She wanted to howl in frustration, but she held back, knowing she wouldn't be frustrated for long if she did what he asked.

"Slower."

"Yes, Master." This time, she bent her knees a miniscule bit. And the dildo slid a fraction of an inch deeper. She leaned back, welcoming Shadow's support and quivered. This was the most incredible experience. Her thighs were trembling a tiny bit from the strain of holding her in position. The rest of her was trembling from the need to drop several inches until that penis-shaped hunk of rubber was stroking all the deepest parts of her. "More, Master?" She wouldn't last long. Not like this. Not physically. She couldn't remember the last time she did squats in a gym.

"Yes. More. All the way down. And touch your clit while you're doing it." He took her right wrist in his hand and moved it around to her front. "Touch yourself, slave."

She bent her knees more, more, more until the dildo touched the opening to her womb. And she drew slow circles over her clit until she could barely remain standing. Her pussy was alternately clamping tight and relaxing around the dildo, sending waves of pleasure crashing through her system.

"That's it. Yes. Now up. But don't stop touching yourself. Ride my cock, slave." He held her waist as she straightened her legs and then bent them again. Up and down. The friction of the intimate caress from the dildo, coupled with her touches to her clit, the soft caress of the chain dangling between her breasts, and Shadow's hot body pressed against her back nearly sent her into an instant climax. Shadow seemed to notice. He pulled her up just before the first spasm of her orgasm rippled through her body.

"No!" he said in a loud, firm voice that told her if she disobeyed there would be hell to pay.

She swore she'd die, but she tried to hold back. Pulled her hand away, squinted her eyes closed, and stiffened her whole body.

Shadow moved away from her. She heard the metal clink of

the chains. Felt the first strap fall away from her ankle, then the other.

"Very good. You're learning quickly, slave."

Again, the willful side of her wanted to snap at his condescending tone. But she kept her sarcastic comment to herself, the thought of her reward casting a new and very pleasant light on the whole situation. Granted, he hadn't agreed to anything. Not yet. But she knew he would. She'd make it so he had no choice. She just had to learn to use what was at her disposal. As a submissive, she still had some power. She'd been too furious to see that at first. But now, with every minute they spent in that dungeon, it became clearer.

Being submissive did not mean she was powerless.

He pointed to another piece of equipment. Something that looked like a genuine stock. She stood behind it. He walked around her back, lifted the top half of the stock, and pressed on her shoulders until she was standing stooped over, her legs spread wide, her neck resting in the center indentation, her wrists in the smaller ones on either side. Then he dropped the top half down and locked it in place.

She became painfully aware of the position her ass was in. Especially when he rubbed his still fully clothed groin against it.

She wished he was naked.

He walked away. Even though she couldn't see that he'd gone, she knew it. She felt it. It was like the warmth had been sucked from the air. When he returned, happy little tingles skittered up and down her back. The heat index shot up a few degrees. "I have a surprise for you."

Went up a couple more.

"You're doing very well today, my slave. So well, I want to reward you again."

She tensed when she felt him touch her bottom. He dragged a finger coated with slick, cool wetness along her crack.

What was he going to do?

The anticipation sent her heartbeat into triple time. Her breathing turned shallow and quick. She heard her own gasps echoing off the stone walls.

Something pressed at her anus. Something small. She concentrated on trying to relax to let it in. She'd never had anal sex, but she'd taken a vibrator inside her ass. On many an occasion. That felt wonderful.

Whatever it was, it slipped inside with little effort, providing a slight feeling of fullness. Not a whole lot. Just enough to make her sigh.

"You like that, do you?"

"Yes, Master."

She felt more pressure, and a second something slid inside, pushing the first deeper. The second one was larger, the sensation as it went in more intense. She moaned. Her knees wobbled. Her face flamed. She wanted release. She wanted orgasm. She wanted Shadow's cock.

He walked around to the front of the stocks, unzipped his pants. His erect cock pushed at the front of his snug black Jockey's.

"Suck my cock." He kicked off his pants. Then got rid of the underwear and positioned the head of his erection at her mouth. His fingers tangled in her hair. He pulled just enough for a pleasant sting to spread over her scalp, adding yet another amazing sensation to the many already plundering her system.

She was nervous as she opened her mouth. Giving head was not her forte. And she had absolutely no control over how deep he thrust into her mouth, thanks to the stocks. She concentrated on regulating her breathing and using her tongue to pleasure him when he pushed inside. He tasted amazing, and she was surprised to find that the very thing that made her current position so scary seemed to make it all the more exciting. She rarely ever got hot while giving oral sex to a guy. But now. Now! After swirling her tongue round and round, lapping, flickering, sucking, slurping, and even taking him deep into her throat once, she was about ready to combust. The things pressed into her anus also seemed to intensify her body's reaction. It was a crazy, erotic, intoxicating cocktail of sensations. Feeling, smell, taste, sound.

Once again, she felt the tension of an orgasm spreading through her body. And wonder of all wonders, he wasn't anywhere near her genitals. She sucked harder, eager to show him her gratitude. To show him how exciting and thrilling he was making this for her.

He gave two quick thrusts and then abruptly jerked away from her. She caught sight of his face when he stepped back. It was flushed a deep magenta.

Standing in front of her, his erect cock mere inches from her mouth, he unfastened the stocks and helped her stand upright. Her back creaked a bit. Something gently struck the back of her upper thigh. She instinctively reached around to see what it was.

A string of beads. Dangling from her anus. Hot juices streamed from her pussy.

"Don't touch those." He led her to a chair with a slanted back and stirrups attached to hold her legs. He secured her to the chair with a single strap above her breasts and fastened a leather cuff around each thigh. Wide apart and open. He stood between her legs and entered her with a swift, deep thrust that sent the air from her lungs in a loud huff.

At last! He was inside her, filling her. It felt so right, the way his cock seemed to reach every part of her pussy, which ached for its intimate touch. He took her hard and fast, hammering in and out quickly. She screamed out in bliss, completely lost in the hunger building inside. Coiling tight. Churning hot.

When he synchronized his hard, deep thrusts with firm strokes to her clit, she felt the orgasm ignite inside. Like a spark setting a room full of gas fumes into flame.

"I'm going to come," she said.

"Yes, slave. Come. Now." He pulled on the beads in her anus, and they came out one, then the other, with a delightful pop.

Her entire body shook as orgasm blazed through her body like liquid fire. Up from her center and out until there wasn't a part of her that wasn't awash with breath-stealing heat. She heard him growl as he found his own release, then heard the sounds of his thoughts echo through her head. Pain and joy, anguish and frustration. Fears and doubts swept through her spirit, dragging it from the high it had sailed to down to a dark, cold depth. She felt the heat of tears sliding down her cheeks.

And then it was gone and nothing remained but her twitching body, slick with sweat and chilled by the cool air, and Shadow's upper body slumped over her.

"Training's over for today."

She stood on shaky legs after he released her from the restraints. "Thank goodness. I don't know how much more I could've taken."

He gave her an evil smile. "That was only the beginning. I have three more weeks with you, my little slave." He traced the line of her jaw and sent her naughty promises with eyes gone dark with lust. "I'm going to make sure every night—correction, every minute—counts."

She had every reason to believe he'd keep his word on that one, although something else left her feeling uneasy. She couldn't put a finger on it yet. It was one of those vague feelings, like a gray mist with no shape. She gave him a grateful nod and smiled.

Whatever it was, she was sure that sooner or later, it would come to her. She'd deal with it when the time was right.

13

A little over a week later, Shadow met his sister at the door. She was even bouncier than normal as she practically launched herself at him.

"Quinby, I have the most wonderful news!" she exclaimed, beaming. He glanced over her head to the rest of the new arrivals. His brothers and several trusted clan members, including a young man he hadn't seen in years, Mikhail Novak, had trailed in behind Tyra.

Well he'd be damned. Mikhail Novak. Their parents had been dear friends, and Mikhail had spent many days chasing Tyra through the castle and terrorizing her with toads, snakes, and other creatures. Then, his parents had sent him away to study at an exclusive private school in Paris. Shadow knew Tyra had written to him a few times, but he'd thought she'd lost contact with him years ago. It was damn good to see him again.

Tyra turned and motioned for Mikhail to step forward. "Quinby, you remember Mikhail Novak, don't you?"

"Of course!" Shadow gave the young man a quick hug and slap on the shoulder. "It's great to see you again. Where've you been hiding? Didn't make it to the last clan meeting. How're you doing?"

Mikhail gave him a trademark Mikhail goofy grin. "Hi, Quin—I mean, Your Grace. Good to see you too." Then he slid a questioning glance Tyra's way.

"What's up?" Shadow asked, catching the silent communication going on between Mikhail and his sister. Was Mikhail looking for a job? Did he need money? Protection?

When Mikhail returned his eyes to Shadow, the happy-go-lucky expression was gone. In its place, a mask of raw nerves. "Well, uh, I'm here to ask . . ." He visibly swallowed.

Shadow couldn't stand seeing the guy suffer for another nanosecond. "Need a job? I'll be happy to set you up with something. What did that fancy school teach you?"

Mikhail shook his head. "No, no. Nothing like that. I'm here for a more personal matter. I, uh . . ." He glanced at Tyra again, and she gave him a subtle nod of encouragement.

What were these two up to?

"Wanted to ask you for your sister's hand in marriage." As soon as he spit out the words, all the tension in his shoulders and face seemed to drop away. "There. I said it." He smiled at Tyra. "I did it."

The brilliant smile she gave him in return nearly blinded Shadow.

He felt his eyebrows lifting. Mikhail wanted to marry his little sister? Wait! His sister was getting married? His sister? "Uh . . ." For the first time in forever, he didn't know what to say. "Damn."

Tyra tipped her head. "Quinby, you *are* going to give Mikhail permission, aren't you? Because if you don't, I'm going to have to whoop your butt."

Mikhail and Tyra. Tyra and Mikhail. Had Mikhail touched Tyra? He had better not have! He'd be a dead man if he had.

"I'm going to . . . think about it. That's what I'm going to do."

Was there anything to think about? Shadow had known Mikhail since the kid had toddled around in diapers. Knew his parents too. They'd been like a second family to him when he was younger.

"Think about it?" Tyra said, crossing her arms over her chest and giving him a nasty glare. "What's there to think about?"

"Good morning—er, evening. Oh, we have visitors!" Shadow's face warmed. A few other parts too. His wife was awake. He turned to find her.

There. At the back of the room. She looked stunning. Still sleepy and rumpled, wearing a short little red robe that barely reached the top of her thighs. She was yanking down on the hem nervously. Her face was maybe one or two shades lighter than the robe. "Perhaps I should go up and get dressed."

"No! Don't you dare walk out now. I need you!" Tyra dashed across the room and gave Regan an enthusiastic hug. "The man of my dreams just asked my control freak of a big brother for my hand, and he had the nerve to say he'd think about it. Can you believe that? We've known Mikhail forever. It's not like we'd have to do a background check—"

"You do a background check?" Mikhail asked.

Shadow glanced at Rolf and Stefan, who were standing along the wall, in identical positions, arms crossed over their chests, an amused smirk on their faces.

"No, no! I'm just joking," Tyra said, waving a hand back in Mikhail's direction as she blabbered excitedly to his wife about boyfriends and weddings.

"Well, I don't know . . ." Regan said, sounding unsure. Her gaze met Shadow's for a brief instant. He felt the connection between them, even though they said nothing. It was like a charge of energy zapping between them. Their bond had grown stronger this past week. Stronger as he trained her. Punished her. Rewarded her.

He wasn't all that happy when she turned her attention back to his yappy sister and broke the bond. "I'm sure your brother has your best interests at heart."

"What?" Tyra staggered backward like she'd been struck. "Is this the same woman who talked me into helping her sneak—" She clapped her hand over her mouth. "I didn't just say that out loud, did I?"

Regan's eyes widened.

"Yes, you did say that out loud." Shadow crossed the room in the longest strides he could manage. He stopped just before he stomped right over her. "Does this have anything to do with your missing phone, Tyra? What is this about helping Regan? You helped her do what?"

"I . . . I helped her . . ." Tyra slid Regan a glance. "Helped her sneak in a snack?"

He didn't buy that for a moment, but as a guy who didn't like to punish anyone without proof of guilt for some crime, he couldn't do anything outside of give her a grunt of disbelief.

He'd find out the truth.

Tyra was in no way intimidated by his grunt. That was extremely clear. "You made the poor girl starve before leaving the States. I felt sorry for her."

He puffed up his chest and narrowed his eyes. "My wife's eating habits are none of your concern. Got it?"

"Yeah, yeah." Tyra shook her head. "I don't think she'd take anything I snuck to her anymore anyway. I think you brainwashed her."

"No, he hasn't brainwashed me," Regan said. "All my brain functions are still fully within my control. Although I have learned to handle things a little differently since coming here. Anyway, congratulations on the proposal. I'm sure your brother will make the best decision for both of you."

Tyra screwed up her face into a mask of disgust. "Girl, where'd your spine go?"

Over the years, Shadow had been a little indulgent when it came to Tyra. But he could not, would not, allow her to insult his wife. "Don't talk to my wife like that!"

"Sorry." Tyra backed away and rushed toward Mikhail, who'd stood back so quietly Shadow had nearly forgotten he was still in the room. "I'll just show my *fiancé* to the guest quarters. We can talk about everything else later."

That girl needed a firm hand, no thanks to him. He hadn't missed the way she'd emphasized the word *fiancé,* obviously rubbing it in. He thought about delivering the needed firm hand on her backside when she turned but decided now wasn't the best time. Once she was wedded to Mikhail, it would be his job. He wished the poor guy some luck there. Wouldn't wish his baby sister on anyone. Little willful imp. "Good idea." He watched them leave. Mikhail looked at Tyra tenderly, took her hand, and together they headed toward the exit.

"Shadow." Stefan stepped forward. Shadow noticed his brother's expression and tone of voice had changed. "We need to talk about a few things. We found out something. Figured we'd better tell you right away."

"Okay." Shadow turned to his wife, took her hands in his, and kissed each fingertip. "Go up and prepare yourself. I'll be in shortly."

"Yes, Master." She nodded obediently and left the room.

Shadow was pleased by his brothers' shocked expressions as they watched her.

"W-what the hell'd you do to her?" Stefan stammered.

"Yeah. You've only been gone a little over a week," Rolf added, looking at him as if he'd sprouted wings and taken flight.

He shrugged, all casual-like. "I showed her the pleasure to be found in obedience."

"Shit," Rolf said, glancing Stefan's way. He shoved a hand in his pocket, pulled out his wallet, and counted out a hundred dollars. Stefan happily accepted them, tucked them into his wallet.

Right away, Shadow knew what that was all about. "You bet against me?" he asked Rolf.

"Not really. I bet for her."

"Anyway," Stefan said. "We intercepted some intelligence yesterday and learned the assassin hired to kill your wife is here, in the surrounding area of the castle. Came in this morning."

"I'm not too worried about it. He won't get to her. She's safe in the castle. I haven't accepted any deliveries that haven't been verified. No poisoned food or bouquets."

"Any word from the police back in the States?" Rolf asked.

"Nothing new. All they know is that the food she left sitting at the store was indeed poisoned. I still don't know if she left without locking the door or if someone else broke in. Haven't wanted to bring it up, since things have been going okay. Now that she's safe, I don't want her being fearful."

"Okayyy." Stefan didn't sound as confident as Shadow felt about his handling of Regan's situation. "Well, let us know if there's anything else we can do. I'll keep communicating with my contacts. They're not high up enough in the organization to know who the assassin is, but at least they have access to some useful stuff."

"Good enough. I gotta find out who the bastard is. He'll pay when I do. I'll torture him until he begs for death. Whoever he is, he's got a lot of nerve . . . and not a lot of brains."

"Actually," Stefan said. "He's pretty damn smart. Look at that bouquet setup. How'd he know how to set up that reaction? How much of each chemical to use? How to store them so that they'd meet at a certain time? Seems like a damn complicated way to kill somebody, doesn't it?"

"Yeah," Shadow agreed. "So?"

"So, you gotta wonder if he's doing it for money or because he gets kicks out of playing with his chemistry set."

"Hopefully we'll find that out. Soon."

"But if the guy's that smart, what makes you think he couldn't get inside the castle?" Rolf asked.

"The guards," Shadow pointed out the obvious.

Stefan shook his head. "I don't think our guy will go that way—by force. He'll get inside. Somehow. And chances are good we won't know about it until—"

"Bullshit!" Shadow interrupted. He couldn't hear those words. No. Just the thought of losing Regan burned like hell.

Stefan took a step backward. "Just looking out for you."

"Yeah." Shadow knew his brother wouldn't say those things if he didn't feel it was necessary. Dammit, he hated hearing them, though. For a little over a week, he'd lived like there was no world beyond those tall stone walls. He'd spent hours with Regan. Talking. Training. He couldn't remember a time in his life when he'd been happier.

His brothers came home, and it all came with them—the troubles. The worries. The bullshit.

He hated being king.

He didn't want to think about it, but what Stefan said was true. The bastard was damn smart. Sneaky. He hadn't barreled through Regan's door, armed with an M16. He sent her fucking flowers with Shadow's name on them.

Fuck, the bastard was more than sneaky. He was gutsy, had balls the size of Jupiter.

Shadow would have to be more diligent, keep his eyes open, his senses keen. Trust his instincts. That was the only way he'd keep them both alive long enough to catch the bastard and stop him for good.

He went to his office, the responsibilities of his position

weighing heavily. He'd put off several tasks this past week. He should get them done now.

He'd reward himself—and Regan!—later. By giving them an extra half hour in the dungeon. Maybe tonight he'd try a little suspension.

"Regan, are you sure you're okay? You don't seem yourself." Tyra plopped onto the couch and watched Regan as she toweled her wet hair. Tyra's soon-to-be husband sat silently by her side.

"I'm good. Really." She adjusted the neckline of her robe. "It's not as bad here as I expected. Though it would be nice to get out of the castle once in a while. The town down the hill looks so cute."

"Okay. I just wanted to make sure. I know how my brother can be with a cat. The guy can be merciless."

Regan fought a smile. Yes, he could be. But she was learning really quickly that she liked that particular trait in him. A lot.

"Hey! I say we plan a trip down to Vled. It is an adorable little town. Not much in the way of shopping, if you're looking for couture, but I hear the food is great for you mortal type of people."

"That sounds nice. I'll talk to Shadow. Maybe if he knows I'm not going alone, he'll let me go."

"I'd be happy to accompany you both," piped in Mikhail. "I hear you've had some . . . unfortunate accidents recently. Are the rumors true? Has someone tried to kill you?"

"You know, since we came here, I haven't heard a word, so I'm not sure." Regan wrapped the towel around her shoulders and ran a comb through her tangled hair. "Personally, I think it's just a very weird chain of coincidences. But I could be wrong."

"I hope you're right," Tyra said. "I like you. I'd hate to see anything bad happen to you."

"It's hard to believe any of our clan members would even think to try to kill our queen," Mikhail added.

"Yes, hard to believe," Regan repeated, not adding the part about how easy it was for Shadow to believe it—and for good reason. Evidently, even if Mikhail had been a close family friend to the Sorensons, some things weren't discussed, like the hazards of being a member of the reigning royal family.

Could he not have known that Shadow and Ty's parents had been murdered?

"I don't want to talk about that anymore." Ty waved her hands in the air. "We're here to ask you a question. In our culture, our weddings are small, private. But I'd like to ask if you'd be my witness?"

"Me?" Regan blinked in surprise. "What does that mean? What's a witness do?" She didn't recall any witnesses at her so-called ceremony with Shadow. Unless they counted the two guys holding her arms, who she learned later were his brothers.

Ty gave her a goofy smile. "Stands behind me and watches?"

"Sure. I'd be glad to be your witness. I'm flattered you asked."

"Well, outside of Mik"—she patted his knee and slid a smile his way—"I've never had any friends." She caught Regan's wrist. "You're the closest I've ever had to a girlfriend. I'm so glad you married my brother."

Regan's heart sank a smidge in her chest. No friends but Mikhail? It was no wonder she wanted to marry him. She glanced down at their joined hands. Gosh, what would it do to Ty when she left? She guessed the young woman would be crushed.

Then again, she thought as she caught Ty giving Mikhail an eyelash flutter, maybe it wouldn't be so bad for her if the timing was right. Like if she left after Ty and Mikhail were married. Then Ty'd probably be too busy with her new life to be bothered by a sister-in-law who had decided to become an ex-sister-in-law.

Right?

Regan forced a smile. "When's the wedding?"

"The next full moon," Ty answered. "Always has to be a full moon."

Full moon? Ugh. Not what Regan had hoped for. That would coincide exactly with when her one month term as vampy queen would expire. Drats. And drats.

She supposed she could hang out an extra day or two, but that was it. She needed to get back to her life. Her store. She had yet to present her proposal to Shadow—the one she'd brainstormed during her free time. He was going to make an investment into her future. But even if he refused she had a good life at home to return to. She hoped vampires went on extended honeymoons somewhere dark—Antarctica?—so she'd be spared the unpleasant task of explaining why she'd be heading back to the States immediately after the wedding.

Despite the fact that she didn't know Tyra all that well, she liked the young woman too. For a dead girl—or was it undead?—she was very full of life.

Regan swallowed a sigh. A young woman who looked at her like she was about to announce Christ's second coming was another complication she didn't need. If she had learned anything this past week, it was that making a clean getaway from the vampire people was not going to happen.

Her getaway was going to be very unclean, unpleasant, from the looks of it.

"That's assuming Quinby gives his permission," Ty jabbered. "Which I just know he is. He didn't want to appear too hasty, that's all. He really likes Mik here. Always has."

Mikhail's face brightened a smidge. "I was so nervous asking him."

"You did great," Ty said with that girl-in-love glimmer in her eye. She lifted her hand to Mikhail's face and stroked his cheek. All of a sudden, Regan felt very much like a third wheel.

That was, until Ty turned to her and said, "I'm sure we'll get the good news no later than tomorrow. I even have my dress all picked out. It's beautiful. You have to see it." She gave a girly sigh.

"I'm sure it is. And I'm sure your brother will give his decision very quickly. He doesn't seem like the type to languish over decisions like some people do."

"Oh no. If there's one thing my brother is, it's decisive." Tyra stood up and jumped forward, giving Regan a bouncy hug. "I'm so excited! Thanks so much! I can't wait! Only a couple of weeks and then I'll be Mrs. Mikhail Novak. It'll be the best day of my life. It wouldn't be the same without you there."

"I wouldn't miss it for anything." Regan gently extricated herself from Ty's rather suffocating embrace.

Ty clapped her hands with girly glee. "Yay! I say we go down to town tomorrow night to celebrate. I'll make all the arrangements. We'll head to—"

Regan waved her hands, trying to cut off Tyra's animated jabbering. "Whoa, girl, let me talk to your brother first."

Ty didn't look the least bit concerned with getting Shadow's permission—this from a girl who said she had no friends because her brother was overprotective. Did she know something Regan did not? "I'll convince him. Don't worry about it." She yanked on Mikhail's hand until he stood. "Come on, sweetheart. We have plans to make. Lots and lots to do."

He offered his hand to Regan. "It was a pleasure to meet you. I'm glad we had a chance to talk, since we weren't formally introduced earlier. Tyra hasn't stopped talking about you since she met you."

Regan accepted his firm handshake. He squeezed pretty hard and pumped her hand up and down like he was drawing water from a very, very deep well. Smiled into her eyes. "Yes, it was very nice talking." She winced as her knuckles ground against each other. She could say one thing for the guy—he didn't have a wimpy handshake. "Easy, easy, there. I'm a mortal. Remember? Those bones do need to remain intact to work."

Ty was already standing at the door. "Come on, Mik. Gotta go!"

"Coming." He released Regan's hand. "Sorry about that. I forget how delicate humans are. Well, I guess we'll see you later."

"Sure. Bye." She watched them leave, then went to the bedroom closet to pick something to wear.

Not much to choose from. Lingerie and . . . lingerie. Black. Red. Pink. Leather. Nothing qualified for going-out-on-the-town type of wear. In fact, nothing qualified for going-out-of-the-bedroom type of wear.

Her lack of selection in the fashion department hadn't bothered her until now. She'd suffered enough humiliation that first night, when he'd dragged her out to the airport while she'd been completely nude. Never in her life had so many people seen her nekkid. At least not since she'd left the neonatal nursery. God, that was awful. So the little scraps of clothing he'd provided, mostly to help her stave off the freaking frostbite—and it was summer!—had been accepted with utmost gratitude. But now, with other men in the building, shoot. She had a feeling Shadow couldn't care less. It was as if she was his . . . trophy.

Gasp! Was she a trophy wife?

Never! Not Regan Roslund.

She reminded herself that the marriage was temporary, so even if she was a trophy wife, it was only for the next couple of weeks. She could live with that. She was at the halfway point now. The time—especially the past week—had gone relatively quickly, much to her surprise.

She selected the negligee that covered the most skin and topped it with the robe, tied extra tight so it didn't gap open.

Couldn't do much about the length. That would have to do for now. She'd just have to make sure not to bend over. No problem. Some makeup, hair. She was all set.

Where was Shadow? He'd told her he'd be up almost an hour and a half ago. He'd never made her wait so long for a meal, not since they'd arrived. She was starving, and she expected so was he. Neither of them had eaten—if what he did could be called eating—before the arrival of their guests.

If whatever was keeping him busy downstairs wasn't important, she was sure he'd have come up earlier. But she was so not a patient kind of girl. Go hunt him down or sit up here and starve to death?

Seemed like a no-brainer to her! She was dying to find out what could be so important it had kept him from his meal. Although, depending upon his mood, she knew there could be hell to pay for leaving their suite without permission. Then again, he'd never specifically said not to come down after she'd gotten ready for him. She remembered it quite clearly. All he'd said was, "Go up and get ready for me. I'll be there shortly."

Hmmm . . .

Shadow was a fair man. He wouldn't whip her for disobeying an order he hadn't specifically given.

She made it out the door and partially down the stairs before she started having second thoughts, inspired by a furious vampire standing at the foot of the stairs glaring at her.

Uh-oh. He looked way more angry than he should. It wasn't like she'd left the castle or anything.

What was going on?

14

"Did I not tell you to wait upstairs for me?" Shadow spat.

"No . . ."

He raised one glossy eyebrow, which stirred her to explain why she thought he hadn't specifically told her to park herself in their suite, which she gathered was what he thought he'd said.

"You told me to go get ready for you," she explained. "And you told me you'd be up soon. But you never specifically told me I was supposed to sit up there and wait. It's been a while, and I thought you might have meant to tell me to come down—"

"You know damn well what I meant," he said in a low voice that reminded her of a dog's warning growl.

A whipping was definitely on the way. A pleasant little ripple shot up her spine.

He snatched her wrist in a grip that made her bones grind together and pulled her through the castle. Past guards—to whom he barked an order for his favorite slave to be sent to him immediately. Past his wide-eyed sister and smirking brothers. Down to the dungeon, which was thankfully empty. He slammed the door behind them and then motioned toward the stocks.

She hesitated for a split second, not because the stocks were particularly unpleasant. Truth be told, she'd already formed some fond memories featuring them.

No, it was the fact that he was overreacting to something that seemed so insignificant that made her hesitate. He'd never punished her for disregarding an *implied* order before.

A quiver of fear raced through her but quickly died as the little voice inside her head reminded her that she trusted Shadow. Since coming to the castle, he'd helped her see the power of submitting. The joy. He'd never been cruel. Never been unjust.

The heavy door opened with a heavy creak.

She knew who that was. The human Shadow called his slave.

Being a girl of the twenty-first century, the moniker still kind of rubbed Regan the wrong way, but who was she to be offended if the one labeled took no offense? If anything, it seemed the woman wore the tag with pride.

In this world of blood-sucking masters and castles and rebellious clan members, there were more bizarre things to deal with.

She took her position in the stocks, deciding she'd hold her tongue for the moment. Even though Shadow didn't seem to have cooled down any, he was distracted. There was something very feral in his eyes as he turned his attention to the woman who'd just entered the room.

If she saw it, she didn't show any sign of concern or surprise.

"Come here, slave," Shadow demanded. He secured Regan in the stocks, then motioned for his source of nourishment—also known as "slave"—to stand in front of her so that the view of one shapely, enviously cottage-cheese-free behind was about all she had.

Now, that was some cruel punishment!

She lifted her chin as high as her restraints would allow, catching Shadow sweep the woman's long hair to one side in preparation for a bite.

Regan couldn't begin to imagine what was going through the woman's head, although she could smell the scent of her building arousal. It was surprisingly pleasant. Musky but sweet at the same time.

The woman's backside started to tremble. Regan guessed Shadow was feeding. Slick juices ran down the woman's inner thighs. She moaned. Regan watched as one of Shadow's hands ran down the slope of her back, over the rise of her rump. His fingers explored the crevice between her buttocks. The muscles lying under the smooth skin tightened, making her rear end look even more perfect than it had just a split second before.

Regan's own juices started flowing as she stood there powerless to move and watched Shadow finger-fuck his slave. Two fingers, then three, plunged in and out, in and out until the woman's purrs of delight turned into shrieks of pleasure.

And then it was done, and she staggered backward, smashing that ass into Regan's face. Regan's cheeks heated until they were nearly as sweltering as her vitals.

The woman was ordered to a piece of equipment that vaguely resembled a piece of playground equipment—four wooden ladders that were secured together to form a backless and frontless box. This box just happened to be within Regan's direct line of sight so she could watch as Shadow told the woman to lift her arms. He tied her wrists up, securing her arms to the top ladder high above her head.

"I was planning on giving you this pleasure, my wife. But since you decided to disobey me, I will give it to my slave." He buckled leather cuffs around her ankles, lifted them up high, and secured them to the chains hanging from either end of the top ladder.

Her legs were open wide. She was suspended in the air by her wrists and ankles.

Regan gasped.

How would it feel to be hanging like that, her legs wide open? So powerless.

Shadow went to the cupboard Regan had labeled his "Little Closet of Delight" and found himself a dildo. He stood to the side—clearly wanting Regan to see everything. He fucked the woman with the dildo until the room filled once again with her squeals. Then, being extra cruel, he released his plaything from the restraints, led her to Regan's favorite piece of equipment—the bench—and placed her in Regan's favorite position, stripped himself naked, and fucked her.

Regan stood by and watched, both a tad more jealous of the woman than she wanted to be, and incredibly turned on. It was something watching Shadow fuck, from eyes wider than the narrow slits hers tended to become once she was lost in passion.

Thanks to her extremely clear vision, she could see his arm muscles ripple under his smooth, dark skin. Tighten and relax as he thrust in and out. His shoulders and back too. His adorable buttocks. Thighs.

Because of her position, Regan couldn't see the woman he was fucking. So she could imagine herself lying there, a spreader holding her thighs wide apart, her ankles chained high over her head, arms out to the sides, wrists in matching leather cuffs.

Saliva collected under her tongue and she swallowed.

She shuddered when a telltale growl rumbled through the room. Shadow was about to come. Her pussy clenched around slick emptiness. She closed her eyes and remembered the last time he'd fucked her, the last time that growl had sounded in her ear, reverberated through her body. The bitter tang of jealousy filled her mouth at the realization that this time another woman would experience that moment when the barriers between them melted away and their minds, spirits, and souls became one.

Sex was one thing. Watching him fuck his slave didn't bother her at all. But the idea of her getting the rest of him . . . Regan's insides twisted into an excruciating knot.

She couldn't open her eyes until she knew it was over. She heard the rattle of metal as the restraints were removed. Heard the hushed whispers between them. Finally, she heard the door hinges creak. The huge metal door closed with a soft gong.

It had been a while since Regan had felt like this, like her heart had been cut out of her chest and squeezed in a vice until it exploded into pieces. Her mind told her she had no right to feel that way. This was a temporary arrangement, according to her own wishes. Shadow was no more hers than she was his. They were playmates. Lovers but not in love. They were tools for each other, a means to get what each of them wanted.

He wanted peace for his people. She wanted a fresh start.

God, this sucked! The pain would not ease up. Not a tiny bit. Why was she falling for this guy? A man who was such an unlikely prospect for supplying her the kind of future she envisioned. This was not happening.

She opened her eyes just in time to catch his gaze before he lifted the top part of the stocks to release her. She saw something flash across his eyes for the briefest of moments. Much too quickly to figure out what it might be.

It was gone long before it registered in her brain.

"How do you feel?" he asked. He'd never asked that before, not even after he'd caned her until her ass felt like it was on fire.

She held his gaze. "Fine. I'm perfectly fine. Why?"

He looked unsure. Tipped his head a bit to one side and studied her with furrowed brows. "That's the first time you've seen me fuck another woman. I had to punish you. You need to know how serious I am about this."

It wasn't easy to look all casual while in stocks, her insides churning, but she did her best. Even managed a bit of a smile. "Hey, we never promised each other we'd be monogamous. I can deal with it."

"You're fine?"

"Yes. I'll be honest with you," she said as she silently rehearsed her lie. "If you were expecting this whole bondage thing to make me fall in love with you, you're in for a big surprise. Because although I'm learning I really, really like it, I'm no closer to falling in love with you than I was the night you dragged me from my store and chained me to your bed. Felt it was time for some honesty."

"Okay. Thank you for being honest."

"I just want you to be prepared for when I leave two weeks from now. I fully intend on leaving, you know."

"Yes, I gather that." He nodded. "Time for your meal. You look pale." He helped her stand. To her surprise, she felt funny this time when she straightened up. Nothing specific. She just felt kind of weak and yucky. Had she been in the stocks too long? The blood settled in her legs, maybe? Or it could be because she hadn't eaten in ages. She was so hungry now, she felt a little sick. "Are you sure you're feeling okay?"

"Yes, already. I'm fine. Just a little woozy, I think, from being hungry." For some reason, now seemed like the time to mention the proposition she'd been entertaining since they'd arrived at the castle. "There's something else I'd like to talk about, though. Get it off my chest."

"Sure. Okay." He kept a hand on her elbow. She was much too aware of that simple touch than she wanted to be.

"It's about this whole arrangement we made. It occurred to me after we arrived that you stood to gain everything from this while I gain nothing once the thirty-night term is over. I don't accept charity. Period. I'd rather sleep on the streets than take a handout. But I am all for a win-win business deal, so I'd like to offer you the opportunity to invest in one boutique in the lovely town of Ferndale upon the termination of our current arrangement, two weeks from yesterday. In exchange, you will receive a percentage of all profits, to be determined at a later date."

If her proposal took him by surprise, he did a damn fine job of hiding it from her. He thought about it for a few minutes, nodded his head, and said, "I think that would be a very wise investment. I'll have my attorney draft something right away." Then he took her into his arms like he did every time they'd finished in the dungeon, and drew her into a tight embrace. This time, it was with extremely mixed feelings that she allowed him to hold her. His skin was cool against hers. The beating of his heart so slow she only counted one dull thump before he released her.

Her head felt a little swimmy when he released her. The world seemed to move every time she turned her head. Her stomach sloshed around in her belly. Her knees felt soft and wobbly.

Was she getting sick, maybe? That was so much easier to accept than the alternative—that she was developing feelings for Shadow. Feelings that might lead to things she hadn't wanted to consider until now.

Nausea gripped her. Twisting away from Shadow, she wretched, dropped to her knees. Dark patches obscured her vision.

Everything went black but, before the emptiness swept her away, she heard Shadow shout her name.

Shadow caught his precious wife seconds before she fell to the floor. Instantly, the hairs on his arms and nape stood on end. Sick panic raced through his body. Something was wrong. Terribly wrong. Why would she collapse? There was no reason for it. Was she ill?

Holding her cradled in his arms, he carried her upstairs to their suite, then called Stefan and told him they needed a human doctor, immediately. The queen had fallen ill.

He sat beside the bed, her hand limp and cool in his. He knew she was breathing. He could hear her even breaths. But with every minute that passed, he sensed she was slipping further from him. When he felt his own strength weakening, he knew she was dying.

By the time the doctor had arrived, Shadow was barely able to stand. His body felt boneless and heavy. His mind dull.

Stefan, who had followed the physician into the room, took a startled look at Shadow and ran to catch him before he fell to the floor.

"She's dying," Shadow croaked. His throat felt dry as sand. "How? What's happened? I've done everything to . . . everything to keep her safe."

"The doctor's here. He'll cure her." Stefan helped Shadow to a chair and stood mutely by his side as the doctor listened to the queen's heart. Shadow watched through eyes that were so dry and gritty it hurt like hell to blink. He was so tired. Tired and cold. Sleep. He wanted to sleep. "Stay awake, dammit!" Stefan slapped his cheek. Hard.

Shadow cursed him. Then, as exhaustion pulled at him again, he let his eyelids drop. The vision of Regan's stormy pain-filled eyes flashed in his head. It was agony seeing that. So painful he had to open his eyes to escape it.

"I'll draw some blood and have it analyzed immediately. She needs to go to the hospital. Her heart rate and respirations are severely depressed. Soon she'll need life support. I'll call for transport." The doctor pulled a cell phone from his pocket and started dialing.

"Thank you, Doctor." Stefan stepped forward. "Let me know what you need from us. I'll help any way I can."

The doctor hung up. "Go, help the medical technicians get past that security. It took me almost twenty minutes to get in this place."

"Sure." Stefan patted Shadow's shoulder. "Stay with us. We need you. We'll get her help. If we can't, you know what we can do. Just say the word—"

"No." Shadow shook his head. "I won't. She wouldn't want that. I know it. She'd rather die. And I'd rather die than do that to her."

Stefan clearly didn't agree, but Shadow hadn't expected him to. To hell with him. With them all. He was tired. Tired of the rebels. Of fearing for his life. Of living for everyone around him.

Maybe it was best for everyone if he died. He let the darkness carry away all the troubles, all the worries. They were gone. Peace at last.

"Wake up, Shadow." Rolf's voice sounded very distant. Annoying, like a fly buzzing around his head. He wanted to stay asleep. Why didn't his brother understand that? "Come on! Open your eyes, you bastard. Your wife needs you. Regan. We all need you. Wake up."

Regan? She needed him. It wasn't easy, but he summoned the strength to lift eyelids that were as heavy as blocks of concrete. He tried to speak, but his throat was too dry. Nothing came out.

Rolf gave him a weak smile. "Fuck, Shadow. I thought you were a goner for sure."

Regan? Where was Regan? He remembered now. She'd been sick. Gone to the hospital. He had to know if she was okay. "Regan?"

Stefan's face took the place of Rolf's in his currently very narrow, hazy line of sight. Distant things were still nothing but a blur. "She's recovering. The doctors say she'll be okay in a few days."

"What happened?" He had to work hard to get the words out. He was so fucking weak. Everything took effort, even blinking his eyes.

Stefan frowned.

Bastard wasn't going to tell him.

"We'll talk about that later," Stefan said. "You just need to concentrate on getting better. Here. Feed."

The slave sat on the bed, flipped her hair to the side, and offered her neck.

He tried to push her away but couldn't. "Fuck that. Tell me."

She sighed and walked away.

Stefan gave him an impatient glare. Didn't speak right away. Made Shadow have to ask a second time before finally answering, "You need to feed if you're going to get stronger. It was poison."

That single word was enough to inspire him to fight the exhaustion pulling him back into the darkness. He forced himself to sit up. The room spun, but he focused on Stefan's face, which acted like an anchor until the sensation stopped. "What?"

"The doctor said it was poison of some kind. Although the treatment they gave her worked, they haven't determined what the exact substance was or how she was exposed to it."

"She needs protection."

"There is a policeman stationed at her door. I was able to convince them that the poisoning was an intentional attempt on her life, even though the doctors haven't finished with their tests yet. Wasn't easy."

"Thanks. But not enough. I need to go." He pushed up and swung his legs over the side of the bed. They felt heavy. Numb.

Stefan gave him a rough shove, sending him flat onto his back. "No, you don't! You're not in any condition to go anywhere. You're as weak as a new lamb, Shadow. I can't let you go out like that."

"Regan."

"I'll go to her," Rolf offered.

"No," Stefan said. "You can't go. You need to stay here to handle that other issue we talked about. Remember?"

"Dammit. Yeah, I remember."

"What issue?" Shadow asked.

"I'll go! Oh, Quinby," Ty said from somewhere beyond his limited vision before either of his brothers could answer his question. Her voice was shaky, filled with worry. He turned his head in the general direction of the sound. His sister stepped closer, her usually animated face dark with concern. She took his hand in hers and gripped it so hard he flinched. "I was so scared. I thought you were going to . . ." She visibly swallowed and glanced to the left at a tall fuzzy blob that he guessed was Mikhail standing farther back. "I thought you were going to die. First Mother and Father. And then you." She dropped her head on his chest. It felt like an earthmover had just parked on his sternum. "You have to take care of yourself. Come sunset, I'm there at Regan's bedside. I'll protect her with my life until the minute before sunrise. Nothing will happen to her. I promise."

"Ty." He lifted an arm that felt like it was forged from lead. "Thanks, but—"

She picked up her head and gave him one of her challenging glares. "You're not going to give me that nonsense about girls not being good at this guarding stuff, because that's a bunch of bullshit."

"Since your brothers are going to be busy with more pressing matters, I'd be happy to go to the hospital," Mikhail offered, stepping closer. "I'd be honored to protect our queen, if you'll allow me."

If there was anyone outside of family Shadow knew he could trust, it was Mikhail. "You'll call me if you see anything suspicious?"

"Yes!" Ty said.

"Yes, my king." Mikhail lowered his head in a show of reverence. "Thank you for trusting me with this very important task."

"We're practically brothers, especially now . . . aren't we?" Shadow said, pulling the corners of his mouth into what he hoped was a smile.

Mikhail and Ty's reaction told him he'd succeeded. Ty jumped into Mikhail's arms, hugged him, then nearly strangled Shadow with an embrace that felt like a hug from an anaconda. Then, chattering about plans to make, she and Mikhail left the room.

Shadow wasn't entirely satisfied with the arrangements he'd made to keep Regan safe, but until he was at least able to sit up without a feather pushing him over, he had no choice. But he still wanted to know what was keeping Stefan and Rolf so busy that guarding their queen wasn't top priority. He blinked at the haze still clouding his vision. "Rolf?"

"Yeah, I'm here." Rolf's face came into view. "You need to rest, Shadow. Don't worry about anything. We're taking care of it all."

"What's so important you can't go? Hospital?"

He turned his head, hesitated before shaking his head. "Just rest. We'll tell you as soon as you're strong enough."

"Fuck that."

"Later," Stefan said from somewhere beyond his vision.

"Fuck that!" Shadow repeated, louder.

"Come on, Rolf. Gotta go, Shadow. Feed. That's the only way you'll be any good to anyone, Regan included."

The slave resumed her position beside him, neck exposed. "Master?"

He did the only thing he could at the moment. He fed, vowing the entire time to make whoever was responsible for poisoning his sweet Regan pay for what he'd done. The bastard would suffer.

He'd been a fool thinking Regan would be safe in the castle. His dear, sweet wife, the love of his life, had nearly died. Because he'd been lulled into a false sense of security. Fucking stupid.

He'd never make that mistake again. Never. He'd make sure she was safe, no matter what it took. As a husband and protector, he'd failed her.

He'd never do that again.

15

"I will find out how she was poisoned, and she will not return until I do." Shadow shoved his objecting brother, Rolf, aside and yanked open his chamber door. He'd been in bed for more than twenty-four hours. He couldn't continue to lie around and wait for the murderer to succeed in killing his target. Whoever the bastard was, he was smart and he had guts. Poisoning the queen under the king's very nose? What kind of man had such nerve?

A determined man, that was who.

"We will start in the kitchens. Perhaps it was tainted food. Nothing but food was brought into our chambers, so it's most likely the source of the poisoning."

"But, Shadow, as of yet, the doctors haven't said for sure whether it was an intentional poisoning. She could've been accidentally exposed to some kind of substance."

"What're they taking so damn long for?" he snapped. "And what do we care? We both know for a fact it was intentional. This is the third attempted poisoning of our queen."

"Yes, I know." Rolf trailed behind Shadow by a full stride as he hurried toward the kitchen. "But if the second attempt was by the application of a toxin to food, why would the assassin attempt the same thing again?"

He stopped midstride. "You have a point. But how else? Where else? The air? She breathes much more frequently than we do. So any gas that we would've been exposed to would've affected her much sooner. Perhaps there was a gas released into the dungeon. That's where she collapsed." He spun on his heel and headed in the opposite direction.

"Or perhaps she was exposed hours earlier and it just took a while for the poison to affect her."

He stopped again. He was still far from back to normal. Feeling worn out, he leaned to the left and let a stone pillar prop him up. "You're not helping me."

"Look at you. You're still very weak. What if the assassin is in the castle?"

"I think we can assume that much."

"What if he makes an attempt on your life? In your weakened state, I doubt you'd be able to defend yourself."

"I don't give a damn. I need to make sure my wife is safe. Since it is still daylight, and I am unable to get to the hospital to see to my wife's safety, I'm going to do everything I can here to find out what happened. What is so difficult to understand about that? I must protect her! I love her!" he shouted. Then, as his words echoed through the room, he closed his eyes.

It was true. He loved Regan. More than life. More than the crown. And her safety meant more than peace for his warring people. More than anything.

She was everything.

"I love her," he repeated, mostly to himself. He hadn't thought it was possible for him to love. Care, yes. But love? To throw away everything that was meaningful for someone else?

Rolf shook his head. "I understand." He stepped up beside Shadow and wrapped an arm around his waist. "Here, use my shoulder to steady yourself. I will help you."

"Thank you." Shadow gladly accepted his brother's offer of support. Together they slowly made their way down to the dungeon. Rolf helped him search every inch of the room. They looked for powders, liquids, pills. They sniffed the air for gas. They looked over the stocks for signs of any residue, since that had been the only piece of equipment Regan had come into direct contact with.

"We should let the police investigate. They have tests they can run, test for tiny traces of chemicals," Shadow said, carefully stepping back toward the door. "Get them in here right away."

"Until the doctors verify that a crime was committed, I'm afraid the only thing they've agreed to do is post a guard outside her hospital room."

"Hire a detective, then. We need answers. We need them now before any evidence is lost."

"Let's go. I'll make some calls. You need to rest."

"I want to catch whoever did this and make him pay. If he's one of us, he'll face the crown's judgment, not the human's. I'll use the Old Ways to teach them all a lesson."

Rolf looked disturbed as he nodded. He pulled the dungeon door closed.

"Lock it. Just in case there is evidence in there and whoever is responsible hasn't gotten in there to clean it up."

"Good thinking." Rolf twisted the skeleton key in the lock, then pulled it out and handed it to Shadow.

Shadow fingered it thoughtfully. Why hadn't he thought to lock the dungeon before? Perhaps if he had, Regan wouldn't be lying in a hospital after having nearly lost her life.

Yes, when it came to protecting the woman he loved, he'd done a very poor job. He'd ignored his brother's warning that she could be in danger. Foolish!

He'd not taken even the simplest steps to see to her safety. Unforgivable!

He'd made it easy for his enemies to almost kill his wife.

There was no word for that one.

He ached to see her. To hear her voice. To touch her.

As if Rolf read his thoughts, he led Shadow toward his chambers. "Come, let's get you ready to visit your wife. I'm sure she'll be glad to see you."

"I wouldn't blame her if she sends me away. I failed. I failed to keep her safe."

"She doesn't look at it like that. Trust me. You need to feed again. I'll call Sasha for you."

He didn't care to feed, completely oblivious to his body's need for nourishment.

Grateful to his brother for helping him through this wretched time, he nodded and lowered himself onto the couch to wait for his slave. All he cared about was Regan.

What would she say when she saw him?

What would he say to her?

Three words came to mind.

When Regan heard the door squeak, she pretended to be asleep. God help her, Ty was doing her best to keep her company, but Regan had endured just about all the jabbering she could handle at the moment. The girl had more energy than the Energizer Bunny and never shut up. Regan had never been able to sleep in a hospital. She'd been in one a couple times. But at least those other times, the only annoyance had been nurses poking her from time to time, the noise of food carts rattling in the hallway, and voices of medical personnel and patients. Not a young woman who was head over kitten-heeled toes with the guy of her dreams who wanted to do nothing but sing his praises for hours on end, ad nauseum.

Quiet. Solitude. Yes, that was all she wanted at the moment. Some alone time. Maybe a nap. A snack sounded good.

"Regan."

That voice didn't belong to Ty. Nor did it belong to her nurse, or her doctor, or the gal delivering late-night snacks.

Shadow.

Her heart did a happy little hop in her chest. She opened her eyes and smiled at him. He didn't exactly return her smile. Kind of, but he didn't really pull it off. He really was a sucky actor.

"Hi," she said when he just stood there, wearing this pained expression that she assumed was meant to be a smile. Looked more like the expression one might see on a constipated toddler.

He took her hand in his, held it like it was so fragile it would shatter in a billion shards if he squeezed too hard. "Regan, I don't know what to say."

"About what? You didn't do this to me. From what I gather, no one did."

"I don't believe that for a minute."

She shook her head. "You still think someone's trying to kill me? You're wrong. At least this time. The doctor told me I had a reaction to something I ate, that's all. No spy injected a mysterious death serum or laced my food—"

"I haven't been honest with you. I need to tell you something."

"About what?"

"Your store. The night you sneaked out. The food you were eating. There was something in it. It killed the dog."

"That dog was on death's door when I let it in. It probably died from something else."

"No." He shook his head. "I should've told you sooner so you knew I wasn't being overly cautious. I've actually been as careless as a guy could be. And it's my fault you're here now, that you nearly died. It's my fault."

She silenced him by pressing an index finger to his mouth. "No. You're wrong. You've just been living with this for too long, the suspicion, the danger."

"No, that's not it. It's all very real. The flowers you received at your home were a deadly trap, meant to kill you. The food you ordered was laced with tranquilizers, meant to either kill you or knock you out so that . . ." He didn't finish the sentence. Just left unspoken the ugly words she knew he'd meant to say. He raked his fingers through his hair. "My brothers warned me that the castle wasn't completely safe, that the rebels could easily get someone inside, but I didn't believe them. I let the assassin into our home. I allowed him to almost kill you."

Something rattled in her brain as he spoke; the memories of the night in the store came rushing back. The break-in. The dog. The second break-in. Her near escape. Had her food been poisoned? Had someone, some assassin, expected to find her lying unconscious when they got into the store? Were they there to finish the job?

She had to admit, it hadn't been easy ignoring the obvious all this time. But a very big part of her hadn't been ready to face the facts, one specific fact, actually.

Someone wanted her dead. And they'd tried several times.

Oh God! What should she do? Would she be safe after she divorced Shadow? Or would the killer still come after her? She'd been scared a few times since that first night when Shadow had surprised her in the store. But never had she been this terrified. This was beyond words. Her insides skittered around like spooked spiders as her eyes darted about the room. When would the killer strike next? Where would she be? Would he succeed?

Suddenly, Shadow's overbearing, über-protective nature seemed like an asset well worth keeping a hold of.

Then something else clobbered her upside the head with the force of a steel baseball bat striking a marshmallow.

She'd ignored the obvious before. And it had cost her a fortune, literally! It was painful to admit now, but she'd known deep down that something was wrong with her accounts long before she'd walked into that bank and been told she'd been cleaned out. Why, oh why, had she chosen to convince herself that her instincts were wrong? She'd be swimming in Manolos now if only she'd faced the facts sooner.

Could she rewind time, please?

"I must tell you something else," he said as he twined his fingers through hers.

"There's more? More bad news?" Already, she felt like the world had been knocked off its axis and tipped on its side. She wasn't sure she could handle anything else. What more could there be?

"Something's happened between us. You and me." Shadow dropped his gaze to their joined hands. "I care for my brothers a great deal. I care for my sister. My people. But there was one thing I cannot say I've ever been able to do." He lifted his eyes. "When you have no soul, you can't love. My people. We have no soul. We weren't created in his image, like humans."

"Whose image?"

"Some call him God. We call him the Creator. Doesn't matter. The bottom line is we were created without a soul." He met her gaze. His eyes were sharp. His gaze intense. "And because of that, we can't love, or so I've always believed."

What did this mean? Why was Shadow giving her a theology lesson now?

Did he think she expected him to love her? Did he think she wanted him to love her? Because she didn't . . . did she? No. She wanted to go back to her safe, blah, old life, with her freaky store and empty refrigerator. She wanted to sell plastic clothes to people who spend way too much money on rubber jewelry and whips and black nail polish. She wanted to find herself. She realized now how useless her life had been, how little she'd accomplished since she'd graduated from college. Sure, she'd filled the time. Her schedule had been jam-packed with stuff. But that stuff had been meaningless. Hedonistic. Shopping trips to France. Skiing in Switzerland.

She'd wasted so much time. She had years to make up for. Getting the store up and running was only the beginning. A way to make other things happen.

She wanted to do something meaningful.

"Shadow, I never expected you to love me. I didn't ask you to. I agreed to give you a month to woo me, not because I was hoping to fall in love with you, but because I was being selfish. I thought I'd enjoy four weeks of sex, fun, good food. You showed me how much I wanted to submit to a man. How sexy and thrilling and powerful being a submissive was. But I told you I want to go home when it's over. This isn't life." She did want that . . . right? To go home. For this to end. To return to real life. Yes? Yes. "I need to go home when it's over. This life here isn't real. A castle. Guards. Vampires. Days spent sleeping. Nights spent playing with you in the dungeon. What kind of life is that? What am I accomplishing? I'm just drifting through the days and nights. Nothing matters."

He didn't speak. He stared down at their hands, fingers still entwined. Slowly, he nodded. "I understand completely."

"Here's something to think about. Not only because I'm being a little selfish here and would like to keep my tush intact. But also because you're in danger too."

He raised his eyes to her. They were dark. Filled with emotions she couldn't begin to read.

"Maybe we ought to think about cutting this arrangement short, for both our sakes. Me, so I'm not killed, and you so you aren't in danger anymore. Obviously, the whole marriage-to-make-peace experiment was a huge failure. The rebels in your clan are using against you the one thing you expected to be an asset—me. I'm no longer good for you or your kingdom. I—

our marriage—has become a tool for your enemies." She said the words and waited. Her heart up in her throat. None of this felt right. Not staying. Not leaving. She was tired. She was confused. She was lonely. And Shadow was there, in the room with her. But he felt so distant. A part of her had to admit that hearing him say he could never love her stung. While what she said had been true, that she'd never expected him to love her, how could she stomach living the rest of her life with a man she knew would never love her? "Do you think they'd come after me, even after we're divorced?"

"I doubt it," he said in a voice so low, she barely heard him. "There's no reason to. Once we're divorced, the connection between us will be broken. Killing you will no longer render me powerless, which is what they're hoping for right now."

There was a really awkward, heavy moment or two of silence. The tension was thick in the air between them, so palpable, she could practically see it. Like a thick dark gook churning around them.

"Do we have to wait until the full moon?"

He shook his head.

More silence. It was almost painful. She hadn't felt this awkward and uncomfortable with Shadow since they'd met.

He straightened up, released her hand, and without saying a word, walked to the door.

That was it? Just walk out? He wasn't going to say anything? Tell her what he thought? What he was planning?

When he left the room, she rolled over onto her side, her back facing the door. She just wanted it all to go away. The emotions bubbling around inside. She felt like a pot about to boil over. Her eyes stung. Her nose burned.

A moment later, as she was dabbing at her watering eyes, she heard the door hinges creak again. Was it Shadow? Had he come back to tell her what he was going to do? Did she want to hear what he had to say?

She twisted her upper body.

He was standing just inside the door, with his sister on one side, her fiancé on the other. She couldn't help noticing that Ty was intentionally avoiding making eye contact with her.

She'd known she'd regret this moment, hurting the young woman who had been not only a jabbering pest, but who had also become a friend. Some things were very hard for her to deal with. Hurting someone, disappointing them. That was a biggie.

Maybe Ty, being a vamp, could never love her as a friend. But she obviously could feel some sort of closeness. And when faced with losing it, experienced some sort of pain.

She wanted to turn back around, to turn away from all this ugliness. Hurting Tyra. Shadow. The pain she didn't want to feel at the thought of going home.

She forced herself to face them.

"We can do this right now. Here. With these two witnesses," Shadow said flatly. Everything about him, his expression, his gait, his posture, was lifeless.

She wasn't crazy about the idea for some reason, but who was she to complain? She was the one who'd suggested they end their marriage early. Had she secretly hoped he'd put up a fight? Plead with her to reconsider? Tell her he loved her and refused to give her up?

Where the heck was this stuff coming from?

This wasn't a sappy romance novel, and she wasn't some weak, spineless heroine who was afraid to face life on her own. She was a strong, independent woman who knew what she wanted in life . . . sort of. And she wasn't the kind of woman who needed a man in her life to feel whole.

"Sure," she said. "Okay. Where do you need me? Should I stand up?"

"No. You can stay right where you are." Shadow stepped up

to her hospital bed and took her hands in his. His gaze parked itself on her eyes for a moment but then dropped.

She felt awful.

Tyra and Mikhail stood back by the door, Regan noticed. Like they were afraid to come closer or something. As Shadow started muttering words in that strange magical language of theirs, Tyra's expression darkened. Even clear across the room, Regan could see her eyes reddening. Tyra blinked the tears away and sniffed. Just as Shadow said a final word, Tyra raised her watery gaze to Regan's for a split second. Then she turned to Mikhail, and wrapping her arm around his waist, pointed to the door.

The choker fell from Regan's neck, landing on her lap.

"I want to go home," Tyra said as Regan picked up the piece of jewelry, fingered one of the intricate swirls.

She lifted her other hand to her neck and watched them leave, then looked at Shadow.

"Only one step remains," Shadow murmured.

"One step?"

"Yes. This." He leaned forward and kissed her. And it wasn't a chaste have-a-good-life kind of kiss. It was a tongue-thrusting, knee-buckling kiss to end all kisses. The kind that was guaranteed to stay fresh in her memory for a long, long time. The kind that would keep her up at night, wondering where Shadow was, what he was doing. Who he was doing it with.

She moaned into their joined mouths, and a funny tingle zapped when her tongue came into contact with his. Like a little charge of electricity. Before she had a chance to wonder what that was all about, a blast of warm air filled her mouth. Out of instinct, she breathed in, drawing that sweet, hot air deep into her lungs. The heat spread through her body, out to her toes, fingertips, roots of her hair.

Shadow broke the kiss way too soon for her liking. "I'll

make the arrangements immediately. The jet will take you back to Detroit in the morning, assuming your doctors say it's safe for you to travel. Good-bye, Regan. And thank you."

"Thank you for what?"

"For three weeks that I'll never forget. Be safe." He turned and left the room before she managed to force any words past the huge boulder blocking her throat, leaving her to her own memories. Memories she sure as heck wouldn't ever forget, either.

"Well, isn't this just great? I'm divorced. And Tyra hates me." She sighed and blinked as tears collected in her eyes. "Good-bye, Shadow. You be safe too. God, this sucks." She gently set the choker on the tray sitting next to her bed, covered her head with her sheet, and had a nice, long cry until her head hurt so bad it felt like her eyeballs would pop out of their sockets.

16

Shadow went home to discover he had no home to return to. The structure that had housed and protected his family for centuries looked nothing like it had a few short hours earlier. The better part of the rear was completely leveled. And the rest that remained standing looked like it would collapse with a slight breeze. The former inhabitants stood in small groups in what used to be the central court, pale-faced and wide-eyed, staring, hands to mouths. Shocked. Bewildered. Injured.

He didn't see Rolf or Tyra, but he found Stefan standing next to one of the security guards. Stefan was pointing at the horizon, which was beginning to get a little dusky. The sun was threatening to rise, which created an entirely different set of problems. They all needed to find someplace to stay. Fast.

He broke into a full run and didn't let up until he was standing at Stefan's side. "What the hell happened?"

Stefan was wiping blood from the corner of his lip. His hair was matted, and he was coated head to toe in dust, dirt, and what appeared to be the remains of their home. "Two explosions. The first one was in the west wing. The second over there, in the main hall."

"Two explosions?"

"Yeah." Stefan staggered a little. Shadow helped him to a bench. "I haven't found Rolf yet. And Tyra. She came back from the hospital right before the first explosion. I saw her heading up to her suite. Haven't seen Mikhail, either. He was with her when she came in."

"Damn!" Shadow just couldn't take any more in one day. The loss of his wife. His home . . . and maybe a sister, a brother, a friend. He couldn't take any more! And if the explosion didn't get them, the quickly rising sun would. Very soon! "I'm going to look for them. You stay here. Better yet, go get in the car. As soon as I find them, we have to go. It's going to be tight."

"Okay." Stefan's shoulders slumped as he dragged his feet in the direction of Shadow's parked car. He was holding his rib cage as he walked.

Shadow took one last look at the eastern sky before dashing toward the rubble that had once been his home. He shouted his sister's and brother's names as he ran. He climbed, jumped, and scurried toward the wing that had once held both of their suites, now nothing more than a mountain of stone and wood. When he didn't find any sign of them there, he headed in the opposite direction. He found Rolf and Mikhail sitting on what had once been the wooden beam that had run the entire length of the great hall's ceiling.

With mixed feelings, he dashed toward them. Relief for seeing they were okay. Worry about Tyra. Was she close by? If Mikhail had been somewhere safe, wouldn't Tyra have been near him and safe too? He now greatly regretted not returning home with them earlier. He'd wanted some time alone. But if only he'd been there when the explosions had occurred. Could he have done something?

"Rolf! Mikhail!" He waved, stopping directly in front of

them. Neither one of them appeared to be too bad off. Dirty but not hurt. Mikhail's face, however, was smudged. Damp lines cut through the gray chalky grit coating his cheeks.

"Shadow," Rolf said, his voice shaky. He stood and, for the first time Shadow could remember in millennia, hugged him. "Tyra," he said, his voice breaking. "She's gone."

Shadow looked at the tears streaming from Mikhail's eyes and knew it was true. Instantly he was crippled by pain so fierce it felt like a branding iron scorching his very heart.

He didn't deny the truth. It was there, in both the men's eyes. He just took them, and holding in a sob, walked them back to his car, gathering as many people as he could as they walked. His slave, the guards, humans, clan members. He helped them into vehicles and directed them to the nearest hotels.

This night was just about to end. And Shadow's nightmare had already begun.

He needed Regan. How his heart ached for her right now. He needed her strength, her arms around him as he wept. He had lost so much this night. Nearly everything.

They checked into a hotel mere seconds before the sun rose. He fed, but not because he wanted to. He fed only because his slave begged him to. He listened mutely as his brothers and Mikhail discussed the explosion with the security guards. The police detectives. Nothing penetrated the thick cloak of icy numbness that encased him. Not words. Not looks. Not touches. He was empty. Defeated.

Later that day, his sister's death was confirmed, along with a dozen other people. Some human. Some clan members. All innocent of any crime but being in the wrong place at the wrong time.

Where was the justice in this world? Why did innocent people have to suffer? When the fire department confirmed the explosions had been set intentionally, he walked around in a blind daze, wondering why. Who had been the intended targets?

Everyone in the castle had known Regan was in the hospital. This time it couldn't have been her.

Who was the target?

Who had done this?

Why?

Despite those questions whirling nonstop in his brain, he didn't have the conviction to finding the answers. He didn't want to talk to police detectives or firefighters. He didn't want to listen to his brothers' hypothesizing. He just wanted to walk away and leave it all behind, take what remained of his family and keep them safe. Somewhere where no one would find them.

He was tired. So very tired.

During the daylight hours, he lay awake, wondering where Regan was. What she was doing. He sent the contract and wired the funds they'd talked about, so he knew she wasn't starving or sitting in a home without lights. Still, he worried about her. The assassin's attack on his home didn't make a whole lot of sense to him. What if he decided to do something equally nonsensical and go after her?

It could happen.

Yet, despite spending days and days worrying, he couldn't get up the courage to call her. Weak. He was so damn weak. He hated himself for it.

What kind of king was he? Couldn't protect anyone, not his family, his wife. Couldn't provide even a decent lifestyle for them. Didn't have a firm hold on the clan. He heard his brothers talking. The rebels were gaining support.

He didn't care anymore. It would almost be a relief if they took the crown from him. Let them come. They can have it.

He decided the family would return to the States.

Ten nights after the explosion, the first night after they'd settled back in their Michigan condo, Rolf and Stefan entered his living room with Shadow's slave held by the arms between them. They jerked her forward and practically threw her at him. She stumbled, landed on her hands and knees before his feet.

Bloody welts marred the smooth skin of her back, all the way down to her buttocks. Her wrists were bloody. Ankles. Her face swollen and bruised.

"What happened?" Shadow asked, stooping and lifting her chin to inspect the bruises on her face. "Who did this to you?"

She opened her mouth to speak, but before she did, Stefan said, "I did."

Stunned, Shadow stood. "You? Why? I didn't give you permission—"

Stefan narrowed his eyes to tiny slits. He pointed at her. "She set the bombs. She killed our sister. That . . . that piece of shit."

He couldn't believe it. This woman had been his slave for years. His faithful servant. Why would she do such a thing? What possible motive could she have?

He looked at his slave's face, searched for the truth, but her gaze was fixed firmly to the floor. "No. You're wrong."

"Are you ever going to learn to trust me?" Stefan pulled a folded piece of paper from his pocket and thrust it at Shadow. "Read this and tell me you still don't believe she did it."

Shadow unfolded the paper and read the letter, written by one of the known rebels. It applauded her efforts to eliminate the enemy and spelled out the method for her next attempt.

"It could be forged." Shadow flipped it over, looking for something indicating where it had come from. A seal of some kind. Something that would authenticate it. "Where'd you get it?"

"A maid found it in her room," Rolf said.

"Could've been planted to implicate her and throw our suspicion off the real guilty party."

"It wasn't found in plain sight," Stefan pointed out. "You'd think if it was planted, it would've been somewhere someone would easily find it."

"Someone found it easily enough," Shadow argued.

Stefan shrugged. Shook his head. "Told you he wouldn't believe us. You have a murderer sitting at your feet. You're the king. It's your responsibility to decide her fate. What will you do?"

Shadow waved the piece of paper in the air. "I need more proof than this to convict her."

"How about a recorded confession?" Stefan asked, producing a cell phone.

"Let me guess, she confessed while you were beating the shit out of her." Shadow snatched the phone from Stefan's hand and punched the button to play back the short recorded clip. "You know I won't accept a coerced confession."

"Just watch it."

He gave his brother a warning glare. He was really pushing it. "I intend to." Expecting to see his slave mutter a weak confession while enduring lashes from Stefan, he watched the hazy picture. Damn things. Never produced a decent quality image. And the voices sounded funny too. It wasn't easy to make out what was being said.

"We didn't lift a hand to her until after she confessed."

By damn, Stefan was telling the truth.

Shadow played the short clip three times, over and over. He had to hear it that many times to believe it. His slave had betrayed him. She'd worked for his enemy. She'd set the bombs. She hadn't even tried to deny it and told Stefan there were many others conspiring. Right under their noses. That they would succeed. That the Sorenson claim to the throne was over. And that the rebels would do whatever it took to make sure a new regime was put into place.

As his law demanded, he regretfully ordered his slave to be executed. For treason.

* * *

If he thought that his slave's execution would bring peace to his people or safety for his family, he learned fairly quickly it wouldn't. Within two weeks, there were two fires in the condo, and he was forced to find a new home for himself, his staff, and his brothers. He intentionally stayed away from Rolf and Stefan, thinking that would keep them safe.

He was wrong.

He tried to gather support from his clan, to counter the vicious and oftentimes untrue propaganda the rebels spread, but the harm had been done. Support for the rebels was growing, for the reigning monarch failing. Shadow called a final clan meeting and faced his opponents head-on in a debate. Even though he presented himself and his side well, he saw his people had turned their backs on him. On the old laws. They wanted change. They wanted what the rebels promised.

If only they could remember the last time this had happened! He wasn't old enough to recall firsthand, but he'd read about it. Every child attending their schools read about it. About the bloodshed and turmoil their people endured. The near extinction.

Yet, they'd made him powerless to stop history from repeating itself.

When Stefan barely escaped with his life after his new home was burned down mere minutes before sunrise, Shadow was forced to consider the only option that remained to him. One that, despite his prior lack of enthusiasm for his position as king, he hadn't ever wanted to seriously consider.

He cared for his people. Truly cared. The decision to abdicate didn't come without a lot of struggle and pain. Guilt. Remorse.

Walk away and protect his family? Or remain on and try to protect his clan?

Most times, he operated under the belief that it was always

best to serve the masses before himself and his family. But in this case it wasn't so simple. The masses wanted what they wanted. And it was clear they'd get it, whether he stood in their way or not. Why make his family suffer any longer?

He told his brothers of his decision. As he expected, they were angry. Frustrated. Yet, much to his surprise, they didn't lash out at him. They took the news with a solemn shake of their heads.

The night before he would make his abdication official, he decided he needed to do one last thing. He needed to go see Regan. He needed to talk to her. He wasn't sure if he'd have the nerve to tell her everything, how much he missed her. How much he loved her. But he knew he had to at least go to her. To make sure she was safe. Happy. That was, if she'd even see him. He knew it was possible she'd moved on with her life, put the few weeks they'd shared behind her. Maybe she wouldn't want to speak to him?

As he drove to her house that night, he was more nervous than the day of his coronation. It was a cool evening. He could smell the hint of fall on the breeze. The sky was crystal clear, and dozens of stars twinkled dimly in the blue-black. The full moon hung low over the western horizon.

Regan's car sat in the driveway, and a light filtered through the curtains on her front window.

She was home.

It felt strange knocking on a door that he'd once walked through carefree, like it was his own. It felt strange standing on the porch waiting for her to answer, not knowing exactly what he'd say when she opened the door.

Hi, do you mind if I just sit and stare at you while you sleep?

No, too creepy.

Hi, I just happened to be in the neighborhood and thought I'd drop by and see how you're doing?

No, too cliché.

Hi, even though I shouldn't be able to, I love you and I don't want to live another day without you?

No, too desperate.

That was just it. He was desperate. That was something he had never been before. He had no idea how to act, what to do, say.

He was sure he'd do the wrong thing. This was stupid. He needed to leave now, before she answered the door. He turned around and jumped from the porch. This was a huge mistake. She deserved to live her life in peace, without a desperate ex-king trailing behind her, dragging his tongue on the ground.

"Shadow?"

Dammit, he hadn't left soon enough.

He faced her. Damn, she looked great. Dressed in a snug T-shirt that showed off her breasts to perfection and a pair of shorts that made her legs look a mile long. "I . . . uh . . . was in the neighborhood and thought I'd stop by?"

Her eyes glittered with laughter. He adored that glitter. "Is that so?" she asked, disbelief lacing her voice.

"Don't like that one? How about . . . I came to tell you I'm sorry."

That obviously surprised her. "Really?" She stepped to the side and opened the door wider in a silent invitation to come inside. "I think I'd like to hear this."

There was no way he could refuse that invitation. It was like inviting a starving man to an all-you-can-eat buffet. His arm brushed her breast as he stepped through the door. It was all he could do to keep from grabbing her, throwing her on the couch, and kissing her senseless. He had the feeling she might not appreciate that too much. Although, by the look on her face, she didn't seem to be too bothered by his surprise visit.

Should he even dare hope she was glad to see him?

Don't read too much into a smile and some eye sparkles. She's happy now with her life. You can see that.

"So, what's this all about, Shadow? Why are you here? Tonight? Over a month after I left Slovenia?"

Yes, why was he there? That was a good question. One he couldn't answer in a few short words. "I . . . um . . . wanted to see how you've been? How's the store doing?"

"I sent my first month's financials to you. Didn't you receive them?"

"Oh yes. I did." He had. But he hadn't read them. Whether or not her store was turning a profit was her business. Even if he had invested a big chunk of his personal savings into it. For some reason, he hadn't felt right reading those documents. It was good business, knowing how an investment was performing. But he didn't want to think of Regan or her store as an investment. As business only.

Besides, he trusted her. With his money. With more than that. He knew she'd never let him down.

Not like he'd done to her.

Not like he'd done to his people. His sister. Everyone, practically.

Regan tipped her head and gave him a curious stare. "Shadow, what's going on? Why are you really here? I know you didn't just happen to be driving by. And I know you're not checking on the store. What is it?"

What did she want from him? What did she want to hear? What did she expect?

"I've made so many mistakes lately. With you. With my clan. With my family. A lot has happened since you left. I don't know if you heard . . ." He couldn't say the words without his throat closing. "My sister . . . she's . . . gone."

Instantly, Regan's expression changed. She pressed her trembling fingertips to her mouth. "Oh no. Shadow. I'm so sorry."

"My home in Slovenia is gone. Destroyed. My brothers both nearly lost their lives, Stefan twice. Has anything happened to you?"

"No, no. Nothing. I swear."

That was the first bit of good news he'd heard in a long time. "Good. I should go, then. Because things aren't settled yet, and it was a bad idea to come here. But I needed to know. I needed to make sure you were okay." He pushed open the screen door.

Regan caught his wrist. "Nothing's settled yet? What're you going to do?"

"The only thing I can. The only thing that will guarantee my family's safety. I'm going to abdicate."

"When? Where?"

"Tomorrow. There's a meeting. At the Hilton. The last meeting I will attend as reigning monarch."

"But what about your clan? Didn't you say that would be bad for them?"

"I can't help them anymore. There are too many now who want this. Either I step down, or I am taken down. The end will be the same. The rebels will take power, and a new figurehead will be put in place. Someone who is either with them or can be easily manipulated by them. Either way, it will be the same. Disastrous."

"So you haven't taken a new wife? To secure your power?"

"And risk another woman's life? No. And I refuse to do that again. It was a mistake dragging you into this. I am sorry I did that." He stepped out on the porch and let the door fall shut behind him. It slammed against the doorframe with a metallic *twack*.

She was standing there, the light from a table lamp behind creating a golden aura around her form. One hand was pressed to the screen. "Shadow."

The image of her standing like that, the light making her look like a golden goddess stuck in his mind for hours afterward.

She was lost to him. But she would forever be his goddess. The light in his dark world.

17

Shadow's mind whirled as he drove back home. Thoughts about Regan, his sister, the terrible crimes that had been committed. He'd spent so many hours trying to piece the puzzle together, figuring out who the assassin was. What was motivating him. Based on his actions, Shadow knew this was about more than un-seating a political figure.

The poisonings—his slave had never confessed to those, so he assumed they'd been committed by the same bastard—the explosions and fires, they weren't the methods of a typical assassin. Granted, the means of killing his kind were limited, but there were methods that were simpler, more effective than a fire. And Regan was human. She was vulnerable to a great number of methods.

What did this guy really want?

Shadow could sense the assassin was always close by. Extremely close. As a result, he'd taken to scrutinizing everyone around him, their actions, words, gestures. Only his brothers were free of suspicion, and Mikhail, who was as close to a brother as anyone. Poor guy. He'd suffered something fierce at Tyra's death, more proof that their people were indeed capable of loving.

Everyone else was a suspect.

Despite the efforts of the police, the fire marshal's office, and Shadow and his brothers, they were no closer to unmasking the assassin than they had been after the first attempt on Regan's life.

He was trying to tell Shadow something. Shadow sensed it. But what? What the fuck did it mean? The flowers. The food. The fires in the condo. The explosions. It frustrated him. It was like the answer was right there, lingering in the back of his mind. But he just couldn't reach it.

He wasn't in the mood to be alone tonight. But he didn't want a woman's company. That would only remind him of Regan, of what he'd shared with her for those few short weeks. He missed her so much it hurt. Everywhere.

He wondered how Mikhail was doing. Since the Releasing ceremony—their clan's version of a funeral service—the guy hadn't been around much. Came to see Shadow once or twice. There was a deep sorrow darkening the guy's face. Dimming the life in his eyes.

Although Regan wasn't dead, Shadow could relate to the sense of loss the guy was feeling.

He drove to Mikhail's place. Shadow'd set him up with a little ranch on the other side of town, in a quiet subdivision set in the center of a wooded area. His brand-new Tahoe was parked in the driveway. A light was on. He was home.

Shadow parked his car behind Mikhail's truck and cut off the engine. Went up to the door and knocked.

Mikhail looked surprised, maybe a little leery, when he answered the door. He wasn't particularly forthcoming with an invitation to come inside.

Shadow felt compelled to explain himself. "I just stopped by to see how you're doing. Haven't seen you in a while, since Tyra's Releasing."

"Yeah. I've been staying home a lot lately. Haven't felt like going anywhere. Haven't been out of the house in days."

"I understand." He truly did. If it wasn't for his work, for the challenge of trying to win back the loyalty of his people, he didn't know what he'd do with himself. "If you need a job, something to keep you busy, I can help you out."

"No, thanks. I'm fine. Just have a few more weeks before the new term starts. Then I'll be busy. Teaching a full load. Thank the gods for the Internet. Allows me to teach during the daylight hours."

"Oh yeah? What're you teaching? I never did ask what you studied at university."

He shrugged. "A couple computer programming courses, Visual Basic and SQL for Business. Anyway, I need this time to . . ." His bottom lip quivered. He blinked watery eyes. ". . . just be alone."

"Okay."

There was a weird silence. Shadow took a step backward. "Marriage or not, you're still part of the family."

"Thanks."

"If you need anything, call." Shadow folded his arms over his chest. Fiddled with a thread hanging from his sleeve. He'd never been any good with words in situations like this. He doubted any words—even the world's most perfect ones—would do any good anyway.

"Will do. Thanks."

"Coming to the meeting tomorrow?"

"I'm going to try."

"Good." He stepped off the porch. "I need to talk to you afterward." He wanted to tell Mikhail what he was planning to do at the meeting, but it just didn't feel like the right time. He waved over his shoulder. "Good night, Mikhail." The front door was closed before he'd made it to the driveway.

His old friend wasn't handling Tyra's death well at all. Shadow wished there was something he could do for him. As he walked past Mikhail's truck, he twisted at the waist to look back at the house, brushing an arm against the front grill of Mikhail's truck.

It was hot. Not just warm, but hot, hot. Like just-been-driven hot.

Shadow turned his gaze to the front door. Hesitated for a moment, then shook his head.

So the truck's engine had just been run? No big deal. Mikhail had probably gone to the store or something, right? Ran an errand. When he said he hadn't gone anywhere, he just meant anywhere to see friends. Anywhere important. Anywhere worth mentioning.

Shadow hesitated next to the truck. He glanced back at the house, caught the shadow of a body at the window, peering out at him.

Mikhail had sure looked damn nervous when he'd first answered the door.

This was one of those times when Shadow was faced with a choice. Either he could ignore his gut instinct like he'd done so many times before, or for once he could trust them and investigate.

There wasn't a lot of evidence to go on here. No condemning letters or videotaped confessions. Still, Shadow didn't have trouble believing something wasn't right.

He didn't want to believe Mikhail was up to no good, but he had to admit it was possible. Very, very, very unlikely, but not impossible.

Shit, when he thought about it, Mikhail would be a perfect candidate for an undercover agent for his enemies. Shadow circled around the back of Mikhail's truck and got in his car. Anyone who knew Shadow would know Mikhail was one guy he'd never suspect. He started his car, drove down the street, around the corner, and then parked on a dead end a couple of blocks away. He put in a call to Stefan and asked him if he thought Mikhail could be working for the rebels.

Stefan told him he was nuts, that Mikhail had been nothing but loyal to the clan and to their family since he was a kid.

Shadow hung up the phone and walked back to Mikhail's house. He'd ignored his instincts so many times the past month—correction, since he'd taken the throne. It was time to heed that internal voice. To trust himself to know the truth.

The porch light was on. Shadow walked around the side of the house, being careful to stay in the darkest shadows, just in case Mikhail was still watching. He stopped at the kitchen window and peered inside. As he expected, the kitchen was dark and quiet. He moved around to the back and, thanking the gods the house was all on one level, peered into a bedroom window.

Mikhail was talking on the phone. And thanks to the fact that he was either upset or angry, he was talking loud. Shadow risked being discovered and pressed an ear to the very bottom of the window.

He got an earful and none of it to his liking. Even though Shadow was hearing half the conversation, he was quickly getting the picture.

Mikhail was being ordered to do something he didn't want to do.

And then Shadow heard the words that placed all the scattered pieces together: "I told you, I do things my way. Bullets are too fucking easy. No. Fire or poison. Those are the only weapons I use. I told you. I spent eight fucking years preparing for this day. Eight years."

Shadow staggered backward.

It was him. The assassin was Mikhail. Fuck! His sister's fiancé. A lifelong friend. Mikhail. He'd set the fires and explosions. He'd sent the flowers. The food.

If your average guy saw red when he was angry, Shadow now was seeing neon crimson. The kind of red that burned a hole through a human's retina.

He wanted to storm in that house—a house he'd fucking bought for the bastard!—and twist Mikhail's neck into a pretzel. He wanted to shove his hand into every orifice the shit had and pull his guts out.

He wanted to make him suffer.

But he had enough wits about him left to know that if he stormed in there, he had half a chance of things going wrong. No, he needed to cool off and think things through. Talk to his brothers. Do this right.

As he drove to Stefan's house, he put in a three-way call to both brothers. He told them he knew who the assassin was. Rolf agreed to come over to Stefan's to discuss their next move.

Once Shadow had his two brothers locked in Stefan's bathroom—the one room he figured would be least likely to have a bug if Mikhail had thought to place any—he told them.

After more than an hour of Shadow repeating every word he had overheard, neither brother was convinced he was right. After two hours of arguing, all three decided they needed more proof. A whole lot more before they could do anything.

They discussed their next step. Stefan suggested they go over and talk to Mikhail, see if he'd slip up and say something.

Rolf suggested they wait until the meeting tomorrow, and instead of Shadow making his planned speech, calling Mikhail out and demanding he tell the truth.

Shadow didn't like either of those plans, but he decided that a combination of the two would work best. If he was going to remain king, somehow he needed to turn his people's loyalties. Somehow he needed them to see he had their safety and well-being at heart. That he wasn't clinging to his crown for his own purposes. And wasn't staging the attacks on his family to justify murdering loyal clan members as the rebels claimed.

This was their only hope. He needed to get Mikhail to confess to the crimes, in front of the entire clan. Could Mikhail, a brilliant criminal who'd been planning murder under their noses, be drawn into a trap?

Shadow was abdicating? Giving up his throne?

Seeing him last night had stirred up emotions Regan had tried like hell to suppress for the past several weeks. Tried, but failed.

There was no denying it. Even though the magical connection between them had been severed that night in the hospital room when Shadow had completed the divorce ritual, there remained a different kind of connection. The kind that didn't break. It stood up against magic spells. And wishes. And logic.

It just was. And it would never go away.

Regan knew that now. She was through hiding from it. She was through fighting it. She was through denying it. She'd gone into the agreement with Shadow intent upon making their marriage temporary, getting what she could out of the deal and then walking away.

She had never expected to be preparing to give him everything, everything she owned. Everything she was. Everything she hoped to ever be. But that was exactly what she would do tonight. She loved him. She had to do this. Even though it meant she'd be permanently joined with a man incapable of loving her back the same way.

She dressed with care. The nipple chain went on first. No bra. A beautiful gown. Makeup. High heels. She did her hair up. Looked into the mirror.

She wasn't physically perfect like Shadow's slave had been, but that didn't matter. She was Shadow's chosen queen. She was the one who would stand by his side. She would help him re-build his people's faith in him, in his family's honor.

She knew her leaving had to have made things look even worse. A king whose wife had left him. A king who could not provide for a wife was not a king who could be trusted to pro-vide for a clan.

By securing her safety, she'd made things ten times worse for Shadow and his family. She cursed her own selfishness.

She'd said she wanted to do something, to serve. Yet she'd walked away from the greatest opportunity she could ever find. Why had she been so blind? Her fear had been like the biggest, thickest blindfold she'd ever worn. Not a single particle of light penetrated it.

There was one last thing she had to do before leaving. She lifted the black choker to her throat and fastened the clasp. A familiar burning scalded her skin, but she bit her lip and en-dured the pain. A few seconds later, it was over, and the choker was fused to her skin again.

Time was getting short. She needed to get to the meeting early, before Shadow had the chance to officially abdicate. She broke land-speed records as she raced to the hotel. Her heart was hopping around inside her like a rabbit on crack as she pulled into the hotel parking lot. Her hands were trembling as she turned the key to shut off the car's engine. She swore she was about to pass out from nerves, yet, she held her head high as she walked into the lobby, through the hallways, and into the filled-to-capacity conference room.

Hundreds of voices filled the room with excited chatter. Something was going on. Something big. Had Shadow already made his announcement? Where was he?

Shadow adjusted his clothes, making sure not to dislodge the tiny microphone from its hiding spot. This spy shit was not for him. But he knew for a fact that if anyone was going to get a confession out of his "old friend," it was him.

For the first time in his entire lifetime, he was aware of his heartbeat. It was fast and heavy, thumping along at a rate that he suspected fell just short of a human's.

He'd followed Mikhail into the building and now into the bathroom. It was a curious place for either of them to go, since neither ever eliminated. That was a human thing.

Mikhail appeared to be waiting for someone. He kept washing his hands, over and over, watching Shadow do the same. Finally, he grabbed a towel and patted his hands dry and left the room.

Shadow followed him as he walked down one hallway after another, until they were right back where they'd started, just outside the bathroom.

"Are you following me?" Mikhail asked. He kept glancing over Shadow's shoulder, toward the door.

"I was wondering when you'd ask." Shadow twisted at the waist to glance behind himself. "Waiting for someone?"

"Kind of."

Shit, he didn't know what to say next. He didn't want to blow this. "Maybe someone from the *Opstand*? The Rebellion?"

Mikhail's eyes narrowed slightly. "Could be." Mikhail sized up Shadow while Shadow did the same. Then he added, "It's too late for you, you know. No sense keeping it a secret anymore. I was wondering when you'd figure it out. Was beginning to think you never would."

Bingo, he had him. Shadow shook his head. "Of all the people. I never suspected you. We practically grew up together. Friends since before you could talk. You were going to marry my sister."

Mikhail shrugged his shoulder. "Not my fault you underestimated your enemy. That's a sign of a weak leader, you know.

You're a weak leader. A weak man. Couldn't keep a wife. Can't keep a nation. You're pathetic. Don't deserve the crown."

"You set those bombs?"

"How'd you figure it out? Not that it matters."

"Overheard a phone call last night."

Mikhail nodded. "So you did come back. I thought you might, but then again, you'd overlooked so many things, I thought maybe you'd just ignore the fact that my truck's engine was still hot. I knew you'd caught that."

"Yes, I did. And I came back. On foot, naturally."

"Hmmm." He looked almost impressed. Not quite. "I guess I underestimated you too."

"We both have made some mistakes lately, haven't we?"

"Could say that."

It was time. Time to push. Shadow sensed it. Mikhail would tell him everything now. He seemed to think it was all over. That Shadow had lost already. "So, you're admitting it, then. You set the bombs. The poison?"

Mikhail hesitated, and glanced at the precise location of the hidden microphone.

Did he figure out what Shadow was doing? Would he answer?

Mikhail gave a grin so evil, Shadow was tempted to take a step backward.

There was a sound, a squeal of feedback from the speakers at the back of the room. And then a voice. Someone Regan didn't recognize. She glanced around, her eyes darting from face to face.

Where was Shadow?

"Yes, I did all those things," the voice on the loudspeakers boasted. "Sent the rigged flowers to the queen. That was a fucking work of art, that reaction. The tainted food was your ordinary poisoning. Nothing special. Although I had my fun. I staged the break-in at her store, because I knew you wouldn't let her go back there unless there was good reason. I planted the menu because I knew she'd eventually get hungry and didn't have any food. I set the bombs. Every attempt was a masterpiece, wouldn't you say?"

"Why? Why'd you do it?" That was Shadow's voice, and instantly Regan knew what she was hearing.

An assassin's confession.

"Because I saw what your family did to mine. I saw how your parents' greed led to our loss. Our ruin. My ruin. You had to be stopped. The Sorensons had to be stopped. Put in their place. The gutter."

"This is about money?" Shadow asked, echoing Regan's thoughts. All this? Because of money?

"No," the assassin said in an icy voice. "This is about justice. Your parents took what didn't belong to them. Our laws didn't deal with them, so I vowed to. And I'm going to finish what I started."

A collective gasp rippled around the room. There was shuffling as everyone in the room turned to stare at the set of speakers suspended from the ceiling, one directly above Regan's head, a second one on the other side of the room.

Then once again silence. They were all waiting to hear what would be said next. Regan held her breath.

"I started the rumors, because I wanted to see you suffer," the assassin said proudly. "I knew it would kill you to watch your people pull their loyalty. To turn to your enemies and walk into a trap that you knew would eventually cause their deaths. It was a glorious plan. And it worked. You're here to abdicate. I know that. Your own brothers told me about it last night. The fools. They fed me information all along. And although a few people want to watch you die by cursed bullet tonight, I decided it would be better to watch you suffer. You need to live long enough to see your people fall into your enemy's hands. To be stripped of everything they had. There's nothing you can do to stop it now. No one believes in you anymore. No one will believe you if you tell them what I've said."

"They're your people too," Shadow said. "Doesn't that mean anything to you?"

"No. Not really. They mean nothing to me. Less than nothing. They turned their backs on me when I needed them. The clan ceased to exist the day my parents died. I doubt any of them remember it. But I can't forget. Won't forget. Ever."

A moment later, Shadow stepped through a door at the rear of the room and walked to the podium at the head of the room.

Regan was stunned to see a smirking Mikhail follow him into the room. Mikhail? It had been his voice she'd heard? Saying all those awful things?

It couldn't be.

Shadow opened his mouth, but before he spoke, she held up a hand.

"My king." Hundreds of sets of eyes turned to her, but only one set truly mattered. Shadow's. She lifted her chin and smiled. "I believe in you. My king and master."

Shadow looked stunned. He looked strong. And he looked damned sexy. But mostly he looked stunned. "One moment, please," he said into the microphone before taking long, land-gulping strides toward her. He pulled her out into the hallway, his eyes searching her face. "What are you doing here?"

"Isn't it my job to stand by your side at clan meetings?"

"It *was* your job. But . . ." He let his words trail off as his gaze fell to Regan's neck. Regan's eyes followed the line of his gaze.

She traced the line of the choker with a fingertip. "I found this and just knew it was the right accessory for this event. Wouldn't you say?"

He caught her hand in his. "What does it mean?"

"It means I love you, and I don't give a damn if I'm ducking flying bullets, exploding floral arrangements, or cyanide-laced Chinese takeout, I want to be your wife and your queen." She watched Rolf and Stefan slip through the doorway. They stood behind Shadow. Watching with curious smiles. "And as queen, I further refuse to accept your abdication. Can I do that?"

"No." Shadow's lips pulled into a tense smile. "Not that I was planning on abdicating, but you're not queen anymore, and even if you were, I could abdicate if I wanted to."

"No, actually, that's not true." Stefan stepped up beside Shadow and set a hand on his brother's shoulder. "A king can only abdicate if he has the support of every member of our clan. Like it or not, that little lady has a bit of power over you now."

"She would, but she's not a clan member any longer." Shadow pointed at her. "We're not married."

"Oh yes, she is a clan member," Rolf piped in. "Even I know that divorce doesn't end a spouse's rights as full member."

This was a very illuminating conversation. "Is that so? I'm an honest-to-goodness, card-carrying vampire?" Regan asked.

"In a matter of speaking, yes," Stefan said around what sounded a lot like a chuckle turned into a cough.

Shadow scooped Regan's hands into his. "Forget about that whole abdicating thing for a moment. Are you sure about this? Really sure? Because as hard as I tried, I couldn't protect you from them. From that fucking bastard in there who thinks he's won."

"You bet I am. I know all about the danger. And I'll be damned if I'm going to let him win. Let's fight him, Shadow. I heard it. Heard what he said. Everyone did. You can beat him now. They know what kind of monster he truly is."

"That was the plan. Though I wasn't sure if it'd work."

"What happened between his parents and yours?" she asked. "What brought all this on? What was he talking about?"

"I have no idea. But I'm going to look into it. If there was some kind of injustice, I'll do what I can to fix it."

"Despite what he's done?"

"He'll face the consequences for his crimes. But I won't close my eyes to an injustice if one was committed."

"You're a much bigger person than me. That's for sure." She admired his strength, his levelheaded objectivity—even while facing an enemy so wicked. She'd had a hard time even looking at Mikhail when he'd entered the room.

"I love you, Shadow. More than I ever wanted to. More than I expected to. I accept the fact that you're unable to love," she added in a softer voice. "I'm good with it all. If you can only give me tenderness and caring, then that'll be good enough. I'll love enough for both of us."

"Actually, there's something I need to tell you in regards to that. And then I've got to go in there and deal with an issue." He pointed at the closed conference room doors. "It's about that love thing. You see, I wanted to tell you before, but I couldn't. I thought it would make things too complicated. I wanted to keep you safe."

What was he trying to say?

"Regan, I love you. Which is why I divorced you. Why I sent you away. Why I have been absolutely miserable without you for the past several weeks."

"You love me?" She couldn't believe her ears. A man who was supposed to be incapable of love loved her? "How? Why?"

He stroked her cheek, and she tipped her head into his hand. His touch was so gentle. So sweet. "You asked me once why I married you. I didn't give you the complete truth. You are the Chosen. Selected by Eudor, the most powerful mage in the world. I think he knew. He knew you are the only woman I could ever love. And I know it now too. Whether we are married or not, my heart is yours."

"It's magic," Rolf whispered.

"Oh my God! I love you." Regan threw her hands around his neck and hugged him as tightly as she could.

"No, I'm just a king, not a god," he joked.

She giggled and slugged him in the belly. "That's a matter of opinion. So . . . does this mean we can . . . You'll be my master? Forever?"

"Come inside." Shadow smiled and turned toward the door, then took her hand and nodded at Stefan to pull it open. "Let's go inside. We have an assassin to punish and a clan to win back. Are you with me?"

"You bet. But is it a problem we're not legally married any-more?"

"Not a problem. It's the full moon. A perfect night for a wedding. So we're making this permanent a month late? What's a month in the scheme of things?" His eyes twinkled as he looked down at her. She adored those twinkles. They were the most amazing, sexy, playful twinkles in the world. "And I must say, this dress is much nicer than the outfit you wore to our first wedding."

Regan happily took her place at the front of the room. And this time, there was no need for Shadow to trick her into asking him to marry her. She willingly and eagerly asked him. In front of his entire clan—less one would-be assassin, who'd already been placed into custody by the local police department.

It was the wedding of her dreams.

The marriage of her dreams.

To the vampire of her dreams.

Regan now knew there was no higher place than kneeling at her king and master's feet. No greater power than submitting her body, heart, and soul to him. No greater purpose than helping him reunite his people. And no greater joy than seeing his love for her in his eyes.

Turn the page for a preview of
PROMISCUOUS!

On sale now!

1

1990

Pajama parties have long been known as a popular event for young girls; it's where secrets are shared, true friends bond, and those who don't quite fit are revealed. The party at 234 Mulberry Court was no different. Five teenaged girls discussed their secret, and not-so-secret, loves. They discussed who'd done "it," who wanted to do "it" and what "it" might be like when it finally happened. In the midst of their giggling and teasing, the one who didn't quite fit was exposed to the unflattering glare of parental microscopic inspection.

The party was hosted by Constance Jefferson. "CJ," as she was called, lived in a well-maintained estate home in the right neighborhood. Her father was a successful and prominent surgeon. CJ was a pretty, shy, and petite sixteen-year old. She'd invited three of her friends from the cheerleading squad at the private high school they all attended: Petra Engles, sixteen, a snobbish child of privilege who was happy to let everyone know her father was the mayor, Debbie Cardena, a buxom, gregarious blonde, also sixteen, and Emily Park, polished, reserved, and mature beyond her seventeen years.

Debbie had called CJ earlier in the day to ask if she could bring along a friend. CJ had eagerly agreed without asking the identity of the additional guest—as far as she was concerned, the more the merrier. However, when she opened the door later that evening to find that Debbie had brought along her best friend, Andie Moore, CJ wasn't certain how her other guests would feel. After the two girls entered the foyer, CJ hastily grabbed Debbie and pulled her down the hallway, whispering intently.

"Why didn't you just tell me it was Andie? You know Petra doesn't like her."

"She's really nice, CJ. It's just that nobody takes the time to get to know her," Debbie replied easily.

Andie, a tall, gangly teenager, with thick, curly brown hair and hazel eyes, took the opportunity to meander along the hallway and admired the décor of the tastefully appointed home, and pretended she didn't hear the whispering about her being there. She didn't care what they said—she was here and that was all that mattered to her. She could pretty much get dimwitted Debbie to do whatever she wanted. Convincing her to call CJ for the invitation had been easy, and she told Debbie not to tell CJ whom she was bringing along. She knew that if her name had been mentioned, she wouldn't be there. Polite manners dictated they allow her to stay and she counted on them relying upon correct manners. Now all she had to do was convince them she belonged as a part of their sphere. Tonight she intended to win them all over.

In the 1950's Andie would have been referred to as being from the wrong side of the tracks. In more modern times, they politely referred to their poorer neighbors as not a good fit. Not a good fit for their social clubs, their organizations, their neighborhoods, and certainly not a good fit to be their children's friends. Considering that Andie did not live in an upper-class neighborhood, and her parentage was certainly in question it was difficult to uncover how she ended up at such a posh high school. The school was discreet enough not to disclose the details.

CJ quickly slipped back into her role of hostess and guided the young women to the family room, where the others were waiting. Conversation halted briefly as they entered the room and then a flurry of whispers could be heard. Determined her party was not going to be disrupted, Connie took charge.

"Hey, everybody, I'm not sure if you all know Andie. This is Andie Moore, one of our classmates, and she's joining us tonight. Everybody say hi," she said in an attempt to break the ice.

Resolute in her determination to win them over, Andie greeted Petra and Emily warmly before choosing the empty space next to Emily on the sofa. CJ began passing around snacks and the five girls easily slipped back into their conversation about school and boys. They watched a few movies before retiring to Connie's oversized bedroom for the night. In the privacy of Connie's bedroom the conversation turned toward sex.

Andie listened to their tales of petting and heavy kissing in silence. She was waiting for her opportunity to impress them with her knowledge and sexual experience.

Debbie admitted she'd let a boy put his hand inside her panties during a date. "He started rubbing me down there and getting all excited. His thing was so big, I could see it through his pants," she explained.

"Well, how did it feel? Did it feel good to have his hand down there?" Petra asked.

Debbie giggled before replying earnestly, "No, it didn't feel so good. I mean, his hands were rough and he was rubbing so hard it was uncomfortable, but he was moaning and groaning like it was so good."

"Did you see his thing?" Petra probed.

"No, but you know he tried to pull it out and show it to me. I turned my head and told him to put that thing away, 'cause I knew what he was going to try next, and I wasn't having none of *that*!" She stated it as though they all knew what "that" was.

"They ain't all that scary once you get used to them," Andie said quietly from her corner of the bed. All eyes turned to look at her.

"You've seen more than one?" Petra asked

"I've seen a few," she replied, and then continued, "Boys aren't any smarter about sex than girls are. Boys experiment more and are more curious than girls, so that gives them the upper hand."

"We can't go around experimenting like boys do, we could get pregnant," Connie said, repeating the mantra told to her by her parents over and over again.

"Yes, that's true," Emily heartily agreed.

Andie took a deep breath; she had important information to share. They would be so happy once she told them, they would be her friends forever. "You can make boys do things for you and give you stuff without letting them put their dicks inside you. And that's the only way you can get pregnant," she advised.

"Like what?" Debbie asked.

"First, like you said, you let him put his hand inside your panties and he really liked it, right?"

"Yeah, he did."

"But you didn't like it so much."

"No, not really."

"That's 'cause he didn't do it right—"

"Wait," Petra interrupted. "Aren't they supposed to be the experienced ones? So, shouldn't they be doing it right, and how would we know?"

"Girls gotta stop being afraid of their bodies. Boys jerk off all the time. That's how they know what makes them feel good, but girls never explore their bodies. If you knew more about your body—you could control any man and any situation."

"I don't think we should talk about this anymore," Connie said nervously, and looked toward the bedroom door.

"No, Andie's right. We're always told to treasure our bodies and keep our legs closed off from boys, but nobody talks about that other stuff. I think we need to know. I don't want the boy to control me. I want to be in charge," Debbie protested.

"In order to be in charge, you have to know what to expect and how it is supposed to feel, and that way you will know if he's doing it right," Andie explained, and began to wiggle out of her panties.

Shocked, CJ and Emily gasped, "What are you doing?"

Petra giggled nervously and Debbie immediately slipped off her panties.

Emboldened by their rapt attention, good and bad, Andie lifted her nightshirt and exposed her pubic area. As though explaining a science project to a bunch of schoolchildren, she used her fingers to spread the lips of her vulva and expose the tiny pink bulb hidden beneath. "This is the clit, and if you rub it the right way, you can have an orgasm," she instructed while lightly stroking the protruding bulb. Soon she was moaning softly and shaking violently as she climaxed over and over.

The girls sat with mouths agape as they watched Andie masturbating and enjoying it. Debbie, who was quickly getting flushed and excited in a voyeuristic way she never had before, eagerly followed suit, but she had difficulty finding her bulb. "Where is it, damn it? CJ, can you see it?" she asked as she spread her legs wide.

"I don't want to look at you like that!" CJ exclaimed. "You guys better stop, or you're gonna get us all in trouble."

"Chill out, CJ. It looks like fun. I want to try," Petra said, and wiggled out of her panties.

Emily had retreated to the farthest corner of the second bed and watched silently, appalled and intrigued at the same time.

"Help me, Andie. I can't find my button," Debbie cried in frustration.

Andie stopped her own self-pleasing and scrambled across the bed to assist in the lesson. Kneeling between Debbie's knees, she guided Debbie's hand to the exact location and showed her how to rub lightly.

Debbie started moaning and giggling alternately at the sensations she was creating in her own body. Thrilled by the prospect, Petra exclaimed, "Show me! Show me!" Andie happily obliged. Soon all three were spread-eagle on the queen-sized bed masturbating while CJ and Emily looked on.

"I think you should stop now," CJ cautioned. She was feeling very uncomfortable and her body was tingling in very strange places.

Debbie, now overly excited and horny, was eager to try more things. "CJ, Emily, you should try this. You don't know what you're missing. What else can you show us, Andie?"

"Well," Andie replied, "if you're really in control, you can make him eat you, and that's so cool. Usually, boys will want you to suck their dicks. But if you suck his, he has to suck yours too."

"Suck what? We don't have anything for boys to suck on—except our tits, and they're always trying to do that anyway," Petra protested.

"Sure, you do," Andie replied confidently, and with a secret smile. "Make him suck your button."

"What!" Petra exclaimed loud enough to cause CJ to get up nervously and check the door. The hallway was clear. This was getting out of control and she was afraid what Andie would have them try next.

"Oh, suck my button! I want to know what it feels like,"

Debbie exclaimed. "Come on, Andie. You suck mine and I'll suck yours."

"Who's gonna suck mine?" Petra wailed, still playing with her newfound toy, as she looked impishly at CJ and Emily.

Andie eased herself between Debbie's legs and spread her vulva with her fingers. She expertly swirled her tongue around the moist pink opening and then flicked the bulb with her tongue.

"Oh, my gosh!" exclaimed Debbie as she enjoyed the feel of Andie's tongue. Andie burrowed deeper and she pulled the tiny sensitive bulb into her mouth and sucked. Debbie's body bucked wildly and her shrill cry of pleasure pierced the stillness of the room.

All the girls froze in place as they waited for the inevitable footfalls of CJ's parents. When no one came, they all breathed a sigh of relief and returned to their former activity.

"You have to keep your mouth shut, Debbie," Andie cautioned, and leaned back on the bed. "Your turn," she said, and lay back on the bed and spread her legs.

Debbie needed no further urging and she buried her face between Andie's legs and sought out the pleasure button. Petra was getting antsy that she was missing out on this extra bit of fun and began to protest.

"What about me? What about me?"

Andie's worldly experience would cause her to make one more bad judgment. "Come on, I'll do you too." While Debbie concentrated on her newfound talent of eating Andie's pussy, Andie showed them how to conduct a proper threesome by having Petra straddle her face so she could suck her button at the same time.

These three young girls in the midst of a taboo, and very erotic, activity was the picture emblazoned on Arlene Jefferson's face as she opened the bedroom door to check on the girls before retiring for the night. Her unearthly scream caused her husband, Carlton, to come running and the girls to scatter around the room.

CJ and Emily began to cry as CJ explained to her shocked mother that she'd tried to stop them, but they wouldn't. Debbie and Petra immediately distanced themselves from Andie, and had the grace to look ashamed.

Andie, who was not ashamed or embarrassed by her body, lacked the humility to realize how bad this situation had just gotten. Her demeanor of nonchalance set her apart from everyone else in the room and identified her as the organizer of the sex fest.

It only took a moment for Arlene to assess the situation and lay blame. Through clenched lips she hissed, "Get that half-breed trailer trash out of my house this instant!"

Humiliation and anger overcame Andie as she realized she was the only one being unceremoniously escorted out of the house. When she was dropped off at her apartment across town twenty minutes later, Dr. Jefferson didn't even wait to see if she got into the building safely as he sped away from the curb. Mrs. Jefferson's withering look was etched in her mind—a look that said she was no better than common street filth. But it was Arlene's parting shot that carried the most sting as Andie passed her on the way out the door to the awaiting car. "You're nothing but a common whore," she hissed, and paused for a moment before adding, "Just like your mother." She then slammed the front door behind her.

CJ, who had followed Andie downstairs, and had been sniffling quietly in the corner, gasped at her mother's cruelty. Arlene whirled around at the sound and her look sent CJ scampering off to her bedroom.

Meanwhile, in spite of the events of the evening, Andie was certain that she'd made some new friends, and it would all turn out okay once the shock wore off. She quickly learned her newfound friends were not her friends at all, for the girls distanced themselves from her. Even the once gullible Debbie no longer had time for her. While the girls never told what truly happened at the party, the whispers of half-breed and trailer trash followed Andie through her remaining year in high school.

It was a humiliation she would never forget or forgive.